The Risk of His Music

The Risk of His Music

STORIES BY PETER WELTNER

GRAYWOLF PRESS

Copyright © 1997 by Peter Weltner

Publication of this volume is made possible in part by a grant provided by
the Minnesota State Arts Board through an appropriation by the Minnesota
State Legislature, and by a grant from the National Endowment for the
Arts. Significant additional support has been provided by the Andrew W.
Mellon Foundation, the Lila Wallace-Reader's Digest Fund, the McKnight
Foundation, and other generous contributions from foundations, corpora-
tions, and individuals. To these organizations and individuals who make our
work possible, we offer heartfelt thanks.

Published by Graywolf Press
2402 University Avenue, Suite 203
Saint Paul, Minnesota 55114
All rights reserved.

Published in the United States of America

ISBN 1-55597-253-5

2 4 6 8 9 7 5 3 1
First Graywolf Printing, 1997

Library of Congress Catalog Card Number: 96-78740

"The Greek Head" has appeared previously in *American Short Fiction 6, Men
on Men 4*, and *Prize Stories 1993 The O'Henry Awards*.

Cover Design: Adrian Morgan at Red Letter Design

Cover Art: *The Double* by Jared French (c. 1940, egg tempera on masonite,
21¾" × 30"). Private Collection, courtesy of D C Moore Gallery, New
York.

The Risk of His Music

I

The Greek Head

OUR WORLD, MINE AND CHARLIE'S, resembled theirs, Don and Roger's, only superficially. It was curious that Don and I both managed record stores, though his was twice as large as mine and three times more successful; that Roger and Charlie were both vice principals at middle schools here in the city; that Roger and I both came from Providence and that Charlie and Donald grew up, if thirty years apart, nonetheless within blocks of one another in San Mateo; that Don and Roger had met in 1946 in a bar located in the same block as the bar in which Charlie and I met twenty-nine years later; and that the first several letters of our pair of last names were the same, Don Ross and Roger White, Charlie Roberts and Sam Whitten. But it was only curious, nothing more. People are constantly taking accidental facts and arranging them into some kind of order, as if to show, in this instance, that the two of us were destined to become friends with the two of them. But that's not how it happened, of course. We saw their "For Rent" sign before someone else, that's all. And, if the truth were told, we didn't really get along all that well, not well enough to be described as truly successful friends.

When an artery in Donald's brain, having apparently already ballooned, finally exploded, I was at lunch with a guy named Rick whose ad I'd answered—eyes wide open and skeptical, not expecting much. Of course, it turned out he was the one to be disappointed since he had apparently believed, when I'd told him on the phone that I was currently uninvolved, that I'd meant "really." Though we'd agreed nothing would come of it, the meal still lasted too long because I had been trying to justify myself to him and to myself at the same time, attempting to explain that all I had meant to say was that I was unhappy. Nor was I home later when Roger first pounded on our door at a time when I'd told him I'd be sure to be back from work in case he heard anything from the hospital. He had heard something. Donald was dead.

I knew that there was no need for me to feel guilty. It was just a mistake, something bad that happened while I was looking for a way out of my life and not paying attention to much else. Still, if you'd asked me how my life was going then, I'd have answered as Don used to when he was down in the dumps, "In low water." I knew one of us, either Charlie or I, should have made the break and gotten it over with long ago. But neither of us had, perhaps because it's so hard nowadays to be certain whether one is behaving rationally or from fear. Charlie figured I was safe, I figured he was safe, so it was OK. We were all right together.

That's just another way that Roger and Don weren't like us, only seeming the same. They argued all the time, too. But the difference is that they were never afraid. They had never been afraid of anything, not of each other, not of splitting apart, not of the world's opinion of them, certainly not of dying. They understood as well as anyone that nothing was forever. But they endured. They stuck it out anyway. They had become famous for lasting. Thirty-nine years they had been together, thirty-nine years and counting, Roger had said when Charlie and I had helped them celebrate their anniversary right before last Christmas.

It was a familiar number by then, they'd repeated it so often, but all of a sudden it seemed a miracle to me. Their entire lives were somehow like the one brief moment when Charlie and I had just become lovers and we'd flown to the Cape to rejoice in our success. All week long the weather was beautiful, mild. We rode rented bikes, swam, walked the beaches, strolled the strip, danced at the Sea Drift, drank too much, made love, were happy, the night sky so clear as we lay back on the sand that it seemed as if the souls of all our just-spent seeds' unborn children were blinking to us from the stars. It didn't last. The first fight after our return to San Francisco almost destroyed everything. Like pilgrims in search of consolation, we took another trip, this one to Seattle. It worked. When we got back, we found the apartment, its garden for our use too.

The days after Don's death, as Roger waited anxiously for Don's sister Susan to arrive, we could hear him pacing overhead, especially at night. It kept even Charlie awake who, if tired enough, could easily fall asleep while having sex. In earlier years, we might have known what to do about Roger, might have known better how to behave and what to say so that we might have believed some of it ourselves. But we had given up speaking about such things or trying to affect the course of grief, Charlie months before me. Don's was the third death of a friend in a year that was barely a month old. The other two had been twenty years or more younger, and their dying had been much more painful, taken far longer, and been terrible to witness. Why waste more useless words on Don's death? It had been easier, much easier, than most. He was almost old. He'd been, he said, a happy man. Wasn't that enough? Let Roger remember all of that and quit stomping down on the floor, on our ceiling, as if it could do any good.

A big and awkward man, Roger seemed to be foraging for food, the refrigerator door opening and slamming shut over and over. Or was it only ice he was after? It annoyed us and was meant to annoy us. I was sure of it. We could hear the anger in it, expressed as well in the clogs he had apparently exchanged for his usual soft slippers, an anger directed against us and our silence, I figured, at our failure to have offered him any comfort. It was funny in a way. For the first time, Roger had to envy us for something more substantial than our relative youth. Unhappy as we were, we still had each other, if we wanted, for a while longer. There was still a party of sorts downstairs, even if it was breaking up. And, momentarily at least, he hated us for having it.

Because of him, we were eating breakfast much earlier than usual. "I didn't know they bothered to carve clogs in a size fifteen," I remarked. "Those things must weigh ten pounds each." It sounded like dumbbells falling in a gym or like furniture dropping.

Charlie said nothing. He was quietly furious. He had just found the new ad I had cut out and boldly circled, and he was refusing to acknowledge it. It didn't puzzle me why I had left it out on the top of the bureau like that, exposed so blatantly under the lamp's light in an otherwise black room as if deliberately to call his attention to it, the way lately he had been calling my attention to the fact that he had masturbated while I was gone by leaving a porno mag or two lying on the nightstand top rather than hiding them back in the drawer where he knew I knew he kept them. The previous night I'd been searching for my one pair of black socks in the back of my bureau drawer, thinking I'd need them for the funeral or whatever. But I didn't put everything back in. That was why I was pretending to look for those socks; I was preparing to pay Charlie back for the golden boys he had been fucking in his imagination yesterday afternoon, if it was only in his imagination since Duane had entered the picture. So it went. We were each trying to let the other know he wasn't necessary anymore.

With one hand, Charlie opened the interior shutters behind the kitchen table. The sky was already a radiantly pure blue, the surprising storm which had sailed through last night having netted up all the junk that usually floats in the air and left in its wake only a few wisps of clouds.

I sipped my coffee. Why does it never taste as good as it

smells? That had been Donald's annoying question nearly every morning when we four were in Baja together on a week's vacation five winters ago.

"Which of these shells do you like best, Charlie?" I prodded. "I think this one is probably my favorite." I shoved it over toward him from the pile in the middle of the table that Roger had arranged as a centerpiece, though it had early become unglued. "What do you think?"

He picked up the shell, examined its shape, so much like a dragonfly's wing and nearly as transparent, and tested its firm, sharp edge, like a knife's. "It's OK. It's pretty."

"Right," I said and stared back out the window. It had been a dumb question on a lousy topic, the centerpiece itself something we kept on display only to please Roger. I'd hated the foul, variously infested town on the southeastern coast where Don had directed us all because it was supposed to be such a great spot for diving. Charlie, of course, liked it. Ever since, each time I had mentioned anything about it, Charlie scowled at me in exactly the same way, as if he owned this one special mask whose sole purpose was to remind me that my bad time there was no one's fault but my own. But that was like Charlie. The bad times anywhere with anyone were always the other person's fault, and he had designed lots of different scary masks to let us know it. Yet the truth is that Charlie is much better company than I am. Nearly everyone says so. I've told him so many times myself.

I glanced up at the ceiling. "Roger seems to have settled down."

"So it seems. Maybe he's gone to bed." Charlie checked his watch. "Finally." He folded our newspaper and laid it on the table next to my elbow. "Talk to him today, will you? Find out what's going on with him. What did that note say? That Don's sister is to be here at least by tomorrow, didn't it? She's next of kin, for God's sake. Roger's got to have his wits about him, even in this enlightened era. Try to calm him down some."

"Why don't you?"

"Because I'm going to work." He took a last swallow of his yogurt drink and stood up.

"So am I."

"Yeah. But not for four more hours."

"So what? I don't get it. What's the big difference?"

"You don't have to get it. Just do it."

"Why are you avoiding him, Charlie?"

"Why are you?"

"I'm not."

"Like shit you aren't," Charlie said. "You're avoiding Roger every bit as much as I am. And we both know why."

"We do?"

"Oh, cut the crap, Sam. You don't want him to know we're really breaking up this time. I don't either. Not now, not yet. It's that simple."

"Are we?"

"What?"

"Are we really breaking up this time?"

"Of course. Don't be an ass. We've been doing it for months and months. I suppose it's just taken me this long to find the guts to say so. Now all you have to do is to find the guts to admit it." He walked around the table to position himself behind me and bent to kiss the back of my neck. I shivered. "No scenes now. We promised, remember? I've got to go. I've got a lazy teacher to bawl out."

"It's still early," I protested.

"I know," he said and left the room.

I sat in my chair motionless, nearly rigid. Outside our window, the city looked dazed, too, as if it had yet to recover its breath from the blow of the storm's wild punch. Twenty or thirty minutes at least must have passed in silence as the sun strolled over a golden flank of Telegraph Hill. Never had a place seemed more beautiful to me than San Francisco at that moment, until Roger resumed his pacing, as regular and as infuriating as a madman's dance.

So I didn't go up to Roger's. I couldn't yet. I was too angry at everything and at everyone, at Donald for dying and messing things up this badly, at Roger for grieving and carrying on, and most of all at Charlie for having walked out on me before I'd summoned the courage to leave him first. I was furious at all of them for their not having asked me whether this was the way I wanted it or not.

To pass the hours before work, I watched two *I Love Lucy* reruns, early ones full of the kind of slapstick and mugging that Charlie hated, and then I took a long, intense shower, soaping my whole body repeatedly to feel the pleasure of washing myself clean over and over again—in the process, however, apparently stripping my pores of all their oil because after I'd dried myself off my skin was like an old man's, like Roger's, old parchment from which all the legible writing had long ago faded.

I stood in front of the mirror, disgusted by my own body, then opened the medicine cabinet door and drenched myself with Charlie's precious baby oil, watching it soak in and bring me back to life like the rush of tide over the body of a beached and dying starfish. It worked. The evidence was that I wasn't so bad off after all. I'd panicked needlessly. There was some semblance of youth left in me, not much perhaps, but enough for a while. Basking in the sunlight piercing through the bathroom window, I almost glowed, the oil covering my body like an unguent that might protect it from the world and time. Before I could dress, however, I had to wipe most of it off with a towel to keep it from seeping into my clothes. So much, I thought, for magic.

I left Roger a note taped to his mailbox, assuring him I'd drop by that night, after I got home. I walked to work. There was still time, lots of time, and the day was too near perfec-

tion to lose altogether, the winter's light pure, the views un-
impeded for miles, all colors everywhere reduced to either
bright blue or stark white, like the Earth in pictures taken
from the moon. Chinese New Year was to be early this year,
apparently. Firecrackers were exploding somewhere up Jones
Street and down Greenwich, too. As I turned to walk up the
steps, a cherry bomb exploded behind me.

Don always dreaded these weeks because the noise reminded him of the sounds of battle and especially of the time
when he was wounded on Kwajalein. That was practically all
he ever mentioned about it, just a little grumbling during the
two weeks or so every year when firecrackers burst all around
us. The festivities didn't bother Roger though, Don said, because Roger had held a desk job in Honolulu for the duration.
Don's eyes gleamed as Roger blushed.

As I paused on top of Russian Hill for a couple of minutes,
standing in one corner of the park on what Don liked to call
"our" hill—meaning his and Roger's, mine and Charlie's—and
gazing northward over the bay toward Marin, I remembered
his saying how the sky here on such brilliant, weightless days
was like the Greek sky he and Roger had seen so often, a
strange, oddly suspenseful sky as if some god were just about
to step out from it. Constantly in Greece, he said, it came as a
shock to discover that eyes so dazzled could see so clearly. He
had winked at me, a bright glint in his imp's eyes, touched
me briefly but firmly where he knew I wouldn't forget his
fingers had been, the running shorts and jock that separated
my flesh from his flesh somehow immaterial for the moment,
and he walked away, never again to make that sort of ad-
vance. Charlie and I had been living downstairs for only six
months. I still don't know what sort of claim Donald was
staking that morning, if any. But recollecting it, I cried a little for the first time about his being dead, until finally I
pulled myself together and hauled ass the rest of the way to
the store.

Only later that night, after I'd closed the shop and turned off all the lights except for the one over the counter and gone in the back to use the john, while I was sitting there in the dark without accomplishing very much, did I think of Don again with that sort of clarity, as if he were standing in the flesh by the door, grinning that half-salacious, half-beatific smile of his, like that time he caught me coming out of the shower. I had stomped back into the bathroom and grabbed a huge towel to wrap around my middle.

"Don't you ever knock? What the hell are you doing barging in here like this, Don?" My hands were shaking, I was so mad.

"You're angry," he said calmly and started to whistle "Danny Boy," which he called "Sammy Boy" to irk me.

"Stop it, Don."

He quit, leaned back against the jamb, and crossed his legs at the ankle, looking quite pleased with himself.

"Care to join us for dinner tonight?"

"It's late, Don."

"But you haven't eaten?"

"No."

Without moving any part of his body, not even his eyes, he surveyed the room. "And Charlie's not here," he observed.

"He's at some gay political meeting. Get out of here and let me dress, will you?"

"What are you ashamed of, Sammy?"

"Don!"

"Charlie's never minded. But then he has a better sense of fair play. It's only a peek I want, after all." I let the towel fall. "Very nice. Sam, Sam," he clucked, "You think the whole world's out to make you, don't you? That's why you're always so on edge, doll, like some sweet young thing out on the streets alone late at night checking over her shoulder to make sure no one's there. But you'd like someone to be there, wouldn't you? Wouldn't you, Sammy?"

I dressed quickly. "Maybe Charlie and I should move out."

"I thought we were going to be friends, we four."

"I'd hoped so, too, Don."

As he two-fingered a cigarette out of his shirt pocket and lit it, I wanted to beg him to stop, but it was absurd to try. Don would smoke even after he was dead. We all knew that, though he did manage to refrain sometimes, like when we were all driving somewhere together. "Listen to me, lad," he said and drew in a lungful of smoke. "You imagine I'm on the make, don't you? Well, maybe I am in a way. But Roger and I are happy. We've been happy together all these years. And do you know why? Do you know why he's really all I want, old fart that I am?"

"I wish I did," I said honestly enough. "I wish I did know, Don."

"It's because neither of us ever expected more from life than what it gave us, including each other. I mean, Roger was pretty spectacular when I first met him. But so were lots of other men, if you get my drift. We just never wasted any time hoping or waiting for something more or better. We made it work, doll. Do you understand me? Is my message clear? We made it go."

"You're not telling me very much, Don."

"You kids," he said, snickering, gazing down absent-eyed at the ember of his cigarette. "You young pups. You know what? I wouldn't see the world as you kids see it for all the hunks in this town. It wouldn't be worth it. It just makes you all so angry, thinking you can have everything and everyone, because you can't. You never could. It's such an elementary truth. Roger and I, we made do," he stressed once more. "Who believes that's enough anymore?"

"I don't know. Don?"

"What?" He grinned at me, his smile as pure and as enigmatic as any virgin's.

"Please don't do this again."

"Do what?"

"Surprise me."

He chucked my chin. "Dinner's at nine," he called behind him as he strolled out the door, turning back briefly only to disentangle his favorite fraying red cardigan from the latch where it had caught.

It was after ten and I was still thinking about Don by the time I wearily walked in the door of our apartment and switched on the light. Charlie had left a note in an envelope on the mantel, but I didn't want to read it. Instead, I made straight for the kitchen, grabbed a bottle of scotch from the cabinet over the sink, and carried it upstairs.

When Roger opened the door, his appearance shocked me. Why was I so disappointed? What had I imagined, or hoped, I'd find? He looked great, clean shaven, casually dressed but dapper as always, his dark eyes bright and quick as a curious child's, no heavy clogs on his feet after all but only his usual well-shined loafers.

"I could use a drink," I said, offering him the bottle. It was less than half full, but it didn't matter. Roger wasn't much of a drinker, either.

He accepted it. "A hard day, Sam?"

"You could say that. I kept thinking about Don."

Roger smiled down at me sympathetically. If he and Don had ever played good cop/bad cop, Roger would have been the good cop, the pal, the buddy, the one with the smile you could trust until you confessed. I followed him into the kitchen where he filled the glasses with ice cracked from the tray and poured enough scotch on top of it to leave room for only an inch or so of water. He tasted it, grimaced, and pointed back out to the living room where, glass in hand, I pursued him to the window that overlooked the deck and garden with their splendid views of the bay. "Such a clear night!" Roger exclaimed.

"Yes," I agreed. "It's swell. Roger?"

"Sam."

"I'm sorry."

"I know you are, Sam." He laid a kindly hand, wide and warm, on my shoulder. "I know you are. Don was cremated today, incidentally. Around noon, I think. We'll sail him out onto the bay in a few days, perhaps Sunday, and sneak him into it, just as he wanted, you and me and Charlie. His family." He withdrew his hand.

I didn't know what to do or to say so I said only, "That'll be fine, Roger."

"Good. Good."

"Roger?"

"Yes?"

"I haven't meant to be avoiding you." When I jerked around to look, he was no longer even pretending to smile, his face creased with a frown like the one teachers use to express disappointment at your failure. "I mean I haven't known what to say. I still don't know what to say."

"Yes," he nodded too eagerly. "It is difficult, isn't it?" He took a sip of his drink. "Come over here," he directed me, indicating the love seat opposite the one he had just flopped into.

A small, restless fire burned in the fireplace to my right. Between us stood a glass-top coffee table covered with the usual art and travel magazines scattered about. But the Greek head sat as always exactly in the center, handsome and proud and serene. I bent over to touch its eyes, as if to keep them from staring up at me.

"You know I wasn't with him when Don stole that," Roger said.

"I know," I said. "You were . . . ," but I stopped myself. He placed his sweating glass carefully on top of an old *Holiday* and folded his arms across his broad chest like someone with a chill. "Only that strange, wonderful woman who had attached herself to us in Perugia. By the time we reached Rome,

Cecille was simply a part of us and our vacation. To this day, I don't understand how it happened. She had broken her leg climbing up to some forbidden monastery high in the Tirol and was on crutches when we met her in that little café. How she had managed to see so much on crutches without our help I never figured out, either. How that woman enjoyed Italy!

"Then, when I got so sick in Rome, Don and Cecille went everywhere together and immediately afterward told me all about it so I might feel I'd done it all, too, been everywhere, seen everything with them. Nine years later, when Don and I returned to Rome, it was so strange because I did have this powerful sensation I actually had done everything they'd told me about. It was Don who was all the time having to straighten me out. 'No, no,' he'd say, 'Cecille and I told you about this place. You weren't here. You were flat on your back in that miserable pensione, poor guy.'

"He was right, of course. And yet it all really was that vivid. The whole city. Cecille and Don had described everything so perfectly it was like life. It was like having lived the words in a book." Roger took another sip from his drink and settled back deeper into the couch's plush cushions, staring into the flickering fire. The apartment was too warm. Don and Roger's rooms, anywhere they were, were always too warm. Yet they were both big, husky men. "I miss him, Sam."

"So do I. So does Charlie," I added as an afterthought. "Already very much."

"Maybe that first trip was our best," he mused. "We felt so lucky to be alive after the war, especially Donald. It had been terrible, but for us in a way it had been lucky, too, since it had brought us to new worlds and eventually here to San Francisco. I'd just finished at State under the GI Bill. Don had made some money at that original store he'd opened downtown. We were in love. I mean that. We were really in love. Neither of us had ever been to Europe before. It was wonderful."

I couldn't look at him. "First trips can be like that," I suggested. "The best. Or the worst. So much is being tested."

"Tested? Perhaps." His eyes seemed fixed on the fire. I could only hope that he, unlike me, wasn't picturing Don's naked body on a pallet sliding into a burning chamber. He had started to cry, very quietly.

"Roger?"

"I'll be all right. In a minute. In a minute. It's just that we hadn't expected it. We thought there would be more time." He attempted a smile. "But I suppose that's only human, always hoping for more time than fate is willing to give you."

I reached over, picked the Greek head up off its stand, and fondled it in my lap. "It's very beautiful, one of the most beautiful, sexy heads I've ever seen. It must weigh twenty pounds, Roger."

"Surely not so much. It's funny, though. We've never weighed it. Think of all the countless things we must have weighed in a lifetime, but we never weighed the head. We shipped it home surrounded by many, many cans of olives that concealed what was placed in sawdust in the center of the box. So I only know what it weighed with the olives, not by itself. Don and I were eating those olives for years afterwards," he laughed, "serving them to guests, too, especially in martinis. We saved one can, for good luck. It's still in the cupboard, the last I looked.

"The Italians were digging up heads and other bits and pieces of classical statues, Greek and Roman, all over the place in those days. It was the war. It had disturbed so much earth that practically every backyard or field yielded one antique body part or another. They simply didn't know what to do with them all. Too many living people had lost parts of their own bodies, or their loved ones, for them to care much about bits and pieces of broken statuary. There are times in history, and this was one of them, when art doesn't mean a thing. Not a thing. So some museums were actually littered with fragments of classical sculpture lying around in basements, in courtyards, in gardens, scattered all over floors. Nobody had the time or the money to do anything with it except pile it all together somewhere.

"I'm exaggerating, of course. Still, it was quite easy, Don said, for him and Cecille to steal this one. She was on her crutches, of course, and had to carry a big bag, more like a sack, draped over her shoulders to hold her belongings, like her wallet and all those mysterious women's things that in those days seemed so indispensable. Don simply waited until the coast was clear, decided upon that head there, lifted it off the cluttered table where it lay with other black marble pieces, and dropped it in Cecille's bag. Then they calmly walked out—or rather he calmly walked out, and she somewhat nervously, she reported, hobbled out behind him. Isn't that amazing? You see, Cecille didn't want Don implicated if she were caught. She said she was convinced that she could easily charm her way out of any Italian jail. I imagine she could have.

"It was to be a present to me, for having missed so much. It's funny. I don't recall feeling I'd missed anything at all. And yet if I hadn't been sick, maybe Don wouldn't have gotten the nerve to pull off the heist. Cecille, well, for her it was a game mostly, something to do so that she could prove she could do it. But Don wanted to accomplish something spectacular for me. For us, I mean. No matter what else might happen to us in our life together, we'd have this special thing no one else like us would own. A real Greek head, early fourth century B.C., Cecille said. Ours, Don's and mine. A work of art for her two Greeks, Cecille said. She loved that phrase. Her two Greeks. Because it was her gift, too, after all, the beautiful thing that remains after everything else has died, she said."

I carefully placed the head back on its stand, the one Don had built for it thirty-five years ago, picked up my drink off the floor, and drained it. "Are you going to be all right? Would you like me to sleep up here tonight? Roger?"

He wiped his eyes. "I must have bored you with that old story."

"Not at all," I protested, though in fact the story had bored me. I couldn't concentrate on it and kept shifting to Charlie, as if he were naked and aroused downstairs in bed. "What did you say, Roger?"

He shook his head. "I said, 'Don't be silly.' I'm fine. Do me a favor tomorrow instead though, will you?"

"Certainly."

"Help me entertain Don's sister. She'll be here around five or so. Come for dinner, why don't you, you and Charlie. Let your assistant handle the store tomorrow night. I'll need to talk to her alone first. But I'd like to spend as little unprotected time with her as possible. She's always blamed me for Donald's 'problem,' as she calls it."

"Blamed you?"

"For making him abnormal or something equally nonsensical. I don't pretend to understand such people. Wouldn't it be marvelous if we actually did have such power? She'll have a fit about the cremation, of course."

"She didn't know?"

"There's a family burial plot outside of San Mateo someplace up in the hills. They all expect Don to lie in it. He said no way. But they didn't believe him. It's strange what some families won't believe, isn't it? I have Don's will to back me up. I've already had to refer to it a couple of times, though I confess I haven't been able to bring myself to read it yet. Don told me the essence of what was in it. That was enough for me."

"You ought to read it," I recommended.

"Yes. Eventually."

"I should go, Roger."

"Thank you, Sam." He stood up and pecked my cheek.

"For what?"

"For conquering your fear at last and coming up. You see, I'm really all right, aren't I? There's no need to be afraid."

"I wasn't afraid."

"And Charlie? He's not afraid either?"

"He'll be up to see you tomorrow, Roger."

"Good." The toe of his shoe poked at the rug. "I guess I'm the odd man out, now, aren't I? Our traveling days together are done."

"I don't see why," I said, though I knew exactly what he meant. "Don wouldn't want your life to stop any more than you would want his to if you had died first," I counseled.

"But I didn't," he said bitterly. "I didn't die first. Good night, Sam." He opened the door for me. "Oh, by the way. What was Charlie doing at home much of the midafternoon? Is he sick?"

"I don't know," I said and almost stumbled out.

I lay still dressed on my bed, unable to sleep and impatient with all the night sounds of the city that seemed determined to keep me awake. I could hear Roger pacing again, more quietly this time, the circle he was making growing smaller as if he were spiraling toward some still center where he and I both might find some rest. The first time I woke up, the light I'd unknowingly left on in the hall, dim as it was, nonetheless nearly blinded me when I opened my startled eyes. After I'd jumped out of bed and switched it off, however, the moon's light bathing the living room was as soothing, as refreshing as the morning sun on those late-summer backpacking treks Charlie and I used to enjoy in the Sierra when we'd hiked high enough to be alone, leaving Roger and Don a couple of thousand feet below, since the rare air wasn't good for Don's heart and Roger was afraid of heights. So it goes. So it went.

Later, I would fall behind, too, as afraid as Roger, while Charlie and Don, to all our surprise feeling stronger again as he got older, climbed far above.

My stomach growled, my head ached from hunger, my toes itched. Propped there on the mantel, Charlie's note seemed not so much to glow in the moon's rays as to be illuminated from within, like a child's night-light. For a moment, long enough for me to reach for it, it consoled me and made me feel safe. But then I read it.

> *Roses are red,*
> *Violets are blue,*
> *I'll be back for the heavy stuff*
> *When the rent is due.*

In the bathroom, I flushed the bits of torn paper down the toilet and tried not to look at myself in the mirror. It was dark enough that I almost succeeded.

Half-stripped of what belonged in it by Charlie, the bedroom smelled slightly of disinfectant, like a hospital corridor. For a well man, however worried, I had been in too many sickrooms lately. Clean the walls and floors, the glass, the tiles, the chrome, the sheets. Take out the bodies. You can't suppress the smell of death. It can't be hidden, any more than old people can conceal the smell of their dying flesh with fragrances or young bodybuilders can hide it beneath their sweat. It was there, too, in the absence Charlie had left behind.

For the first time in nearly three days, I heard Roger walk the long way down the hall to their bedroom, tucked back in the part of the house that cut into the hill, for their flat expanded considerably beyond ours. He moved slowly, almost staggering across the floor as if something heavier than the weight of sleep drew him on. A door shut. Then the whole house grew quiet, as if it, like me, had been waiting for Roger to find his way back to bed and rest.

Though the night was chilly, I undressed and walked out

onto the deck naked, as Charlie and I would sometimes do to make love on a couple of air mattresses, pretending we were back in the high country. The moon had just slipped out of sight. Directly overhead an airplane flew, its red warning lights flashing, and banked toward Japan. Early last September, Don and Roger had tried to talk us into going there with them the next summer. Don said he thought he'd almost forgotten enough about the war to enjoy a visit. Roger maintained all he cared about was seeing a real rock garden—not an imported one, since theirs was obviously missing something—but that if he had his way they'd be going to the Dordogne. Charlie jumped at the proposal. I was less certain. I had been promising myself someplace alone with Charlie, though I didn't know why or where.

Now there would be no trips. I hunkered down and gripped the deck's railing with both hands to keep from toppling over, a sudden gust of emotion blowing through me without doing much damage. I wanted to feel sad, I really did. I wanted badly to feel sad about something real, at least about Don's death or Charlie's leaving. I needed to grieve, but I couldn't. Real sadness, I thought, had to be like fierce desire, a thing of the moment, doomed not to last, but nonetheless profound and enduring in its effects. I believed that once Charlie and I had experienced such passion. It hadn't lasted much longer than the first six months, if that long, and yet I thought we could live off it for the rest of our lives. Apparently I had been wrong. We had both been mistaken. But, if I couldn't love him anymore, I wanted at least to feel the sorrow that was supposed to follow his going. Then I could grieve for Don, too, clinging to the memory of each of them as to a lost hope.

I slept poorly, went to work early, left the store early, having put my best clerk in charge for a few days. While waiting downstairs for Susan to arrive, I pictured her as a tall, gaunt woman dressed in severe black, a handsome woman, handsomer than her brother, her hair the same iron gray as his, her eyes dewy, her lips atremble, her fingers still nimble enough, however, to turn the pages of a will with care. As usual, my fantasy was wrong. A car turned into the driveway and parked. When I peeked around our living-room curtain, I saw a short, dumpy, henna-rinsed, slightly comical-looking old bag dressed in a white frocklike dress dotted with cute little blue birds. She was so pudgy that she had to use both hands to haul herself up the stairs. Once on the stoop, she stood there panting, the loose skin on her neck quivering like a biddy's wattle, and she repeatedly poked at the buzzer with an uncertain finger. She was still breathing too hard to speak when Roger opened the door for her.

Less than an hour later, Roger stamped down on his floor three times, paused, then pounded down three times more, the usual signal that he and Don were ready for me and Charlie to come up and join their festivities, whatever they were—drinks and dinner, a sample of a just-discovered Burgundy, fresh brochures from their travel agent, more recently a new movie on their VCR. They wanted us to share in nearly everything they bought and participate in almost everything they planned because, Don enjoyed saying, they were that rare phenomenon, a one-couple couple and thus truly monogamous.

Neither Charlie nor I ever got around to telling either of them how uneasy that attitude made us. Instead, we simply went along with it, coasting, since we liked them and since they, unlike ourselves, were always so full of plans. Yet Roger's coded stomping on the floor had early on irked us both, perhaps because it sounded too much like an official summons and Charlie and I resented all such commands, all orders, anyone's telling us what to do. Someone's telling somebody, the wrong somebody, what to do was the origin of all the world's revolutions, Charlie remarked one afternoon, glancing up at our throbbing ceiling. I was positive that it was the origin of most of the trouble between Charlie and me. Or maybe Charlie and I just didn't have the patience for the long haul.

Roger clomped down again, this time, however, only twice and with so little force to it, so weakly, that the message it sounded seemed more like a plea than a command. When a few seconds later he met me at his door, he boldly shoved me back down a couple of steps and dramatically shut the door behind him, his pale face as sad as a mime's. He was panting. "Sam, oh Sam," he said. "You wouldn't believe what I've been going through with her." He gestured behind him.

"Try me."

"She's a . . . a . . . a Baptist," he finally managed to say. "Can you believe it, in this day and age? I mean, she believes in it all."

"That spells trouble, Roger," I warned.

"She's already informed me three times that she intends to leave all her money to the church and has recommended at least as often that I do the same, for the good of my soul. Why do I have this feeling that she thinks the sooner I go to perdition the better it will be for everyone? What a gabby woman." Roger wiped his brow with his handkerchief, his eyes blinking too rapidly. "You know what I think? I think that old bat is going to contest the will. I think she believes it's her Christian duty. Christian duty," he spat. "Can you imagine?"

I didn't try to hide my surprise. "She's read it?"

"She's reading it," Roger sighed. "She insisted."

"And what about you? Have you? Have you read it yet, Roger?"

He shook his head nervously. A lock of hair, dirty white like raw cotton, fell over one eye. He pushed it back. A truly handsome man, it occurred to me once more. "I've wanted to, Sam," he said. "Really I have. It's only . . ."

I tugged coaxingly at the sleeve of his blue dress shirt. "Only what, Roger?"

"I'm not sure. It sounds so silly to say it out loud. I've been afraid, I guess."

I took his hand gently in mine. "Afraid?"

"Of surprises. I didn't want to discover any surprises. Isn't that strange? After all these years, after forty some years of Don's and my having been together one way or another, in good times and bad, I'm still not completely sure of what it is that we were together. And wills are such absolute things. You understand. There's no going back and changing them, is there?" He glanced over my shoulder. "Isn't Charlie coming, too? I had been hoping he'd be here as well. I need all the support I can get."

Though I had been expecting it, the question nonetheless startled me. I pulled my hand back and, awkwardly shifting my body away from his, began to fall backward, grabbing for the railing. Roger caught me by the collar of my shirt and held tight until I regained my balance. "Well," he said. "I suppose that answers that question."

"Does it?"

"Yesterday, wasn't it? Yes, it must have been only yesterday. He was carrying too much out for just a trip. But I suppose I pretended not to notice. Give him a day or two more," Roger advised. "Then, if you don't hear, call him. That's what I always did with Don, the few times he left me. That's what he did with me, the one time I left him. You know where he is?"

"Not really. But I can guess. He's at Duane's, I'd bet anything. Or at some other blond's with muscles you could see rippling through his clothes."

"Maybe. But maybe not. Give him a day or two more. You boys will be fine. A day or two more is all," Roger repeated, gazing down the stairs wistfully, as if he were wishing he were waiting for someone to come back in a day or two

more. "That was all that Don ever needed when he got restless. Well." He took a deep breath. "Ready for Susan?"

"No," I said, grinding my index finger into his stomach.
He sucked it up tight.

She sat at the dining-room table, her overfed purse resting
next to her right elbow, her broad, bulging bottom spreading
out over several pillows that lifted her up closer to the document she was reading as she whistled through her teeth, her
lips moving to no word's shape, her chubby little fat-girl's
legs dangling, shoes kicked off, nearly a foot above the car-
pet. She licked the point of the pencil and laid it down, smiling as if her best friend had just entered the room. "Why,
who's that? How nice, Rog. You didn't mention anything
about company coming."

"I'm not company. I'm Sam Whitten," I said, holding out
a hand to her. "I live downstairs."

"Why, that's nice, I suppose," she said, ignoring my offered handshake and returning to the will to examine it
further. "Let's see. Donald mentioned someone who lived
downstairs to me once. From San Mateo, too, he said, over on
Thirteenth Street, just two blocks away from where we was
born, him and I and our little sis. But it wasn't you. It was . . .,"
she paged through the document, "yes, sir, here it is. I remember now. It was Charlie Roberts. Charles Simpson
Roberts, it says here. Oh, Donald was full of high praise for
this Mr. Roberts. But I guess he must have moved out," she
said to me, smiling for all the world as if I were her darling
grandchild, "because you live there now. That's what Roger
just told me was the case, wasn't it? Wasn't it, Roger? This
man lives there now."

"Yes, ma'am," I said, pleasantly enough, I thought.
"Charlie Roberts moved out."

"Isn't that just the way of the world?" she said, smiling
brightly, as if this were the sunniest thought she had had all
day. "Here today, gone tomorrow, what starts in joy, ends in

sorrow. You've got to put your trust in the Lord, Sam Whitten. My poor brother Donald didn't, don't you see, and so everything in this foolish document"—here she gave it a shake in the air—"everything in it is Roger this or Roger that except for this Mr. Roberts once and not one mention of Jesus in it at all. Not one. And He's our only salvation. Well . . ."

"'Well' what, Susan?" Roger inquired, his voice quivering, though whether from nerves or anger more, I couldn't be sure.

"Well, some things will have to be changed, I reckon." She had begun to hum the big tune from *The Blue Danube*.

"Could I fix you a drink?" Roger asked me.

"Nothing alcoholic for me," Susan sang.

"Orange juice?" Roger offered her.

"Fine, fine," Susan smacked. "A glass of cold orange juice would hit the spot."

"A jigger or two of vodka in mine, Roger," I said.

"At least," Roger agreed. Susan wrinkled her pug nose at us.

"How do you spell 'genealogy'?" she quizzed me the second after Roger had left the room.

"What?"

"How do you spell 'genealogy'?"

"G. E. N. E. A. . . ."

"Oh, heck," she said. "Most people spell it with an o. Let me ask Roger again. Roger?"

"Yes?" he called back.

"Susan wants you to spell 'genealogy' for her," I said.

"I just did fifteen minutes ago," he said, exasperated.

"Just do it, Rog," I recommended.

"G. E. N. E. O. . . ."

"You see," she said, winking at me.

"I guess I'm not 'most people' then, Susan."

"Well, neither am I. I'm a genealogist," she boasted, pronouncing the *A* with great care. "I have traced my family's history back seven generations."

"Good for you," I said.

Roger marched into the room, drinks on a tray, and sat Susan's down on a coaster next to her purse. She sniffed it to confirm that hers was the one without the alcohol. "We got rights to Texas oil property," she bragged, "if I can ever get my no-good, no-account grandson Dickie interested in it. Little Bernard, my son by my first marriage, he couldn't care less either. One day I'll be sitting pretty and they'll all be coming begging, you wait and see, though I've already been blessed beyond my hopes and dreams, amen." She began to flip back and forth through the will again until she'd found the section she wanted and reread it, humming all the while some tune that sounded remotely like "Stranger in Paradise." "You answer me this, Rog?"

"I'll try, Susan," he said from his seat way across the room near the fireplace. I was standing to his right, straddling the living room and the deck, leaning against the edge of the open glass door, watching her warily.

"What's a Greek head?" she asked, her eyes glued to the words which her fingers repeatedly underlined. "Don't it sound gory?"

I scurried over to the coffee table, put down my glass, and lifted it up to show her, stand and all. "This," I said almost proudly, holding it aloft for a few seconds and then carefully setting it back down again.

"Well, it's his," she said, without having bothered to pay it much attention.

Roger blinked once. Otherwise he didn't flinch, he didn't blanch, he didn't falter in any way. He simply quit breathing. "What?" I said.

"It's his," she said and checked the will again. "That Charles Simpson Roberts. The one from San Mateo I was recollecting Don having mentioned before. Oh, the few times we talked and yet Don always had high words for him, all right," she clicked. "I remember now Don's singing his praises, going on about how lucky he was to have such a fine neighbor. What is it, anyhow? Some kind of old art? It looks broken."

"You're kidding, right?" I said to her. "You can't be serious. I mean, you have to know how valuable this is, don't you?"

"Valuable?" She smiled at me scornfully. "Son, only your soul is valuable. Well," she sighed, as if closing up shop, "I reckon I've seen all of what I came to see. It saddens me to think on it, but I guess poor Donald is burning in hell today. He led a wicked life, and who can question the justice of the Lord? It's my duty now to make sure he gets a decent Christian burial in any case, owing to how he might have repented in the end without our knowing it. My poor brother needs at least that kindness, Roger."

"There's not going to be a burial, Susan," Roger said flatly, moving only his lips and jaw, the rest of him motionless, rigid, purple with anger.

"'Course there is."

"No, there's not. I had him cremated. Yesterday. In accordance with that will of his you supposedly have just read."

"There's not a word in it," she said. "Not a word about any cremation.

"There must be."

"Not a word. Read it yourself," Susan challenged him.

"Oh, God. Please," Roger exclaimed and covered his face. Susan blandly hummed to herself the melody of the "Emperor's Waltz," her compact out as she layered more powder on her already overpowdered face.

"We're going to scatter his ashes in the bay, Susan," I informed her, for the nasty fun of it. "Roger and I. In a few days. We're going to take Don's ashes out in a small box and dump them into the currents of the bay. You should come along."

"Please, Sam," Roger muttered, his head still in his hands.

She slid down onto the floor and effortlessly bent to pick up her shoes, which she carted over to the love seat to put on.

The Greek head caught her eye. "Heathen work. Devil work. We've been warned," she said, dismissing it at a glance. "Mind my words, the Lord chastises. I don't know why Donald wanted such a thing in his house. Do you know, Roger? It's all so puzzling."

"No," Roger said, shaking his head in a kind of amazement. "No, I don't know." He sat upright again. "You're not staying for dinner, Susan?"

"I think I've changed my mind, Rog." Her shoes back on, she heaved herself up and straightened out her dress, picking at one of the blue birds on its design as if it were a spot she was trying to remove by peeling it off. "You took my brother," she said to no one in particular, certainly not directly to Roger, neither anger nor hatred nor emotion of any other kind in her singsong voice. "And now I can't lay him to rest in that hill where Mom and Daddy and my Frank and our little sister and all the others lie so peaceful. So I guess I'll just drive on back down to Foster City." She checked her tiny gold watch. "It's getting late for a tired old woman like me. You're going to be old, too, even you," she warned me. "It's time for you to be making your case before Jesus."

"Oh, do shut up, Susan," Roger snapped, leaping to his feet.

She chose not to hear him. "You play the piano?" she asked me. She'd wandered back to the dining table to retrieve her purse and seemingly had just noticed the baby grand that stood far to the other side of it.

"No," I said, bewildered. "Why?"

"It would be so sweet to hear a little piano music now," she said. "Donald always did play the piano so sweet, don't you agree, Roger? He could have had a major concert career if he had wanted one. A major concert career. But what did he do instead but waste his God-given talent selling records of other people playing trash. Frittered his life away is what he did. It don't make any sense. I never did hear another human being who could play so sweet."

"You loved Don a lot, didn't you, Susan?" Roger offered.

She was swaying back and forth to some imagined music in her mind. "He was my baby brother. I blame that war. It took him from us and unsettled him and changed his way of thinking. He had been such a right-thinking boy. And then he was called away to fight and came back to . . . ," she looked around the room, her eyes bleary, ". . . to some other place, and none of us ever saw him again, not really. He would have been better off dead, Daddy said, killed on one of those islands. We all said so. Something bad happened to him that made us wish it. Something did." She'd found her keys. Roger opened the door for her. "Help me down, Roger," she directed, slipping her free arm into his. "These stairs frighten me." Her wandering eyes settled on me for a moment. "What you'd want with that ugly old head is more than I can under-stand," she said, clutching the railing with her other hand, her purse swinging from the crook in her arm and bumping against her bosom. They had maneuvered almost halfway down. "Why did Don give it to him anyway?"

"He didn't," Roger said.

"My brother was a strange man," Susan said.

"Yes," Roger agreed. But Susan wasn't listening. She had started to hum "Autumn Leaves," her voice pitchless and warbling, weaving back and forth over the tune like a drunk trying to walk a straight line.

"Well, at least that's over," I said to Roger to console him when, a few minutes later, he joined me out on the deck. The sky was bands of lavender, silver, lace.

"Poor Susan." Roger collapsed into a lawn chair and closed his eyes, his head sinking into his pillow.

"You feel sorry for that dotty old bitch?"

"No." He held his head between his hands as if it were throbbing beyond any relief. "Fix us both another drink, will you, Sam? A real one this time. Something brown, not too translucent, with a kick to it."

When I handed him his, he sat upright to accept it, pulling the back of the lounge up, too.

"So," I said.

"Yes."

"How are you feeling?"

"Peculiar."

"Is that all? Aren't you furious?"

"I don't know," Roger said, stretching out. "I was just thinking about that time on the Hoh River trail when you and I didn't want to cross that ledge and stayed down at Elk Lake and Charlie and Don hiked the rest of the way up to Glacier Meadows by themselves. Remember? How long were they gone? Two days? Three days? I wondered at the time why you were so unpleasant about it. It was hardly the first time they had taken off on their own. But it had never bothered me until I saw how much it was bothering you. So when we got back to the city I asked Don about it."

"And?"

"He said he loved both of you. He loved me first. And then next he loved you, meaning you and Charlie together."

"And?"

"That's all," he said easily.

"That's *all*?"

"It was enough, Sam. I didn't press him any further. Why should I? I was satisfied by what he said. It would have demonstrated a lack of trust to ask any more. You have to have faith, you see. Otherwise, it's no good."

"I see." I squinted out toward Alcatraz where the light had begun to revolve in the gradually thickening dark. I didn't see. "You're kidding yourself, Roger."

"Am I?"

"Admit it. He left the head to Charlie, Roger. He left the head to Charlie."

"Yes." He set his drained glass down on the floor. "As Susan would say, it's puzzling."

"Not to me."

"No, I suppose it isn't to you." He struggled out of the lounge chair, joined me where the deck's stairs led down into the garden, wrapped an arm around my waist, and would not let me pull away. "You know, Sam," he whispered, "Don and I always worried about you and Charlie. You were both very good companions to us, of course. We always enjoyed your company immensely. Our last ten years would have been greatly diminished without it. Yet we found you two to be very strange because, although you were both lovely boys, neither of you seemed to be able to feel anything permanent about the world. I don't know how to explain it, but try to understand that even if Don and Charlie did have some kind of fling together, which I doubt, it can't matter now, don't you see? I mustn't let it. I mustn't have wasted my life."

"Don't let him have it, Roger," I whispered back.

His fingers loosened. "It was mine. It was my gift."

"That's right," I prodded.

"Why would he have to give it away?"

"That's the question, all right."

"To Charlie?" He gazed at me through the shadows, utterly bewildered and dismal.

"To Charlie," I underlined.

"It isn't true," he said quietly.

"You were the one who didn't want to read the will. Why not? Did you know?"

"It isn't true."

"Get rid of it."

"Nothing happened."

"Get rid of it. Get rid of the head. Don't let the bastard have it."

"Nothing happened, I said."

"Sure. Get rid of it. Sink it in the bay with Don."

"Don't turn your anger on me, Sam."

"That's why Charlie moved out three days after Don died.

That's why. Why should he stay any longer? His lover was gone."

"Don't, Sam. It's nonsense. Preposterous nonsense."

"Nothing happened," I mocked.

"It didn't. I know it didn't. Don wouldn't. Neither would Charlie."

"I know all about worst fears, kiddo. They always come true. Sacrifice forty years to him and his need to be flattered. See if I care. I sacrificed only ten. What idiots we all are."

"Get out, Sam." Roger had retreated to the glass door and had already pulled it halfway closed. "Now."

I stepped onto the first stair down. "Sure. That's right. Blame it on me. Kill the messenger."

"I mean it, Sam."

"Do you want to give it to him or should I? Some lawyer's going to have to check it all out, you know. Tell him it's gone. Tell him it disappeared. That's the thing to say. Don't let Charlie have it, Roger. It's yours. Get rid of it. Sink it."

"Now, Sam."

"Drown it. What the heck? You couldn't stand to look at it again, could you?"

He slowly shook his head. "No," he said and slid the door all the way closed, backing into the room so that he wouldn't have to notice the Greek head in the place of honor where it had sat for decades.

I lay on our bed, on the guest bed, on the couch in the living room, clutching the dark. Nothing worked. I got up, turned on a lamp, rearranged books from one shelf to another, separating mine from Charlie's. One of them, a hardback Durrell, was Don's. I set it aside, then placed it on the stack with the others that I knew weren't ever mine. Some kind of pain grabbed the back of my neck and yanked on it, like a not-quite-legal wrestling hold just before a fall. I jerked on the lamp's chain to turn it off, nearly stumbling over a pile of paperbacks in the process, and fell against the wall, the cool of its plaster like smooth marble against my face.

In the hall, a sliver of light shone around the perimeter of the closet door. Charlie must have left it on yesterday. He was always leaving lights on somewhere. But why hadn't I noticed it earlier? Maybe he had been back today, too, while I was up at Roger's, though that was highly unlikely. Why would he have come back here? It didn't matter. Whenever, he had knocked over one of the boxes of letters and postcards we saved there. Or had they spilled out as he searched for one particular card or letter? That couldn't matter either. I might have done it myself, after all, and forgotten.

I picked a handful up. "Our winter was less productive than I had hoped it would be. We have been seduced by the lawn furniture. James studies his law books. The weather is blissful here. And yours?" Another: "Yesterday Delos. Tomorrow Rhodes. Then on to Turkey. Don is exhausted but looks forward to seeing his first camel caravan. So do I. Miss you two. All best." Or another: "The one hurtling off the cliff like Greg L. is mine. The one waiting his turn in the white bikini is Al's. Hi! This island's just what the doctor ordered, guys. It's like no one alive has ever been sick. Al says he could live forever. But what the hey, huh? We've had our fun." One more: "You two have got to be the best tour guides in that crazy town. Thanks for the sack space. That couch is better than my bed back home. Really! Don't apologize about the guest bed's being occupied. Actually, I got in it once. That Tom is wild. Did he tell you? It gets lonely here in Kansas. I wish I could have stayed out there for good. But I guess I'm needed where I am. Needed? Lord! Love ya."

I didn't leave right away. I flipped through several more cards, the pictures on each one like photographs taken by the same uncurious tourist's camera, always aiming for the obvious, for the cliché, so that you'd think the world was everywhere equally dull until you flipped the card over and read

the message, only to find out that instead it was merely hope-
less and sad. I tossed them all back into the box. Whatever I
was going to do, I knew I couldn't stay all night confined by
these walls. I was too angry, at Don and Charlie, of course,
but at Roger and myself as well, furious at all of us for not
being better at life than we were.

I clicked on a light in the bedroom and retrieved from the
back of my dresser's top drawer the fragment of the page
from the personals I had torn out about a month ago, on
which I'd jotted down Rick's number when he called after receiving my letter. When I phoned, Rick was surprised to hear
from me again, of course, and cool to the idea at first. But,
when I told him that Charlie and I had really split up this
time, he agreed to meet me an hour and a half later at a bar
we both knew in the Haight just a few blocks from my store.
The thought of seeing him again actually revived my spirits
for a while.

I neither changed nor showered as I usually would have. I
didn't have to. Since Charlie was gone, there was nothing I
needed to shed. Though I hopped on a bus for the middle
part of the trip through a risky part of town I didn't feel
much like braving in the night, it still took me over an hour
to get there. Rick was already in the bar when I arrived, just
as I hoped he would be. He didn't seem to recognize me at
first, but that was all right because it wasn't recognition I was
after. First he said how pissed he'd been about my having lied
to him during our first conversation on the phone. But when
I explained to him about my life now, not having to lie at all
this time, he said he guessed he understood. Then he smiled
like a man who knew he had just been lied to again, even if
only a little, and who plainly had decided he wouldn't mind.
He was used to it. We were all used to it. No big deal.

In the morning, I wandered home slowly and stopped at a
travel agent or two to check out their new brochures. There

was a special to Catalonia that looked inviting, and another to Tibet that, though still very expensive, promised the ultimate in exoticism, and a third to the Marianas that Don would have avoided at all costs, and a fourth to Great English Gardens, and a fifth for a cruise to Alaska and a sixth for another through the Panama Canal. All specials. Every place was special, every place on sale. I gathered them all up and carried them home, studying each off and on along the way, wondering what it was that Don and Roger had hoped to find by traveling. If Don knew, he never told us. I would have to ask Roger one of these days, before it was too late. Whatever it was, however, they plainly hadn't discovered it any more than Charlie and I had, because in a way they were even more restless than we were. If Charlie and I needed an occasional strange body, Roger and Don had demanded whole strange new worlds, none of which was ever quite strange enough to hold them there. So maybe it wasn't so surprising that in the end Don had settled for an ordinary faithlessness after all, just like the rest of us.

Back at the house, I knocked on Roger's door to see how he was doing, but he either wasn't home or, mad at me, didn't answer. Sitting on the stoop off the street, I watched the mailman slowly work his way up it, a buckle on the strap of his bag catching the sun and reflecting it brilliantly, like a shiny new silver dollar back when we were kids. Maybe there would be a letter from Charlie.

I perched myself eagerly on a higher step for a better view since Charlie had said recently that our new mailman was by far the best looking in the city. When I asked him how he knew, he didn't answer. "There couldn't be much competition," I said, and he responded, "Maybe not, but check him out anyway." OK, for Charlie's sake, I'd check him out. But the letter carrier passed me by, not even delivering any junk mail and carefully avoiding my eyes, as someone accidentally encountering a funeral party will avoid the eyes of the mourners, eager to get on with his business and not wanting to be implicated in their grief, however slightly. As usual, Charlie had been right. He was a babe, his calves and thighs bulging like plates of armor beneath those floppy dull gray trousers they make them wear.

But, because he hadn't opened our gate, come up the walk, mounted the steps, my life would go on just the same, unchanged. So why did each tick of my old windup wristwatch seem dimmer, until at last there were no sounds left at all? Although the chill wind off the bay quietly prickled my skin, it did so without once whistling through the gutters. Not hearing anything, not a thing, I sat there, arms wrapped around my knees, and stared happily into the silence, watching it grow steadily brighter as the sky does in mountain valleys long before you see the sun. One of the neighbor's scruffier cats scaled the front railing, slunk along the coping of the wall, pounced, and landed in my lap. I could feel it purr, I could see it meow when I yanked its stubby tail, but there was no sound.

It wasn't that I had gone deaf. I had simply chosen silence. As if by magic, I had been able to still the world, especially the raucous world of my own body, and keep it hushed for a while. I stood up, unbuckled my unwanted watch from my wrist, and read it, astonished at the time. Back inside the apartment, I dropped it into the hall wastebasket, grabbed a chair from the kitchen table, set the chair on the deck, sat down, and, wondering if blindness might be equally liberating, stared briefly up at the heavens, the whole sky in flames, all of it, save for the huge white disc at its core, burning with the clear, clean blue translucence of a Bunsen burner. In the back of my eyes, orange and red dots began to swirl and collide, battering one another, but I refused to blink.

"Don't," I could hear Don advise me as if he were actually

there. I didn't have to see him to know it was him. I could smell him and his cigarettes, and almost feel his knobby fingers grip my shoulder.

"All right," I consented, though I lowered my eyelids slowly, as if I were gradually letting down shades in a too-sunny room. The bitter, acrid odor of those French cigarettes he liked so much—the ones with the strong Turkish blend of Turkish men's sweaty pits, Roger used to joke, holding his nose—left an aftertaste in my mouth. Then all the city's shrill noises swelled up once more into my ears. It was rush hour already. How had it gotten so late? Hours must have passed. I breathed in deeply, but the air had changed again. Now it mixed dry earth, fetid water, and redwood and cedar chips with a hint of gardenia sweetness and the sour odor of too many neighborhood cats. Another cat, different from the one earlier, bounded into my lap, digging two of its claws into one knee. With a wicked swipe of my arm, I knocked it off. When it hit the brick wall, it squalled like a baby.

"Meditating?" I heard Charlie ask. "Is that what you do when I walk out on you? Sit around and meditate? That and attack cats?" Standing just inside the sliding doors I had left open, he was sweating hard, back pressed flush against the kitchen wall, the sleeve of his sport shirt ripped at the shoulder, exposing a bad bruise.

"Something like that," I said. "Who's been beating up on you, Charlie? Duane?"

"This?" He examined the spot. "I tore it on that new hook in the closet, the one with the sharp point you've been complaining about. Which of course made me lose my footing. Which made me collapse into the corner of that wardrobe of yours. So I fell. Backwards. You mean you didn't hear? You really haven't heard all the racket I've been making? I've been so noisy, chum, I might as well have been building this house all over again."

"You're moving back in then, Charlie?"

"Sure. I figured the point's been made. What the hell, huh?"

"That's nice. What point?"

He flipped something off one finger with his thumb. "The same one as always. You know. The one that says we'd better stick together because anyone else we'd choose would be that much worse. Incidentally, you certainly have been acting strangely for the last couple of hours or so. I figured it was some sort of quiet fit you were throwing for my benefit that we'd have to talk about later."

"Uh-huh. Maybe I don't want you back, Charlie."

"Of course you do, booby," he said, gnawing on a fingernail. "Nobody else would put up with you."

Roger peered over the upstairs railing. "Is that Charlie I hear?" Charlie stepped out onto our deck to offer him a little salute and a click of his heels. "Welcome home, lad. I thought I heard you hard at work down here. I just got back myself," Roger offered as he joined us, "from an important trip. A most important trip. It feels wonderful to be so free of it, much to my surprise."

"Oh? Where to, Rog?" Charlie said. A swallow landed on the head of the statue of Eros that stood as if to pee in the middle of the dry birdbath. The swallow immediately flew off again so that another could pause briefly after it on the same spot. Once the second had departed, it was followed by a third. While I waited for the fourth, Roger positioned a white wrought-iron lawn chair at almost exactly ninety degrees to my left, much closer to Charlie.

"So, welcome home," Roger said to him again. Crossing one leg over another, he fixed the crease in his trousers.

"Thanks," Charlie said, blushing. "I'm sorry, Roger. Please forgive me. It was a lousy time for me to have run out on you. I guess I just got scared there for a couple of days. Certain . . . problems between me and Sam came to a boil. I had to go away and think."

"I understand," Roger said. "I really do quite understand." There was a sharp, slightly rusty edge to his voice though. He two-fingered a cigarette from his shirt pocket and lit it. It was one of Don's cigarettes and he lit it with Don's lighter. "Yes, you needn't tell me, I know," he said, acknowledging our stares, "it's an odd time in my life to start so disgraceful a habit. But it comforts me. I thought of it last night after our discussion, Sam, and it comforted me some. There are so many little things that I didn't like about Don, which now, of course, I find myself missing. Remember that, you two. Sometimes what you disliked, even hated, is no easier to lose than what you've admired or loved. It makes it no easier to sleep recalling one more than the other."

Charlie reached to pick a pebble from the ground and pitched it into the pond where it hovered, suspended in green scum for several seconds before it sank. "We must clean that soon," Roger suggested, "and buy some new goldfish. It would be nice for the spring."

Extinguishing one cigarette, Roger lit another. "I don't inhale. I'm afraid to inhale."

"That's good," Charlie said.

"Don always inhaled. Deeply. He did everything deeply. Don Profondo, I called him. Did you know that?"

"Yes. I think so," Charlie said.

"That was Don. If you're going to fight, really fight. If you're going to love, really love. If you're going to smoke, really smoke. So he smoked like a fiend."

"Say. Isn't that one of Don's sweaters you're wearing?" Charlie observed. "I've never known you to wear bright red before, Roger. It looks good on you, really good. You should keep it up. Very sexy."

"Do you think so?" Roger said. "I suppose I've always been too conservative. Don always complained that I was too conservative, that I should take more chances, more risks. And I thought maybe I should put his things to some use.

Just a few things, of course. I'll give a lot away. I'm making a list. But I've always liked this old sweater. It's Italian."

"It looks Italian," Charlie said, admiring it some more. "It has that flair."

"But I won't give everything away," Roger insisted.

"No, not everything," Charlie said. "Why should you?"

I shivered. In the shade, the air had become cool and damp. Overhead, several flocks of swallows were flitting this way and that seemingly without direction or purpose, like radarless bats, beating their wings all the more furiously, I surmised, because there was no sense to it.

"Not the Greek head, for instance," Roger said, that dangerous cutting edge returning to his voice. "Not that. I've taken care of that." He took a puff, long, leisurely, and pointed, and would glance neither to his left nor to his right. We were both being told something. Charlie started to speak, hesitated, and looked away uneasily.

"Look behind you," Roger said to Charlie, who sat hunkered on the bricks. "How beautiful even the shabbiest of our westward facades become at sunset. They seem to be clutching at these last rays of light like some miser his gold, just as it's to be taken from him. It's why we go to museums, Don used to say. To get some of that lost gold back, the lost gold of the sun. Don was a wonderful traveler. Well, you know that. You can appreciate that, how well he saw everything. He was the most impartially curious man I've ever known."

"Yes," Charlie acknowledged.

"Don Impavido, Cecille would call him. I've missed her so much these last few days, regretting all the more the rupture that both Don and I felt was nearly unhealable between her and us after she married her second husband, a piously conventional man who couldn't help expressing his disapproval of us in numerous petty ways. Don Intrepido was another of Cecille's names for Donald. I especially liked that. Don Intrepido."

"What about Don Giovanni?" I scoffed.

"What is your problem exactly?" Charlie said to me.

"Hardly," Roger said. "No. Don was no Don Juan. To me he was pure pleasure, a fine lover, but he was no Don Juan and he knew it." The night had blackened the lines on his face and deepened them so that it appeared Roger was wearing a mask that, as he smiled, turned comic, a satyr's mask strangely befitting him.

Charlie had taken a cushion from a deck chair and was leaning back upon it, propped against the pond's brick wall, an unopened six pack next to him. When had he brought the beer out to the garden? What was happening to my ability to observe things? Did all men become handsomer, like Charlie, in the dark of night and shadows? If so, did that explain why Don liked black marble best? Something deep inside of me had finally started to hurt.

"Charlie," I called to him. He grinned and pitched a can over to me, carrying another to Roger. I opened mine gingerly, spilling none.

"Rog?" he prompted. "You said you took care of the Greek head. What did you mean, 'took care of it'? Because Don wanted me to . . ."

"Please," Roger interrupted him, holding his hand up as if to warn him to stop. "Let me finish what I have to say first." With the toe of his shoe, he squashed his cigarette into the ground like a hated snail. "You see, Charlie, I just got around to reading Don's will last night. Sam already knows all about it in a way. I'd been putting it off and putting it off because the prospect of reading it frightened me. You'll know what I mean some day if you're the one that's left. But once his ineffable sister Susan had perused it, I felt compelled to do so myself at once. And of course she was completely wrong about the cremation. There it was, all spelled out quite clearly, just as Don told me," Roger said to me without taking his primary attention from Charlie. "That woman is either dinghier than I thought or crazed by religion. But about the Greek head, which she had no personal interest in, she was nonetheless exact. And I don't understand it. I simply can't understand it, Charlie. Can you? You do know what I'm talking about, don't you? You must."

Charlie flipped his empty can into the open trash barrel hidden under the upstairs deck. "About the head? I know that Don left it to me to take care of, if that's what you mean. Is there something else I'm supposed to understand, Roger? Because, if there is, I don't . . ."

"I'll be plainer then. The question is this. Did you or did you not have an affair with Don, as Sam so cruelly insinuated last night? Or is 'insinuate' too benign a word for what you did, Sam? Explain it to me. Why did he leave it to you, Charlie? It was the possession of ours we both loved most, our symbol and his most precious gift to me. Yet he left it to you. Why? I have to ask. I have to ask, Charlie," he pleaded.

"Of course you have to. It's my fault. It's all my fault, Roger," Charlie apologized quietly. "I should have come to you first. Days ago. Right away. You see, Don didn't trust you."

"Didn't trust me? Of course he trusted me. I never gave him the slightest reason not to . . ."

"I don't mean it in that way, Rog," Charlie said.

"Then how?"

"Yes, how?" I interjected.

"Oh, do be quiet, Sam," Roger said. "You've done enough harm. Please, Charlie. How?"

"He didn't trust you to give it back," Charlie said, casually popping the top on another can and setting it aside to dry his hands off on the front of his shirt. "He told me what he was going to do a couple of years ago, that time he and I went on up to Glacier Meadow and left you guys behind at that lake. He swore me to secrecy, of course, because he knew how you'd resist the idea. Don't you see, Roger? For three and a half decades, Don apparently felt guilty for stealing that thing, for having taken it from its own soil and secluded it here in this house so far away from where it belonged among all those other beautiful things the Greeks had made in Italy. He didn't want you to know, Rog, but he longed to send it back. That was to be my job only because he said you loved it too much. You understand? You loved it too much. So did he, almost as much as you did. That's why he knew he'd never get enough nerve to do it himself. And he wouldn't ask Sam over there because he figured Sam would probably just go ahead and hold onto it, pissed that anyone should have to give anything up. Don said he knew I'd do it if he asked me since he believed I didn't cling to things. I don't think he meant that as a compliment, Roger. It was just something he'd observed, like he knew you'd never read his will until you absolutely had to.

"I have the address and all the instructions written down in my desk at the office at school. I thought I'd lost them, but I found them last evening when I snuck in here while you two were upstairs talking.

"Please don't worry, Roger. It's yours to keep until, well, you know . . . I mean, all this I'm telling you now isn't written out in the will because Don only wanted to make sure it got done some day, that's all. And he thought that meant I'd have to be made the head's legal owner. He knew I'd explain everything to you. It was only that my timing was off, I should have been here to tell you. Don said he would rest easier knowing that it would find its way home eventually. I promised him I'd see to it. That's all. So," Charlie said, slapping his hands together. "That's the story, Rog. Believe it."

Roger stood up, his back cracking, and walked cautiously toward the stairs like an old man, the gentle breeze after sunset blowing his hair about so that it glittered like sea grass in the moonlight. He reached for the handrail and grabbed it firmly. "I do believe you, Charlie," he said softly. "I believe you and I believe Don. It's so strange. This afternoon, I was so maddened by jealousy, I packed it up in a crate all by my-self and drove it to the parcel service, and shipped it back to that museum in Italy. I didn't want you to have it, you see. Better them than you. So I don't blame Sam, despite all his unfortunate insinuations. Not really, no more than Othello could blame Iago. The doubt was in me, the anger was in him, the two matched almost perfectly. That's all.

"Don would be laughing now, that great belly-walloping laugh of his I always found so sexy. He would be enjoying it, the irony of it, I'm sure. It happens only rarely, but some-times worst things can come to good in the end. It's our one hope. Good night, gentlemen," he said, waving at us both. "I'm very tired all of a sudden. We'll talk more tomorrow?"

"Roger!" I stopped him. "I'm so sorry. I . . ."

"Yes," he accepted. "Good night. Oh, only one thing more," he said without turning around again. "Did it ever strike you as odd, Charlie, that Don thought the head was his to give back? Well, never mind. Good night once more."

Charlie and I stood opposite one another, waiting, as we had so often waited, for the glass doors above to slide closed. "I'm sorry for so much," I said to him.

"Yes. I know," Charlie said. "So am I." He pointed up-stairs. "Our voices carry. We should go inside. Come on inside now, Sam. Come help me finish my unpacking."

The following Sunday, the three of us poured Don's remains into the bay, each taking his turn holding the ciborium-shaped vase as, once the rented boat was safely stabilized, we scattered the ashes into water and wind. The night before the weather had soured, and it stayed bad all morning, the clouds immediately overhead dirty gray and feathery as a pigeon's wings, the bay's water surging up over the gunwale cold and bitter, the boat rising and falling over and under surprisingly high swells. But none of us was sick. We were too sad to be sick for so little reason.

As we coasted back into the marina, though, the sky cleared and the sun shone brightly once more. While we had been on the water, Roger had retained his composure, but the minute both his feet touched land again, he collapsed into Charlie's arms, sobbing. After we'd driven him home, we brought him a brandy in a warmed snifter on a silver tray and talked to him about his plans for a trip to the Dordogne next summer. We offered to go along. He listened politely to our enthusiasm and smiled and said, No, no, no. It wouldn't do. It was time for him to be alone now. He thought he'd sell the house and move to an apartment somewhere out in the Richmond, a smaller place, easier to keep up and closer to his school. He wondered if we'd like to buy the house. But Charlie and I couldn't afford it, we said, and our future together— this came out almost in unison—was simply too much in doubt. Roger smiled, his kind way of acknowledging that he knew better than we how doubtful or sure it was.

Charlie and I helped put him to bed and spent the rest of the afternoon and evening in his apartment looking through photograph albums we'd never seen before, which Roger had been reviewing the previous night.

"Let me see that first book again," Charlie said to me. I passed it to him. "You know," he said, studying several early photos, "Don was right. Roger really did look like that Greek head when he was young. What a beauty. And so serene."

"I wonder if he really gave it back," I said, "or if he only hid it some place where he can look at it whenever he wants to."

"You're joking, right? Of course he did. Of course he sent it back. Roger doesn't lie."

"I wouldn't have," I said. "Don was right about that."

"Me neither," Charlie laughed. "Or maybe I would have. I don't know. I did promise him."

Back in the bedroom, Roger cried out Don's name once, then again. Charlie rushed in to check on him. When he returned to the living room, he was crying a little, his cheeks flushed and damp. "He's still asleep," he said, "all squeezed over on one side of the bed as if Don were still lying next to him. It's good that he's going back to work tomorrow."

"Yes," I said. "Very good. Pass me that album with the green binding, would you, Charlie? Look," I showed him. "We're not in this one either. And this was Baja."

"Let me see," Charlie said, taking the book from me, flipping through the pages himself, as surprised as I had been.

As we moved from album to album again, what unfolded before us with increasing clarity was the joy of Don and Roger's life together, each trip, each special event, each important occasion carefully documented by the camera, as if to suggest that some day its meaning, not apparent at the time perhaps, would be discovered by people like Charlie and me. And yet Charlie and I seldom showed up in the pictures of the last ten years. We found ourselves in some of them, of course, and it was obvious that Charlie or I had taken many. But we agreed that we thought there should have been more, that we remembered having posed for many more, and wondered in whispers what had happened to them.

"My Faithless, Faithful Friend"

I COULD USE A REAL FRIEND, someone who knows me better than I know myself, who could tell me about my life and help me understand better whether what I've done was good or bad. "You try to be a good person," Jay said to me that July Fourth we spent together in Laguna Beach over twenty years ago, "but, like most people, you just can't face things as they are."

"And you can?" I answered him.

"A soldier has to, Todd. There's nothing more real than war. Except some music maybe. Maybe."

"Vietnam's changed you," I said.

"It's changed everyone."

"It's made you a snob, Jaybird."

"Has it? Sorry."

"I do try to be a good person, Jay," I insisted.

He looked directly at me. His remarkable eyes, though unprotected by sunglasses, didn't have to squint beneath the blazing noon sun. "Try harder. You're my best friend, Todd. I love you like a brother. But you act sometimes as if the world were a place we'd all just made up."

Maybe so. But I wonder if Jay ever understood how hard I've struggled to live up to what he expected of people, especially his friends and lovers. Just this morning I was considering how I wouldn't be able to stand myself or bear being alive one second longer if I felt that the worst of what Larry believed about me had been true, true about what Larry would call my soul. He told me once he believed my soul was in serious danger.

For at least ten years now, all funerals, like the very old or the very sick, have come to look and sound the same to me. I've tried to pitch in and do my part. I delivered food, cleaned houses and apartments, sat up all night with the dying and held their hands. I drove them to see a waterfall, a redwood grove, or a field full of poppies one last time. I took care of their pets afterward, just as I'd promised, and found them good homes. Yet my heart wasn't really in it. And I knew they knew my heart wasn't in it. Why else did none of them ever leave requests that my name be mentioned or my deeds be remembered at his funeral or memorial service?

I was so disturbed by this gap between what I meant to be and how I was seen by others, made evident to me again by the failure of my name to be mentioned during the service for Patrick Hanrahan, that after it, head down, I smashed right into the back of a man who was walking out of the church. "Sorry," I muttered, passing around him on his left.

His arm reached out to pull me back. "Todd?" When I turned around I saw it was Kit Major. "I didn't know you were a friend of Pat," he said. "You look really upset."

Outside, the sun was so bright on the stoop we both put on our sunglasses. "I am upset," I said. "He was a client. Awful word, isn't it? For a few months. I don't think we quite clicked. He wanted solace, the spiritual kind. It's not a comfort I have to give. I think I ought to stop doing this work for a while. Recharge my batteries. You two were friends?"

"Once upon a time." Kit followed the arc of a plane flying overhead. "We lost touch. Years ago."

"Lost touch? Oh, I see. Boyfriends."

"Sort of. For a while. Long before I met Jay. How is Jay, Todd? No one I know ever hears from him anymore. I suppose that's deliberate."

"I bet he's ready to see you by now," I said. "So many years have passed since you went your separate ways. Not even Jay can stay angry forever. Indignant, yes. But not angry."

He shook his head. "He ordered me out of his life. It hasn't always been easy, but I mean to stay out. Jay can be a strict enforcer of the law, Todd. You should know that as well as anyone."

"Maybe it's time for you to disobey his laws. I do it all the time. He's dying, Kit."

"Damn." He kicked the toe of his shoe hard against the cement. "God damn it to hell."

"What was the last piece the organist played, do you know?" I asked. "It was touching. You could see how everyone was moved by it."

"Jay would have known. He'd be able to tell us like that," Kit said, snapping his fingers.

"I wonder, Kit. Do you think it's all Jay's responsibility? Or do you ever blame yourself for the silence between you two?"

"That's not a question I think you should be asking, not unless you want to hear yourself included in the answer, Todd," he shot back and, thrusting his fists into his suit pants' pockets, stomped off.

Watching him vanish around the corner of Eighteenth Street, I remembered having brunch in a patio restaurant on Castro with him one Sunday when Jay was in L.A. on business for his firm, a little more than seven years ago. Once Jay introduced me to him, I knew I would have traded a year or more with any of my exes for an afternoon's romp with Kit Major. He sat back in his chair, his legs crossed, his hands clasped behind his head like an executive at his desk making a decision, and stared at me with those famous eyes of his—blue like the water in a Hockney painting of a pool you want to strip off all your clothes and dive into. Beautiful men always make me feel an ache deep inside I have to defend myself against.

"These little cotton candy pom-poms," I said, flicking my forefinger against one that dangled from a spoke of the umbrella that was shading us, "remind me of my family's summer home on Hilton Head. We used to stick lots of umbrellas just like this one in a row down the beach to the water so we could walk all the way to the ocean always in shade."

"Last time you told that story you said the house was on Pawley's Island."

I twisted around to find the waiter so I could ask for the check. "Did I? You've got a good memory, Kit."

"Better than yours. A person needs to keep the details of his stories consistent. It makes them more believable."

"I'm sure you're right," I said, blushing furiously. Yet what I had been telling him earlier about working to win the vote for the Negroes in my hometown was true. I had saved the old Spring Willow newspapers to prove it.

"Jay says you're really a cracker, Todd. Sort of white trash."

I attempted a sip of my iced tea. "Jay should know."

"It's nothing to be ashamed of. I don't mind. Really. In fact, that hearty redneck look of yours kind of turns me on." He smiled at me in a way that seemed meant to inform me he hadn't really minded all that much a lot of things I'd said or intimated, that afternoon or earlier.

"Jay's my best friend," I protested feebly.

"Yeah," he said, grinning like a cat. "I know."

Kit and I together betrayed Jay only that once and never said a word to anyone about it. No one, not even Larry, knew for a fact that anything had happened between us. Once was too often, of course. And for Kit there were other lapses, some more public than others. Sometimes I felt so much guilt for what he and I had done to Jay that each time Kit strayed again it might as well have been with me. What had Kit ever really felt for me? I found myself disturbingly wondering all over again as, after Pat's funeral, I hiked over the hill to my store to fetch the old photograph of Toscanini I'd found and saved to give Jay. "He wasn't worth it. He isn't worth this pain," I recalled Jay almost shrieking at me just a few days after he'd ordered Kit out of his life for good.

"That's what the Trojans said about Helen," I reminded him.

"He gave me his word he wouldn't, that he wouldn't again." Jay had started to sob, as much from rage as grief.

"He loved you, Jay," I said, wanting to comfort him. "I know he did.

"I'm not going to take him back this time," Jay announced to me proudly.

"I'm not saying you should. Just don't confuse what Kit has done with a lack of love, because that would be unfair to him. Believe me, I know what I'm talking about." But I don't think Jay heard a word of what I was saying.

Photograph in hand, I climbed back over the hill to Jay's place and mostly managed to put these old thoughts about Kit out of my head, relieved to be rid of them. I don't know why, after all those months of Larry's being at Jay's almost night and day, I still expected to knock on Jay's door and have someone else answer it. As soon as the first KS lesions appeared on Jay's face and back, Larry appointed himself Jay's guardian, protector, custodian, lay nurse, and interpreter. It was clear to everyone except Jay that inside him Larry had already lit Jay's perpetual flame and in everything he did he bore witness that he would never let it die. A man's bewilderment, especially if it were a matter of the soul, always attracted Jay, and no one appeared to be more bewildered than Larry. Having dropped his dog collar on the altar of the Church of the Celestial Snooze, as Larry called it, he flew to San Francisco the next day. A month later, he discovered his new reason for living was standing next to Jay at The Stud.

Larry invariably claimed not to remember my having been there too, standing on Jay's other side. Since Larry wasn't my type at all, I didn't try to hear his story over the dance music. Jay had just graduated from Hastings, having enrolled after his last tour in Vietnam. Like Larry, he was starting a different life. From the first moment, Larry adored him as fervently as a disciple worships his savior and distrusted anyone who had been among the chosen before his conversion, accusing them of a lack of ardor. Once Larry learned that, of all his many friends, I had known Jay the longest and best, he suspected heresy in me most of all.

Larry cracked the door open, blocking the entrance with his broad body. "He's sleeping," he whispered. "He's having a rough day."

"I hear music, Larry."

"You know he sleeps to music."

"Larry," I said, forcing my way in.

"Why don't you ever call first?"

"Calm down, Larry."

"Michael and I could have used some help on Saturday, Todd, when we brought him home from the hospital. Where were you then?" he grumbled. He fastened the chain back on the door behind us. "What's that you're carrying in the envelope? Did you remember the note paper?"

I slapped my palm against my forehead. "No. Christ, I'm sorry, Larry."

"You carry stationery at that store of yours, don't you?"

"I promise I'll write myself a reminder," I said, escaping down the hall.

With the door open, Jay was lying on the covers of his unmade bed, wearing only the bottoms of the bright blue pajamas he'd always favored. Though darkly hairy as ever, his once-strong chest had sunken into his rib cage. The lesions might have been stamped on his skin with the ink used to imprint the grade on meat. "Larry said you were sleeping."

"Not really. You're dressed in mourning again. Whose?"

"No one you knew."

"Where's Larry?"

"In the kitchen, I think."

"The man's a saint," Jay said, settling deeper into his mound of cushions and pillows. "Really. I don't deserve him."

"Here," I said, handing him the picture. "I thought you'd like it. It was in a glitzy frame I bought from a dealer in Menlo Park. I've replaced it with one of those pictures of Lawrence Welk playing his accordion that sells any frame you put it in. I'm very grateful to Mr. Welk."

"Thanks," Jay said, examining it. "I saw him conduct once, you know."

"Lucky for you."

"Not Welk, asshole. Toscanini. My father took me when I was just a little boy. I remember sitting way in the back of the balcony at Carnegie Hall and listening to Beethoven. I don't know how he afforded it. Maybe someone gave him the tickets. But my father worshiped Beethoven. And Toscanini."

"What's this music you've got on now, Jaybird? It sounds depressed."

"It is depressed. It's Strauss's *Metamorphosen*. He was very, very old when he wrote it. A way I'll never be. He composed it right after the war, when so much he loved had been devastated, a whole culture blown to bits, thank God. Why should I care what a man so unmindful of real horror feels about the death of his precious *heil'ge deutsche Kunst* as that monster Wagner called it? Yet I find it unbearably moving. My father used to say that while he was fighting in the Pacific he missed only his wife and Beethoven. I think I know better now what he must have meant."

"My father was an orderly in a hospital in Charleston during the war because, when he was sixteen, he'd accidentally shot off three of his toes hunting for possum. He'd stand on the hospital roof at night and scan for enemy planes. He bragged that he'd seen and reported fifteen. But he never saw one."

"I remember how in college you used to say he fought in North Africa against Rommel. Beat him, too."

"Of course. Why wouldn't I make up a story like that? Your father was a real war hero with pictures and medals to prove it. I wanted you to like me. I always ended up telling you the truth, didn't I? In every way that matters, Jay, I've always been honest with you."

"Right. For nearly all fours years of college I believed you'd gone to some fancy prep school. Woodberry something."

"Didn't I show you my Spring Willow Hootin' Holler yearbooks eventually?"

"Only after I'd found them hidden under the bed. And later. All those stars you claimed you slept with. What about them?"

"You wanted to believe it too, Jaybird."

"I've never understood this need in you to be admired," Jay said, "to be envied."

"It's only human," I said, "to want life to be more exciting than it is."

Without a word of forewarning, Larry carried in a tray with three steaming mugs on it, pushed aside a pile of dirty clothes with his elbows, and set it on top of the dresser. Why did this interruption irk me so? Without thinking, I blurted out, "I saw Kit this morning."

When Larry offered him a mug of hot chocolate, Jay squiggled his nose and shook his head. "No thanks, Larry. I threw up again just a half hour ago. I need to give my stomach a rest."

"He'd like to see you," I continued. "I'm sure of it."

"I doubt it. In any case, I don't want to see him," Jay said. "Not ever again. Is that clear, Todd?"

"Jay wouldn't be sick today if it wasn't for Kit Major and his philandering," Larry declared to me as if it were a fact so indisputable I wouldn't dare challenge it.

Jay effortfully twisted his body toward me and scratched a scab on his forehead. "How did he look?"

"Terrific. As usual. Stunning, in fact."

Jay groaned. Larry said, "It isn't fair."

"I wish I could have been more like the Marschallin," Jay said. "Offered my sad but wise 'Ja, ja,' and let him enjoy his Sophie. But I had to make a fuss. I had to yell and scream and break things."

"You loved him," I said. "You still love him."

"No, he doesn't," Larry said. "Kit wasn't worth Jay's love. He was always too busy checking everyone else out to see how lucky he was."

Jay said, "The last face I'll see in my mind's eye as I'm leaving this Earth will probably be Kit's. What a waste of my last moment that will be." He nibbled at the loose skin at the end of his thumb and held his hands out palms up into a patch of afternoon light that fell from the window. "You know how people used to say that the fingernails of the dead keep growing after their demise? What really happens is the skin shrinks back exposing more of the nail. I'm tired, Todd. You'd better go."

I checked my watch. "You're in a morbid mood today, Jaybird."

"What sort of mood should I be in?"

"Rumor has it that it helps to be hopeful."

"Rumor also has it, Todd, that the best orgasm a man will ever experience is at his hanging."

I bent over to kiss his forehead that for weeks had tasted salty as sea water. "I'll see you soon."

"Any last words for me?" Jay challenged.

"I'll remember the writing paper the next time."

"Notice how cagey they all are," Jay said to Larry. "They'll say anything to avoid saying 'Get well.'"

I stepped backward toward the door. "I like where you've moved my favorite photograph."

Jay rolled away from me to face it. "I wanted it where I could see it better."

"I'll be back in a day or two," I said, leaving quickly, not expecting either Larry or Jay to answer.

That photograph was the first thing of Jay's I remember seeing, hung prominently displayed over his desk in the dorm room we were to share for four years. His father had taken it during what Sol Jacobs proudly referred to as "his war" while he was part of the Second Marine Division on Saipan in 1944. A smooth, putty-colored sky hovers over a jagged sliver of land that juts out into a bay where ships float on a wire-thin horizon. The shore line is flat, jagged, sandy, and weed-infested. Naked boys, perhaps twenty or so, bathe in the water or wash their clothes. One scrubs a squatting boy's hair. Another, kneeling in the sand, pounds his pants clean. Behind him, one soldier, crouched over, presses his elbows against his upper thighs while another swings his pants to dry them in the air. They are young, lean, tanned, their hair uniformly close cropped in the marine manner.

I once asked Jay's father whether he'd taken the picture before or after the big battles. He said he couldn't remember. But Jay later admitted his father could remember well enough. He just didn't want to talk about it outside of family.

Yet the scene he had captured seemed to me to be a kind of idyll as blissful as a dream, free of all horror. I would stare at it and think inside its world was everything I had ever wanted or would want. The way Jay gazed at it made me wonder then if he also desired what I had seen in it, though after Vietnam he never looked at it in the same way again.

Jay maintained that he volunteered for Nam because he loved his father and what his father had fought for. Sure, Sol had been called *Jew boy*, *yid*, and *kike* while he fought. But words like that, he had assured his son, would vanish in the future. This country, he declared to me when I had attacked it during the early years of the war in Vietnam shortly before Jay signed up, this country is good and decent. "Sure it is fal-

lible," he had said during a dinner I was sharing with Jay's
family in their tiny apartment in Brooklyn. "Sure it makes
mistakes, its leaders lie. Plenty of them. Look at the Rosen-
bergs. But its heart means well and is generous and full of
promise. It's only bad luck that has kept me down. But my
son Sherman is going to make it. Sherman is going to fulfill
our dream," he said, beaming.

"I didn't know your father still called you 'Sherman,'" I
remarked to Jay.

Jay just smiled the way people say cats smile—the way,
much later, I would see Kit smile, too—and cut deeper into
his fish. "It'd kill me if anything bad happened to that boy,"
his father said.

I kept thinking of that picture during the first weekend
Jay and I spent together after he'd gotten back from his last
tour in Nam. We wrote to each other a lot while he was away,
each of us telling the other things, true things, we'd never
had the nerve to say face to face when we were in college.
We'd agreed to meet in Laguna where I'd heard all the pretty
boys from West Hollywood, Westwood, Malibu, and the
like—those who most wanted and deserved to be seen—
migrated in flocks for the Fourth of July. By Sunday, there
must have been nearly a thousand or more men squeezed together within one acre of bar and beach where the canyon
road runs perpendicular to the coast highway. The sun was
pounding inside through every window and door and gleaming outside like a heavenly spotlight on each body, singling
out each perfection in turn, as if everyone in that miraculous
crowd were alive only to be gawked at, pointed to, praised,
pursued like some rare and beautiful tropical bird that flashes
wonderfully across the sky. As we stood knee high in the Pacific wearing only the briefest of bathing suits and bent over
to splash cold water on our bodies, I turned to Jay and said,
"I feel like I've walked into that photograph of your father's."

He looked over at me and did not try to conceal his exas-

peration. "You don't know anything about it," he said and
headed back to the bar without me.

How many of those Laguna boys are still alive and now,
like me, middle aged? The plague is our war, I said to Jay before he fell sick, but he shook his head "no," though without
getting mad. Those astonishing bodies from the past, whatever has become of them, are like a snapshot in my mind.
Since the light in those days was much too bright for any
image to come out totally sharp and clear, they were fuzzy as
if already a little faded even when they were new. But for a
few hours that weekend I felt a happiness so piercing that I
repeatedly had to remind myself that it wouldn't last.

Maybe that weekend was the best moment of my and Jay's
life together, not that we did so much that deserved to be
memorable. Heads bent down, we explored the beaches and
searched for bits and pieces of plastic buckets, chunks of life
preservers, handleless children's scoops and shovels, deflated
beachballs, split Frisbees, patches of shredded beach blankets, combs, goggle straps, wooden or plastic chips from
beach chairs, any human detritus. Once the boxes we were
carrying were full, we marched to the nearest green waste
cans and poured it all in. One lifeguard, thinking we were
part of a cleaning patrol, complimented us on our good work.

Jay built the most elaborate, yet tiny, sandcastle I'd ever
seen, constructing its ramparts and keeps from minuscule
shell fragments and its drawbridge from driftwood slivers.
He named it "Castle Obsequious." As a dune buggy full of
kids passed us on the left, one of them tossed us a beer from
their cooler and skirted around us, throwing up sand. Even
absorbed by his work on the castle, Jay caught the can on the
wing. I lay on the beach as the sun burned white on white
sand and felt my flesh sweat itself clean. When the rays
pierced me hot as metal, I sat up and rested my chin on my
knees, my hands gripping my ankles, as the sun slowly refined away everything in the forge of my body except that

pure molten desire which all the rest of that long afternoon my eyes poured into the mold of every beautiful boy who passed by. But to me none of them was more beautiful than Jay had become since his return.

He glanced up from where he was working, breaking my stare. "Don't look at me like that, Todd. What I need from you is friendship. Just like always. Especially now."

"But I'll always be your friend, too. It wouldn't change anything. We can always return to normal. I promise."

"No. I don't want sex to confuse things between us ever."

That night, exhausted from so many hours spent under the sun, we lay separated by the space between our beds, and he talked to me about the war. Except for certain inadvertences, he'd never mention it again. "My father had this workroom in the basement of the building where we lived. It was small and grungy, but he liked it there because it was his place, just his. When I was seven or so, he started to take me there sometimes when he was working. He'd plop me down in a corner to watch him work and expect me to be still.

"In that corner were three things: a galvanized pail, a tin basin, and a cracked dish containing a lump of yellow soap. I played with them, pretty much contented until I started to bang the basin against the pail. I was a strong little son of a gun and made a terrible racket. So he swatted me one across the face for being not so much disobedient, I think, as disrespectful. That's what I remember best of my father from those days. A pail, a basin, a dish, a piece of soap, and a smack across the lips.

"I think now I probably can guess why he hit me so hard. There are noises that never used to bother me that I can't stand anymore, Todd-a-o. Like trucks backfiring or those cherry bombs exploding outside in all this celebrating. What's there to celebrate? Jay the patriot, what a laugh. That's why I couldn't hang around in that bar any longer with all those guys preening, all the blood rushing out of their brains into their dicks. They don't know yet that the body won't ever forget anything that happens to it. I still can't sit comfortably with my feet crossed, one foot facing another person, because I was told the Vietnamese regard it as a high insult. I won't write anything except in black ink because the Corps allowed only black ink. You've seen how I walk as if the next step I take will be my last, my eyes having missed that trip wire or piece of vine or thread of spider webbing that sets off the booby trap.

"The worst enemy were the mines. I saw boots with the leg in it shredded at the knee, a buddy ripped open from the top of his head to the tips of his toes, forty-seven holes in him bleeding everywhere. Once you've wandered the corridors of the First Hospital Company in Chu Lai you no longer believe in the Earth's ability to keep from exploding. Another buddy's brains splattered all over my nose and cheeks and when I touched my face the gray pudding dribbled onto my fingers. I saw pigs rooting among corpses charred by napalm. While I was watching white phosphorous shells set fire to a village, I tripped into a ditch with bamboo stakes crisscrossing it and would have been impaled if Steve Compton hadn't caught me as I fell. Chickens were squawking, water buffalo bawling, pigs squealing. I started to scream.

"When I woke up the next morning, the sun shone like a bandage over my eyes. I got drunk and smoked so much grass that the world started to reel like the wheel of a wreck flung high into the air by the force of a collision. I felt good, the way it made me feel good to know I'd gotten used to the smell of burning shit and the stench of feces and lime in a latrine. I'd gotten accustomed to waste. Why should death matter in a world of waste?

"A couple of days later I got thrown temporarily into Long Binh jail, busted with some crazy clown from the Black Berets who'd told me some stories that were the last things I wanted to hear. But what the VC and the North Vietnamese were doing was worse. Protest all you want to, Todd-a-o. But maybe some day I'll tell you the true story. It felt better in jail. Not safer. It wasn't safety I was after. Just better. Right somehow."

He stopped and checked his watch in the orange glow of the light from outside our motel room. "Go on," I urged him. "You want to talk, talk. I'm listening."

"No. That's enough. Let's get some shut-eye." But neither Jay nor I slept that night.

The next day, as we drove the Ventura Freeway north to San Francisco, past shining chrome office buildings, past the crystalline glassiness of shopping centers, past the broken-mirror glitter of high rises flickering in the sun, we played a game we had invented during college and called "Name that Color." I pointed to a house, perched contentedly on a hilltop.

"Cape Cod brown," he said.

Then he indicated another house a little further on. "Just the trim?" I asked. He nodded. "Petal pink and frosted mint. Now it's my turn. The mission-style one."

"I assume you want just the trim around the taffy stucco?"

"That's right."

"Buttercup and fudge. Now you. How about the roof of that gas station?"

"Rose beige. The posts are faded antique green. Turn around quick. See the Caddy at the pump?"

"Lilac, with an orange sherbet roof, recently repainted. How about the van up ahead?"

"The ivory gray one?"

"Nope, that's way too easy. I meant the one in the left lane. The one tailgating the Creamsicle Toyota."

"Toasted almond."

He squinted. "Maybe. More like butterscotch."

"And the two rear panels."

"Easy. Canary yellow," Jay said.

Playing our old game again was my way of telling him I was happy he was back, and his way of saying he was happy to be back. We were like kids on a field trip excitedly yelling out the number of cows they'd counted in the passing countryside, their attention given completely to the present. For the present was where we had silently promised each other the night before to try to live for the rest of our lives. The problem was that I really did believe in that present. Jay didn't. He remembered and hoped for too much. He always would, even as he lay dying.

As I left Jay's house, I sensed Larry watching me from the yard where he'd gone out to water the garden or to perform some other chore. The air shimmered gently, not quite gathering into a breeze, an iridescent lavender seeping through the sky's rich iris blue. Throughout Jay's garden, which Larry and Mike had managed to keep up—front, side, and back— golden poppies glowed, scattered in patches like weeds. Fuchsias and camellias bloomed. Bougainvillea bloomed, spreading across the roof and over fences and through trellises. Roses, peach, amber, ruby, or honey colored, bloomed. Scotchbroom, daisies, calla lilies, and brilliant scarlet salvia, hollyhocks, and nasturtiums all bloomed. Everywhere flowers extravagantly, passionately bloomed. I carefully severed a rose from its bush with my thumbnail and stuck it in the lapel buttonhole of my jacket to rid my suit of some of its aura of gloom.

Larry called that night just as I was draining the spaghetti for the carbonara. As usual, he didn't bother with "hello." "I've been ordered back to work," he said. "Jay says I've been doing too much, which means he's probably sick of me. So I've organized a schedule. Mike Alexander has volunteered his Mondays and Shirley Masterson has Wednesdays free. Don Rose and his lover will alternate Thursdays and Alec Tolliver said now that he's semiretired he needs to do something worthwhile with his Fridays anyway. I'll continue all weekends, of course. I couldn't not be there at least that long. So that leaves only Tuesday without someone, you see."

"What's the matter, Larry? Couldn't you find anyone else?"

Without hearing them, I could sense his fingers drumming on the counter by the phone. "It's no secret to anyone that I don't like you, Todd. But at the moment, for Jay's sake, that's not the point."

"What is the point then? I've done this lots before you know, Larry. I'm making my contribution. I care. And Jay is my best friend. There's no question. Of course I'll take the day off."

"Fine. Thank you so much," Larry drawled. As if it were an afterthought he then added, "It's Jay who asked me to ask you. I wouldn't have on my own. Not because I don't like you but because I don't trust you, Todd. There's a difference between the two sentiments that I wish you'd try to understand."

Larry may have left the church, but the church never left him. Whenever he entered a room, you'd swear he was still a priest swinging his censer back and forth, his button nose whiffing the smoke as if he were floating on the trail of some exotic perfume. Shortly after we'd met, I made the mistake of telling him that he reminded me of the sort of holy man who'd get caught with his cassock up around his waist while he fondled an altar boy. "Why, you miserable atheist," he snapped at me and slapped me in the face. I almost settled it with one strong blow to his stomach, but Jay stepped between us. "I know all about your kind," I informed him. "My mother's father was a fancy Episcopalian bishop in Charleston who had about as much real faith as you do, Larry. You're all just big-city high-church hypocritical snobs," I said. He didn't believe what I'd said about my grandfather, of course. I didn't really expect him to. My face has Holy Roller written all over it, though I reckon I've got Baptist ears, too big for my size. Jay later told Larry that, though my grandfather had been a preacher, all right, he was the kind who believes gibbering nonsense is a sign of grace.

I argued to Jay once that the real reason Larry left the priesthood was that he found hate to be much more redemptive than love. Jay's response was that I mistook his struggles with jealousy for dislike.

"Jealous? What's Larry jealous of? Our friendship?"

"No. Or I don't think so. He's jealous of you, Todd-a-o. Of your freedom. What he'd call your recklessness. In a way, he envies you it because it's so far away from anything he could be himself. He thinks it makes you happy, even when we both know it doesn't, don't we? I suppose people who are chaste in their hearts, if not in their bodies, whether they mean to be or not, will always envy the promiscuous a little. But what gets much less noticed is how people like you envy Larry."

"The only thing I envy Larry for is his wardrobe."

"Wait and see," Jay said, almost smirking, and winked.

The Tuesday morning after Larry's call, it was Mike, thank goodness, not Larry who opened Jay's door at my knock. His clothes were mussed, his hair was unbrushed, and he was rubbing his eyes. "I woke you up," I apologized.

"Not exactly." He checked his watch. "Jesus, I've got to run."

"A long night?"

"Endless. Diarrhea mostly. Once he didn't make it to the john on time. He was embarrassed to tell me and tried to clean the mess up himself. I found him by the side of his bed not squatting but . . . what do you rebs call it?"

"Hunkering?"

"Hunkering and barely able to breathe, holding on to the mattress to keep from toppling over. He's still spitting a little blood. His doctor said we should bring him in for more tests. But Jay refuses to allow any more tests. All night he kept playing *Death and Transfiguration* over and over. Boy, is that ever a bloated piece of music. Do you know what it's like to listen to that piece twelve times in a row? I almost got diarrhea myself."

"I've forgotten what it's like to have to listen to it once."

"When I asked Jay to turn it down so I could maybe try to get some sleep, he just looked up at me mournfully and said that he'd decided at last that Strauss really didn't have a clue."

"I don't hear any music now. He's sleeping?"

"I hope so," Mike said. "Come on back with me to the kitchen. Larry laid the medication out on the counter in exact order and instructed me to teach you the system."

After Mike had left, I sat on Jay's favorite chair, a white linen love seat he'd bought fifteen years ago when he and I had gone to Gump's together on a shopping lark. I read the paper I'd brought with me by the living-room window. When I glanced up, I could see my face in the mirror that had been my gift for Jay's and my twentieth anniversary, as I called it, two decades to the day having passed since we'd met, a couple of impoverished scholarship students at a rich boy's school, only one of whom admitted to needing the help. I'd found the frame at one of those estate sales I'm constantly going to, looking for cheap treasures to fix and sell. I'd restored it for him, filling in the nicks and cracks and painting it with a gilt so fine people frequently mistook it for gold.

While Jay slept, I cleaned up the kitchen, careful not to upset Larry by moving anything from its assigned place, did a load of laundry, and dusted the furniture and all the old things Jay loved to collect: blue porcelain, cloisonné plates, kachina dolls, ginger jars, and a menorah rescued from a Budapest synagogue by a relative who had fled just before the war. Books, records, and more recently CDs lined his walls throughout the house. I never understood Jay's need to save things. After I'd read a book, I'd sell it or give it away. Once I tired of music, I'd trade it for something else. But he kept everything. Old clothes he never would have worn again anyway, including his uniform, crowded his closets. Cracked and chipped dishes, cups, and crockery sat in piles in his kitchen cabinets.

"Mike?" Jay called out in a thin voice while I was stuffing freshly washed towels into drawers in the bathroom. I could hear him slowly rolling over in bed. "Oh, it's Todd. I forgot," he said as I entered the room. "I almost peed in my bed. I tried to get up but I couldn't. Help me, will you? My body doesn't seem to have any strength left in it at all this morning."

I thrust my arms under his armpits and steered him toward the john. His cock—long, thin, and rigid—pressed against his loose pajamas. "Is that a pistol in your pocket," I said, "or are you just happy to see me?"

He almost laughed. "They say hearing and hard-ons are the last to go even with all this medication I'm taking. You wouldn't believe some of my dreams or how grateful I am for them."

I held him as with one hand on the basin he balanced himself and with the other he guided his stream into the bowl. "I was visiting a client at SF General a mess of months ago," I said. "He was thin as a toothpick and struggling for breath while he was lying alone on a gurney in the hall because they hadn't opened a room for him yet. But when this really cute orderly passed close by him, he somehow got enough air into his lungs and strength in his muscles to whistle. I wanted to kiss him."

"Why didn't you?"

"I should have. Steady now," I said as I guided Jay back down the hall. "You interested in breakfast?"

Back in bed, he squinted at the clock on the dresser. "Better make that lunch. I'm not hungry yet, not for food anyhow. The Strauss recordings are on the second shelf of that record cabinet there," he nodded. "Find the *Four Last Songs* with Karajan and Gundula Janowitz.

"Now put it on the player, please. I can control the rest from here. And stay or leave. I don't care which. I've decided to give Strauss one last chance."

But after the third play, Jay shook his head sadly. "Maybe if I were eighty-four. But it's all too beautiful and my forty-five-year-old senses are not ready to sink in slumber. Once more though," he said, clicking the remote.

"You going to play that again?" I inquired later as I brought him his lunch. "This is the sixth or seventh time in a row, Jay."

"I wonder how many times I had to listen to 'Baby Love' or 'Please Mr. Postman' or 'The Man That Got Away' over and over back in college."

"All great music," I said. "Each and every song a classic. How's your turkey?"

"Sawdust." He dropped it back on the plate. "Maybe you're right. No more Strauss." He pushed the off button. "It's all a fraud. He's just trying to cheer himself up."

"I should have given you my precious Motown collection," I teased him, "instead of selling it to Roy MacDonald that time I couldn't quite make the rent on my shop."

"I hate that crap. I truly do." Jay closed his eyes and covered them with his right forearm. "I dreamed about Kit again last night, a happy dream this time. We were in bed together right here. I don't think anyone else ever understood just how good the good times between us were. Yet I was just thinking how strange it is that all of the men I've had sex with Kit is the only one I ever still dream about. The only one. It's as if I lived a monogamous life."

"That's not strange, Jay. Not strange at all."

"Maybe not to you. But it was me he lied to, me he repeatedly cheated on, me he left for that cheap piece of trade Bryant. He should rot in hell."

"Sherman, Sherman. You loved him. You love him. How many times do I have to remind you? And Bryant wasn't cheap. That little fling cost Kit you. If there really was much of a fling," I added. "I always argued you overestimated its importance."

"It's the same old song," he said. *"Odi et amo.* Larry's right, as usual. Why should I care if I never see Kit Major again?"

"Larry's hardly a disinterested observer, Jay."

"And you are?"

"Give me some credit. A lot of time has passed." Jay turned his head toward me and opened his eyes, snorting. "I don't fib about important things, Jay. Or lie. Or tell stories. Don't completely deny those years you spent together. Not now. See him."

"No. That's the end of it. No more discussion."

"Fine. Be unforgiving. I'm going to take a walk down to the deli and buy us some better food. What would stimulate your taste buds?"

"I don't care."

"All right then, what music do you want me to put on before I leave?"

"The annunciation of death scene from *Die Walküre* with Martha Mödl."

"Be serious, Jay."

"I am serious. How much more serious do you want me to be?"

"Bad choice of words," I said, taking off.

How little I understand about pleasure. After that first Tuesday with Jay, I found I looked forward to my twenty-four hours with him more than any other event of my week, our friendship having almost reverted to the organization and predictability it had had during the early years at school, though Jay in his illness had become totally dependent on others. Shirley Masterson and I compared notes on Wednesday mornings as Mike and I did on Tuesdays. Alec Tolliver phoned me to chat every weekend. Don Rose, his lover Joshua, and I shared our first meals together ever. It was like having a host of old friends and a social life I could count on. Unsurprisingly, only Larry never called or made a gesture toward me.

One morning before he left for work, Mike remarked that Larry Pratt had found his true calling at last, the rest of us being there only to assist him in his vocation, mostly ignorable unless we made a mistake. He was already preparing Jay's plans for the memorial service.

"I wish he'd butt out," I protested, "stop making decisions that are not his to make."

"Larry's not the only one guilty of that particular sin," Mike said, "if Larry is guilty of it at all."

"Meaning?"

"What about you and Kit, back when he and Jay were still together? You don't think Jay didn't see what was happening practically in front of his eyes? Did you two think he was blind?"

"That's not you talking. That's Larry, the class snitch. You think he might have tired of his lies by now."

"The man was a priest, for God's sake."

"A mad and sex-crazed monk." The lupine had grown so much during the previous week that tall spikes of it reared through spaces between the pickets of Jay's fence, the front of which was covered with lantana, thyme, and six-hills-giant. "Has Jay seen how beautiful this is?"

"Yesterday," Mike said. "Scoop and I drove him down the coast to San Gregorio where he and Kit used to sunbathe a lot. The beach was almost empty. He cried."

I cocked my head. "What's the music *du jour*?"

"Mozart's Piano Concerto No. 23."

"I wonder what that means."

Mike shrugged. "Ask Larry. He's the authority on Jay's moods."

"On my way over here, I could see Mount Diablo without a speck of dust or a hint of smog in the air. For an instant, the

Earth looked so blessed that it felt like a gift just to be alive to see it. Do any of us have the right to feel happy anymore, even if it lasts no longer than the beat of a pulse?"

Mike flung his jacket over his shoulder. "Just make sure you give Jay his bath today. Shirley says you forgot last Tuesday. She also thinks you may have forgotten one dose of the DaunoXome and two of the acyclovir."

"No way. Whoever forgot, it wasn't me. I follow Larry's instructions to a T."

"Apparently the count was off when the nurse checked last Wednesday."

"What is this? Put the blame on Todd day? It could have been anyone. Nurses make mistakes too. So does Larry, believe it or not."

"I'm sure he does." He gazed out toward the street. "Isn't that Ken Costanza's place where the Open Hand truck just pulled up? I saw him at Cass Benedict's party only two weeks ago and he seemed fine. It's unbelievable. Do you believe it, Todd? Does anyone?" He swung the gate closed behind him. "I'll see you later."

When I walked into his room, Jay was propped up on a pile of pillows, the pink section of last Sunday's paper lying open unread on his lap. He stabbed at the remote to lower the music's volume. "If it's Todd, this must be Tuesday."

"It's me, all right. How are the old peepers, Jaybird?"

"A little hazy. It's getting hard to read." He swept the paper off him and onto the floor. "Mozart's lost it," he said, cutting the music off altogether. "Too much order, too much grace, too much clarity, too many bittersweet dreams of a world that won't ever be. Come sit next to your old roomie, Todd. I need to talk to you."

As Jay's cat's bell jangled under the open window, the birds flapped their wings and squawked. I pried off my loafers and lay next to him on top of the sheet that partially covered him. He weakly slapped my lap. "So tell me, Todd.

How does it feel to be well?" I didn't answer him. He looked thoughtful for a couple of seconds, furrowing his brow. "Too hostile a question? But all questions are hostile when asked by a dying man. Last Sunday, I quoted La Rochefoucauld to Larry, one of his censored maxims. 'In the adversities of our best friends, we always find something which is not displeasing to us.' Then I simply asked him, 'True or false?' He got quite flustered, as I'm sure you can imagine."

"What did he say?"

"I'm much more interested in your answer, Todd."

"You always load your tests with trick questions, Jay."

"I'm surprised to hear you say that."

"You confessed to me once that every time one of your buddies got hit in Vietnam, you said a silent prayer thanking God it wasn't you."

"Not every time."

"That's what you said."

"If I did, it's not what I meant." He grabbed my hand and squeezed it hard, with more strength than I would have expected him to be able to show. "I'm afraid. Something I've never felt before started last night. I could feel it growing inside." He gripped harder as a birch limb scratched against the upper window. "Offer some consolation, some reason not to be afraid."

"I don't know what to say."

"Of course you don't." Air hissed out between his teeth. "Why should you know? After four thousand years of human ruin, no one knows what to say to the dying anymore."

"You want to talk to a rabbi?"

"I hear enough piety from Larry, thank you. Like most saints, he can be a royal pain in the butt some of the time." He was watching a fly crawl around the fixture in the ceiling. "Do you think Kit ever loved me? Not that it matters anymore. I was just wondering."

"Yes. What else have I been saying all these . . . ?"

"And you thought so then? While Kit and I were together?"

"Of course. You remember how I . . ."

"But you didn't let that stop you, did you, Todd?"

"I could kill Larry Pratt. Who else has he been bad-mouthing me to? Why start this up all over again? Why doesn't he let it rest? What does he want?"

"What I want is the truth this time, Todd. One owes to the dying nothing less than *la verité*."

"What's important is that Kit always said 'no.'"

"You have no right to tell me what's important, Todd."

"I'm your best friend, Jay. I always have been. I always will be."

He squeezed my hand. "Yes. Yes, I'm afraid you are. As poor old Marke said to Tristan, 'my faithless, faithful friend'."

"We had good times together, didn't we, Jay? Those weekends in Laguna, the ski trips to Incline, that month we spent biking through Oregon. And all those dinners! Christ, how many meals do you think we've eaten together, not counting all those crummy meals in commons when we were both waiters? And those nights in the bars, each of us waiting hour after hour for Mr. Right?" I laid my hand on his bony shoulder. "There've been hundreds and hundreds of good times, buddy. Thousands."

He touched a patch of KS that had thickened almost into a lump under his left eye. "Did you ever really make it with any of those movie stars you bragged about?"

"One."

"Which one?"

"Guess."

"You didn't."

"I did."

He made me repeat the story twice, to see if any of the details got changed in the retelling, I'm sure. Or maybe he really enjoyed it. "For the first time in months," he said after

I'd told the story for the third time without any significant variations, "I almost feel like jerking off."

"I could leave the room."

"Almost."

Without moving his head, he let his eyes survey the room. "Everything's going to have to be sold. My mother's been even more broke since Sol died, and my sister Miriam never made much of herself. They've had sad lives. They should be here, but I don't want to punish them for their having been so foolish about my life. Larry has agreed to handle the auction and the sale of the house. But I want you to have something, Todd. And, unlike Herod, I won't make you dance and strip for it."

"Pardon me?"

"Salomé. She asked for John the Baptist's head."

"Good for her," I said, "but I'll settle for your father's picture from Saipan instead." I bent over to touch its frame where it hung, next to the picture of Toscanini I had given him, close to Jay's bed.

"I told Larry that's what you'd want."

"Did you put it down in black and white, Jay?"

"I trust Larry's word."

I nibbled my lower lip. "You've forgiven me, Jay."

"I had to, didn't I? A long time ago."

"Nothing really happened. Nothing important."

"How many times did I hear Kit say the same words? About how many guys?" His fingers touched my eyes. "Don't cry, Todd. None of it means a thing. I can't let it mean anything. Not now. I don't want to die angry or bitter or hurt. It would be like losing my soul."

All afternoon, I watched each pill he took with special care and kept count on a piece of paper, but by night he had grown morose and much frailer than he had been in weeks. "Mozart was a serious mistake," he said as I fed him mashed food for dinner.

"What music is this now?" I said. "It's awful."

"Awful awful?" he said. "Or wonderful awful?"

"Just awful."

"Shostakovitch, the Second Piano Trio. War music."

"I don't like what's happening here, Jay," I said. "I'm going to call the nurse. Your face has lost all its color. And your temperature is way up."

"You're scared," he mumbled. "Todd's scared."

"Damn straight."

A drop of blood squeezed out of the corner of his mouth. I wiped it away with a napkin. "So am I. I've never been so frightened in my life, not even in Nam where everything got wasted. But not me. He whom life does not destroy grows stronger. I had to wait twenty more years to waste away." His eyes shone with fear. "Tell me there's something else. Tell me there's more life somewhere, I don't care where, just somewhere not oblivion. Lie to me if you have to. I won't mind."

"I can't, Jay."

"The one time I wanted you to."

"I love you, Jay. The first time I saw you in that dorm room I said to myself, 'Friends for life.' I've made mistakes. Too many. I'm sorry for each and every one. But so it's been. Friends for life, through thick or thin. So it will be, forever. I swear it."

"You've always used the word 'love' too easily." He closed his eyes. "But thanks. That was pure Todd. Sentimental as all hell and almost believable."

"What happened after you called?" the nurse asked me two hours later.

"He started to scream."

"For how long?"

"Forever. Fifteen minutes. Maybe less, maybe more. I wasn't checking my watch, Dorothy."

"You'd better call his friends. Fast."

Alec arrived first, pale and barely breathing, followed by Mike and his boyfriend Scoop. I couldn't reach Larry until he'd gotten home from the symphony, but Don Rose and his lover walked over as soon as they heard the message on their machine, and Shirley said she'd felt it coming in her heart all day. Before Larry left his place, he phoned several of Jay's other friends who had asked to be there.

I told none of them that the first person I'd called had been Kit. I suppose I had been planning to call him when the time came ever since I'd bumped into him at Pat Hanrahan's funeral. A roommate said that he didn't expect him back soon and didn't know where to reach him but would tell him as soon as he got home, not going to bed himself until he had. All night, I watched the door or listened for the knock.

Dawn rose still more beautifully than it had the day before, the birds chirping and singing as after a storm. A sprinkler system that skirted the tall L-shaped fence that formed the border of the backyard next door sprayed water over the lawn like an elegant fan. Stripped to the waist, wearing only cutoffs, the neighbor's boyfriend painted a picnic table by the birdbath. I stared at him until he looked at me and blinked. A ruddy, nickle sized pimple scarred his back. Otherwise, he was perfect. A car, passing by outside, blared rap. A horsefly flew into the living room through the open window.

Alec fidgeted with the drawstring for the curtains. "I saw a man blow up yesterday at another man, hollering and stamping his feet, because the object of his abuse had intended to purchase a few more than ten items at the express lane in the grocery store. I can't explain to myself why I found the incident so deeply unsettling." He gazed outside. "What times we live in!"

"I wonder what our lives would be like," Mike said, "if none of this had ever happened. If the virus had just stayed up in the trees with the monkeys."

Shirley sat perched on a hassock, petting Jay's old cat. "You look tired, Todd. Maybe you should take a nap."

"Has someone called Bruce Coburn at Jay's firm?" Don asked.

"Larry did," I said.

"And Mitch Schlesinger?" Scoop suggested from the floor where he was turning the pages of the morning paper.

"He's out of town," Alec said.

"He'd want to be here," Scoop said.

"What's this music?" Shirley inquired, pushing the cat away and standing up.

"It sounds like an outraged dirge," Alec said.

"I can't imagine this is the music Jay wants to be hearing now," I said. "What is it anyway?"

Larry walked into the room from the hall. "What difference does it make what it is?" he said like a man overcome with fatigue. "It's Allan Pettersson's Seventh Symphony."

"It's very upsetting," Shirley said.

"I don't like it either, Shirley. I never would have chosen it. But, please, I know what I'm doing. Jay and I discussed this just last Saturday. It's what he wants, I'm sure of it. Excuse me. But who is that standing by the door?" Everyone turned around.

"Well, praise the Lord!" Alec exhaled. "It's Kit. It really is."

"You're not wanted here," Larry stated as calmly as his anger allowed.

"That's not what Todd's message said," Kit responded as evenly.

Larry spun back around to confront me. "Todd? What lie did you tell him, Todd?"

"I want to see him. I want to talk to him, Larry," Kit said.

"For heaven's sake, let him see Jay," Don said. "Where's the harm?"

"And violate what Jay has repeatedly expressed to me? Not on my life."

"I don't give a shit about your life," Kit said. "All the years

Jay and I were together you bad-mouthed me to him. Why he always had to believe you, I'll never know. But this time I'm going to have my way." With one arm, he shoved Larry aside.

"Oh no, you don't," Larry said, grabbing the back of Kit's shirt. "You can't. Maybe yesterday. But not now, not when he is no longer able to express his own wishes."

The side of my hand chopped the back of Larry's forearm in a way that was meant to hurt. With a cry of real pain, he released his grip. "Go on, Kit," I said. "I'll knock him out if I have to." But I didn't have to. "Melodrama queen," I said, sneering at Larry as Kit walked into Jay's bedroom alone and closed the door behind him.

A half hour later, I tapped on the door. Kit was sitting in a chair next to the bed, holding Jay's hand in his lap. "He knows it's me. He didn't speak, but I'm positive he knows it's me. He smiled once, Todd. He's glad. He knows it's me still here, holding on."

I studied Jay's face. "I'm going to call the nurse in now, Kit. All right?"

"Sure. Sure."

When I brought her back, almost everyone crowded into the room. "He looks like he's still listening to the music," Alec observed.

"I'm relieved he asked to see me," Kit said. "I'm so relieved."

"Is that what Todd told you?" Larry whispered across the bed. "And you believed him? Todd?"

"Hush, Larry," Don said.

"It's what Jay wanted in his heart," I said. "I know him better than you, Larry. I knew what he wanted but couldn't break his crazy rules to say."

"Will you two fight this battle elsewhere," Shirley said, "or kindly shut up."

"You better put his hand down now," I said to Kit. "He's gone." The nurse glanced over at me and nodded.

"Maybe some of you wish it had been different. But Kit was the love of his life. He belonged here," I said to the group huddled outside on the walk as the men from the funeral home prepared Jay's body for removal.

"You did it to get back at him," Larry yelled, intervening from across the yard. "I'll never speak to you again."

"For what, for heaven's sake?" I said, throwing my arms out in exasperation.

"You weren't his best friend. You were hardly his friend at all," Larry shouted at me. "He confided in me the way he wouldn't dare confide in you. I knew his wishes better than anyone. Everyone here knows how Kit mattered more to you than Jay. You wanted to make Kit grateful to you, didn't you? Didn't you, Todd?" he challenged me. "What you never could see was how Jay had to struggle to forgive you for what you did. He was just too decent, too merciful a human being ever to confront you with all he knew and felt about you two and your ways in all their sordid details. He was the only genuine Christian I've ever known. But not even Jay could forgive everything."

"Please, Larry," Don said, "You're talking twaddle."

"It's way out of line," Joshua added.

"It certainly is," I said.

"Go back in the house," Don said, "have a drink. You could use one."

"Would everyone kindly stop telling me what to do?" Larry demanded. But he walked inside anyway.

"Well," Alec remarked, exhaling. "You know what they said about Tallulah. A day without her is like a month in the country."

"I never did understand what Jay saw in Larry Pratt," Don said.

"Consistency," Shirley suggested. "Fidelity. A kind heart. I don't know. Larry always seemed to me to want to be so much better than he is. I think that's a remarkable trait, don't you?"

"Sure, Shirley," Mike said. "Come on, guys. Give Larry a break. Think of all he's done these last months, all he's given. He loved Jay, pure and simple. He's grief stricken."

"We're all grief stricken, Michael," Alec said. "But he's the only one I've seen tear at his hair like a prima donna."

"Jay was always loyal to people who were loyal to him," Mike said.

"Why do you always take Larry's word for things?" I asked. "Why do you always take his side?"

"Where's Kit?" Scoop inquired. "I wanted to say 'hi.' I always thought he was a terrific guy. A great dancer, too."

"He left," I said. "Or Larry drove him off. At least he didn't have to listen to this latest nonsensical tirade."

"Was it nonsense? All of it?" Mike questioned me.

"All of it," I answered defiantly. "I loved Jay, too, you know. For longer than any of you, including Larry Pratt."

"Well," Alec said, moving off. "I think that's enough talk. Too much, really. Let's hope when next we all assemble our spirits will be more temperate and the day a little calmer and more forgiving, if no less sad."

"Larry suffered with Jay. Every second Jay was sick, Larry suffered," Mike muttered, also walking away.

As everyone expected, Larry took charge of Jay's death with the same attention to detail that he had summoned to supervise Jay's dying. Jay's remains were shipped back to Brooklyn two weeks before the memorial service that took place on Jay's lawn. Larry had moved the stereo and speakers to two windows in the back of the house so everyone could hear the music he said Jay had requested be played. People stood in small groups or by themselves, scattered over the grass as the fog broke over the hills behind them. We were to

listen, Larry announced, to the second movement of Schu-
bert's last sonata played by Artur Schnabel, recorded in 1939
after he'd fled the Nazis; the Allegretto from Beethoven's
Seventh Symphony conducted by Arturo Toscanini; and Max
Bruch's *Kol nidrei* performed by Jacqueline du Pré and Gerald
Moore. Except for the music, which I barely noticed, I had
never heard a neighborhood so still. After the third selection
ended, Larry read a thank-you note that he said Jay had dic-
tated just a few days before he died during the last Sunday
Larry had spent with him alone. He mentioned Shirley, Don,
Joshua, Mike, Scoop, Alec, and his nurse Dorothy Chan, of
course. He thanked quite a long list of other friends who over
the years had added so much to his life, several of whom had
died before him. He spoke lovingly of his family. Larry didn't
fail to read his own name last, of course. But mine, to no
one's surprise, least of all my own, never passed his lips. Not
once. Neither did that of Kit, who stood through the whole
service off to one side almost behind the sycamore holding
and gently stroking Jay's old Siamese. When I turned to look
again, hoping that he might acknowledge the bond we
shared in Larry's erasure of us both, both Kit and the cat had
gone, presumably together. Kit had always paid more attention to it than Jay had, and it deserved a good home.

The day before Jay's belongings were to be auctioned, I
went to the house to claim my photograph, but Larry turned
his back on me and refused to speak. It was Mike who informed me that he was almost certain that Larry had already
sent it back to Miriam, along with a lot of other mementos,
saying it was what Jay had wanted done.

"But that's preposterous," I said. "Jay's sister is so ortho-
dox she'd never display a picture like that. She never understood why Sol had taken it in the first place. Nudity offends
her, Mike. All of it, of any kind. Jay told me so himself. She'll
probably burn it."

"What's done is done. Fight it out with Larry, if you want

to. But it won't get you anywhere. It never has, has it, Todd? But," Mike assured me, "I'll try to pilfer something else for you. You deserve it." His eyes scanned the living room. "What would you like?"

"That mirror," I said hesitantly. "But it's not what I really want. Jesus, I despise Larry Pratt."

Life has taught me never to believe in coincidence or fate or to trust in luck, whether good or bad. Yet on the same day Mike delivered the mirror to me, as I was hanging it on my living room wall, Kit knocked on the door for the first time in seven years. After I'd let him in, I asked him to step back to the other side of the room and advise me as I attempted to straighten the frame.

"There," he said as I moved it a half inch to the left. "Perfect."

I slapped my hands together. "Good."

Kit gazed into it like a child staring in wonder at the surface of a still pond, as if seeing his reflection for the first time. "The day after you gave Jay that mirror, he looked into it and asked, 'Which shall I choose? Poetry or music?' It was a line from a Strauss opera he said he loved too much and had made me listen to over and over until I almost liked it. Then he turned around and hugged me. 'What a stupid question,' he said, 'when I've already got both.' I wish it had been true, for my sake as well as Jay's. I'm here, Todd, because I want to thank you. For lying to me."

"No problem," I said. "I do it all the time."

"But your lying to me was really the truth, wasn't it? Wasn't it, Todd? We were both so stubborn, Jay and I."

"Everyone I know is stubborn," I said. "It seems to be a human trait. You're looking great as ever, Kit. You keeping company with anyone these days?"

"I'm a loner, Todd."

"You weren't always."

"I think I was. Jay never understood that. I loved Jay

more than I've ever loved anyone, I guess, but he wanted too much from me. He expected me to be true in a way that went against my nature. I always felt judged by him and found wanting. You know how it was."

"Yes. Yes, I do. I could use a friend, Kit. I was hoping it might be you."

"And have Jay's friends suspect the worst about us all over again?"

"I wouldn't care."

"Yes, you would. Let's not make old mistakes new, Todd. It was bad then. It would be worse now."

"You're still the best-looking man I ever laid eyes on, Kit Major, and I've always been a fool for a good looker."

He bowed. "Why, thank you for the compliment, Mr. Lawler, sir. But I think," he said with a stage French accent, "you are not being entirely honest *avec moi*." He paused. "Tell me, Todd. Why has Larry Pratt always hated us so, from the moment he met us almost, you even more than me. Maybe I deserved his rebuffs. But why you?"

"Because Larry imagines he knows me better than I know myself. He's deluded by some misguided trust in his own insight. Or maybe he does understand me better than I do myself. I really don't know why, but he and I tugged and pulled at Jay like two selfish children with a doll we both claimed to love more than anything in this world. Jay was right, 'love' is a dangerous word in the wrong mouths. More than dangerous. Cruel."

At the door, he offered me his hand. "So long, Todd. Thanks again for daring Larry's wrath."

"But that's my point, Kit. I didn't do it for you. I didn't do it for Jay. I did it for myself," I said as if confessing, not bothering to stop to think whether my confession was true or not, however honest it felt at the moment I uttered it.

Why had I called Kit? Ever since Jay's death, I have been able neither to stop asking myself that question nor to answer it. Had I really intuited Jay's wishes, expressing them overtly when he could not bring himself to break his own law and speak them out loud? Or had I rather been seeking Kit's attention, wanting to make him grateful to me and so trying in this perverse way to woo him, as Larry more than suspected? Kit had looked into Jay's dying face and seen a smile he took as a sign of his forgiveness, of his reconciliation with the man I have little reason to doubt he truly loved. But what he saw was not what I saw, for I suspect that, by the time Kit reached him, Jay had already passed beyond the possibility of his recognizing or forgiving any of us anymore. His spirit had vanished. His face had become as unyielding as a death mask. Even if by calling Kit I'd meant to do only good, I'd waited too long. I'd failed. Once more, I'd failed Jay.

Only this morning, less than half a year after I last saw Kit in the flesh, I discovered his picture on the obit page of the local gay rag. No one had told me he'd even been sick. I didn't read what had been written about him or risk learning whether Jay's or, what was much less likely, my name was mentioned. I couldn't bear it. But so clearly seeing his face revealed to me all over again how terribly I missed Jay and how happy it would make me feel just to walk a beach with him again and wade in the quiet surf, as if he and I both were washing away the grime of battle while other naked men around us did the same.

Every time I try to hold onto it with my mind, though, the picture fades just a little more. I'm losing the details and, thanks to Larry, lack the means by which to recover them. How I hate him for robbing me of Jay's father's photograph. Yet most nights, I sit alone in my spare living room, staring down at my phone, and wonder whether, despite all his obvious foibles and faults and his many duplicities, I should call Larry Pratt to ask him if he would be willing to let bygones be bygones and talk with me. I can hear Jay laughing now at my having to hope for so strange a friendship, one he had more than once predicted I would some day need. Maybe, I keep thinking, if I could persuade him, I could persuade myself that what my dangerously demented old preacher grandpaw called my "precious soul" has not been already forever lost, doomed to perdition and endless grief because of a lack of faith. But I don't dial Larry's number. I'm almost certain that I never will.

Hearing Voices

"TREES," he hears his mother saying, lying on her deathbed years ago, "I always missed the trees. I think heaven must be full of trees. Do you believe in heaven, son? You must, you know. For my sake, you must."

Kevin shakes his head to clear it and his mother's voice vanishes as a sweetness drifts through the morning air like the fragrance of a nearly odorless flower that only the sun brings out. On a neighbor's line, clothes whip briskly in the breeze. A wasp's shell dangles like a tiny marionette from a web threaded between limbs of a bottlebrush. Stalking weeds with the grace of a prowling cat, Joe clips and prunes a back corner of their small garden. His tanned skin, spotted with freckles of umber varnish, is as soft and lustrous to the eye as suede to fingers. To Kevin's left, the table and benches they have just finished painting dry on the deck. On the second floor of the apartment building behind them, Jerry Castile talks almost nonstop into his speaker phone, his voice surprisingly loud and sharp. Even with the windows closed, Kevin can often hear Jerry talking much of the day and part of the night, as if his body, as it shrunk, changed into words he had to use to try to keep it from shrinking more.

Another phone rings insistently on the other side of the fence. Billie Holiday sings through speakers propped on the desk in the room behind him. The only music Kevin cares to hear lately are recordings of long-dead singers, their voices eerily present and full-bodied despite persistent scratches and ticks that mar their surfaces. Kathleen Ferrier is his current favorite, especially her live performance of the *Kindertotenlieder*, but Wagner performances from the '20s and '30s almost equally obsess him, the singer's physical presence astonishingly clear to him from the voice alone. He would have liked to play them as loud as they must have sounded in the theater, but his and Joe's flat is squeezed so tightly among the many other flats and apartments that border the small yards that divide one building from another that he rarely dares to do so. Especially on hot days, people's voices and other noises seemed inescapable, penetrating floors or walls and seeping through windows, whether open or closed. Sometimes he could hear snippets of conversations long past as well, the voices of the dead occasionally medleyed together into brief monologues, not all of whom he could identify. When hearing voices like that frightened him, he reassured himself by noting that none of them gave him orders or instructed him to harm himself or others. Perhaps it was only memory, as little bothersome as an occasional ringing in the ears he could safely ignore.

Kevin gulps more coffee out of his mug and sloshes it around in his mouth, trying to dissolve the sugary grease left by two jelly doughnuts and to flush the aftertaste down. The liquid leaves its own unpleasant flavor, however—a mixture of chewed paper and granular jelly beans, like those he used to buy at the dusky five-and-dime he visited as a kid whenever he rode with his father in the pickup to town. Once, perched on the roof of his father's shed, eating jelly beans out of a paper bag, he watched an electrical storm shatter the great bowl of the Texas sky. Thereafter their grainy sweetness became almost inseparable from a sense of danger and excitement, and whenever he heard thunder rumble he could taste jelly beans in his mouth.

Joe stoops over, picks up a large clay clod, flings it whooshing into the air, and holds out his arms as it disintegrates above him and falls back to Earth in fragments, covering him in a shower of dirt, some of which sticks to his sweaty skin. "The sky is falling!" he shouts like a mischievous child. A scrub jay caws somewhere in the lemon tree. Two warblers splash unperturbed in the birdbath next door.

"Glad you took the day off?" Kevin asks.

Joe rests the hoe against a post. "You bet. What a waste it would have been for me to spend a day like this looking out that plate-glass window hoping some poor jerk will come buy a car he probably can't afford."

"Tired?"

"Sure. Aren't you? But this morning it feels great."

The night before they had celebrated their ninth year together by getting pleasantly tight in a bar close to the wharf. Sitting side by side in a booth upholstered in bright magenta vinyl, they stared at ships anchored hundreds of yards offshore or up at the TV over the bar, saying nothing, smiling a lot. As they drank their beers, gazing peacefully at the brazen, garish colors of the TV and listening to all the men's voices hoarse from smoke and their love of gab, they held hands. But, after their third round, the noise drove them to the quieter deck outside where, except for one couple in their early twenties huddled against the cool night air wrapped in one coat, they were alone. In the bar behind, one man shrieked with laughter, another gruffly shouted him down, and the jukebox started to throb to a wailing country song. Joe and Kevin leaned against the broad railing and wordlessly toasted one another with their lifted bottles. The fog was returning, a thin gray web, looming and impalpable. "If only everybody could live as happy as us," Joe said, "just like this, forever."

Kevin folds his newspaper into quarters and sets it aside, trying to recall what he's read, having to work to remember one story, all of them having seemed curiously unimportant when he compared them to the stories of those he knew who lived around him. Joe shakes the dirt off the roots of a weed, tosses it into a pile, and chops at the ground with his hoe. "I've got to get back to work if I'm going to meet that deadline," Kevin says. He glances toward the complex to his right where a stereo blares on. "Damn that asshole. Why does he always have to play his music so loud? Listen up, Luke Medlin!" he shouts, not expecting to be heard over it. "Disco's dead!"

Only a large pantry before Joe rebuilt it, Kevin's office is behind the kitchen. With his editing work and Joe's job at the dealership, they usually make do, though some months are harder than others. The last two have been especially dicey, the rent paid late. Sitting at his desk, having turned off the Billie Holiday, Kevin opens the unbound typescript, a New Age self-help book on grief that plays its one message as monotonously, as repetitively as a little boy banging his drum. "Life is organic," it says. "Death is an illusion. Every living thing achieves its place in the cosmic harmony, the song of all creation. All is gathered at the heart of being, only to find its spring again." Kevin would like to red-pencil large chunks of it, cross out whole paragraphs or pages, but his initial anger at its ignorance or deliberate avoidance of the world's horror has slipped into boredom, in part because his job requires him to read so much like it. Yet sometimes he finds himself wishing that at least some portion of these stupid books were true. How comforting, how reassuring it must feel to believe that part of oneself survives the body's rot. Since he first shuddered as a little boy at the inevitability of his physical ruin, he had hoped for some sign that death was not the end of everything. But none had come. Perhaps it was that absence that made him vulnerable to nonsense. Pushing the manuscript aside, he lifts the shade behind his desk to peep out at Joe, who's raking a boxed section of the garden, preparing it for herbs.

They had met on a rainy night just after Kevin had discovered his car's tires had been slashed in an alley near the bar where he'd gone to drink and cruise. Other cars had had their windows shattered. He was holding the collar of his jacket tight around his neck to try to keep the cold water off his chest and shoulders and staring down in helpless fury at the sidewalk, almost blinded by his hair that the rain had washed over his eyes, when he heard a voice behind him saying, "Want a ride home? There's no point in anyone's trying to change those tonight, not in this weather. Might as well wait until morning." He hadn't gotten a good look at Joe's face until they'd walked into the kitchen where Joe's roommate was eating a bowl of ice cream, his eyes wide with delight, smiling at them both.

Kevin lets the shade drop and listens, eyes closed, to the sound of Joe's raking and humming. Taking a deep breath, he resumes his work, deleting words, changing sentences, shifting the structures of paragraphs with a mindless attention that leaves plenty of space for other words, ones he doesn't mean to hear yet can't prevent. *What you don't know about cars is appalling son now suppose you got into trouble out in the desert the fan belt broke say what would you you couldn't even . . . Kevin Kevin look I told you that snake would still be there do you think it's dead don't touch it I wouldn't touch it with a ten foot here use this stick . . . that hurt Kev but it felt real good too I like touching you kissing you licking you all over up and down . . . you know the beach is almost deserted now we could sneak around that cove and look how beautiful the water is the waves like falling pearls pouring out of a shell the sky like jade pale green jade . . . how nice your body is I'm not good with words how beautiful with shoes on nothing more funny Kevin . . . I'm so sorry to be causing so much trouble son complaining all the time we live too long do you know that Kevin nobody should have to live too long beyond the sun Kevin it's in my eyes the shade please draw the shade.*

As the noon siren sounds, it jolts him to attention. The neighborhood's congregation of dogs howls. Shortly after both the sirens and the dogs have quit, Jerry starts to scream wordlessly, then hollers, "I don't want to, I don't want to, you can't make me. You can't!" His voice is shrill and frightened, like that of a child forced to do something or go somewhere against all the determination of his will. "I won't. I won't. No, Jorge, no, no."

When Joe taps on the window, Kevin leans over to open it. "How long has this been going on? Poor Jerry."

"A few days. He must have broken half a dozen plates on Tuesday. Threw them out the window onto the bricks. Plants too. I dropped by yesterday to ask Jorge if there was anything we could do. He said probably not since Jerry has started to distrust anyone who was ever close to him. They scare him worse than strangers even. Except when he's talking to them on the phone. It's people's bodies that frighten him. Or anyway that's what Jorge thinks."

Joe glances over at their apartment. "Jesus. The poor fucker. It makes you wonder what's in store for us."

"Don't," Kevin advises.

"Yeah, I know."

A shrill whistle sounds antiphonally between the walls. "Jorge gave it to him. To call for help," Kevin explains. "But now he's blowing it nearly all the time."

"There's nothing wrong with his lungs."

"You wouldn't think so, would you?" In the apartment, the curtain is slowly closed and the window shut, barely muffling the next scream.

"God help him," Joe says. "I'm all sweaty, Kev. I'm going to take a shower. Want to join me?"

"No can do, Joey. Two more chapters of this madness to go. Is that our phone or Gary's? I can never tell when this window and his are both open."

Joe pokes his head around the corner of the house. "Ours. I'll get it." He races across the deck and down the hall. "Hello?" Kevin hears. A long pause follows. "What? You've got to be joking, right? You can't be serious. Not with you I don't!" Joe slams the phone down so hard it rings like an ear after it's been boxed.

Curious, Kevin walks through the kitchen into the hall. "What was that about? Your face is almost purple."

"I answer the phone and, without so much as a 'Hello' or 'How do you do,' this guy asks in a sort of dreamy stage whisper, 'You want to jerk off?' "

"What?"

"You heard me. No small talk or nothing. Just launches straight into the main bout. Didn't even ask me my name."

"Had to have been a wrong number," Kevin suggests. "Or maybe he just keeps trying numbers until he gets lucky. You're upset over nothing, Joe. It was a mistake, that's all."

"You're the one that's home all day. You ever get a call like that before?"

"I would have told you."

"Maybe we should get our number changed. Have it unlisted."

"Why? Be serious. After just one obscene call? Forget it. It won't happen again. Who would risk a rejection like that a second time? Take your shower, Joe. Relax. Let's both play hooky and go to the beach, what do you say? Let's get away from it all, all this noise," Kevin says, pointing back to his office.

On the deck waiting, he listens to the sound of the water splashing against the shower stall. When he was a kid, he loved walking barefoot down gulleys along the dirt roads that bordered his father's farm as the rain washed the air clean of dust. For two years, his father had let him keep a wild rabbit in a hutch he'd built himself near the barn. Whenever Kevin set it free, it would hop among the beanstalks or nibble on cornsilk tassels or the hay where the cows nuzzled. On the day he found it dead, the dew on the morning glory tendrils was white as salt and the tree limbs were weighed down by the heat as if heavy with rain. A blind horse his father had chosen to spare had stomped it to death, scared by thunder. Kevin dug its grave too shallow during the downpour and the rabbit washed out. He cried so miserably his father had had to bury it the second time and to satisfy Kevin he said a prayer over it, waiting until several days later to remark, "Animals don't have souls, son. Only people have souls. And I'm not so sure about all of them."

While Joe, humming to himself, dries off, the phone rings again. It stops and starts once more. Joe opens the bathroom door, a beach towel around his waist. He gazes down at the phone, chewing his lower lip, but does not answer it.

The next day, a little before noon, irritated as if for the first time at the manuscript he's still editing, Kevin scrawls across the page in pencil, "Whoever believes in reincarnation, spiritualism, transmigration, or any other form of life after death is an ignorant fool who knows nothing about biology or the laws of physics." Annoyed with himself, superstitiously not wanting to believe so absolutely in his own disbeliefs, however, he carefully erases the sentence. Yet even as he tries to continue to work, he cannot keep himself from speculating about the identity of yesterday's caller. Maybe it was Tom Hannan, that sunshine blond from last year's cooking class whose nose had a seductive bump in it and whose smile was cute as Raggedy Andy's. Or perhaps it was Rick Tarantino, the office manager at Harper's downtown who looked like a soldier in a Renaissance painting of the crucifixion, a real Roman whose stony beauty was only enhanced by the indifference with which he seemed to observe all the suffering around him. Or could it have been Austin Trask, Ted Kinard's ex, who had flirted with him more than once at recent parties? The prospect that it might have been Austin was turning him on so strongly that he thought he might have to masturbate before he could return his attention to his work. Such fantasies often took temporary possession of him when-

ever his work was boring him most and seemed to him no betrayal of his love for Joe. They were a distraction, that was all,
and undoubtedly yesterday's caller had been no one he knew.
Besides, even if someone were desperate for sex, what purpose was served by using the phone? He would certainly
never place such a call himself, for more reasons than he
cared to enumerate.

Yet when, shortly after the noon siren has sounded and
died away, he hears the phone ring, he dashes the short dog-
leg from his desk to the hall to answer it, his heart thumping
in anticipation. He picks up the handset cautiously, like a
burglar using a handkerchief to keep from leaving finger-
prints.

After a few seconds, the silence on the other end is broken
by an almost inaudible, "Want to jerk off?"

"Who is this? Austin?"

"No names."

"Rick?"

"I said, no names."

"How did you get this number?"

"You have a nice voice. Deep. Sexy."

"Why are you calling here?" Kevin demands, though in
his stomach he feels the thrill of being on a carnival ride for
the first time as his companion, against his protests, laughs
and rocks the gondola of the ferris wheel as it reaches the
zenith.

"Listen. You want to come with me, don't you? Don't
you?"

"No. I don't know. I shouldn't." Kevin fidgets with the
phone's coiled wire and glances out the glass door to Joe's
garden. When he looks up, he sees that Jerry's window is
open and the curtains are being effortlessly drawn shut. He
hears the whistle followed by Jorge shouting, "Just a second.
I'll be there in just a second."

"I notice you haven't hung up," the voice cajoles.

Something in the facelessness of its sound, his inability to picture the man's body clearly in his mind, excites Kevin further, more than he would have imagined possible. He tugs on the cord so that he can retreat to the hall's darkest corner. "I've never done this before," he whispers. "You start."

In bed that night, lying snuggled next to Joe, Kevin considers confessing, being forgiven, and then forgetting about what now seems to him a sordid, solitary, and inexplicable episode; his fantasies for once had led him beyond his strength to resist. But instead he holds Joe tighter, touching him passionately until they make love with a frenzy, a wordless abandon that startles them both. Afterward Joe falls quickly to sleep, but Kevin, restless and apprehensive, finds himself listening for the phone, fearful that the man might call back, even in the middle of the night, revealing everything to Joe.

At the breakfast table, nibbling on a toasted bagel, he reads Joe's note: "Last night was great. Our life together gets better and better. I don't mean just the sex. I mean everything. Love ya. I won't be home too late." Standing on the deck in his ragged boxer shorts, Kevin scratches his chest. A fat crow squats on a high limb of the acacia and caws at a cat black as itself that stares up at it from the fence, licking one paw. When he hears the phone ring, Kevin shudders, ashamed, but laughs at himself as soon as he notices the sound is coming from Jerry and Jorge's apartment. The coffee he's drunk has made Kevin's stomach feel emptier, his nerves more jittery and on edge. Try as hard as he will, he can't dislodge yesterday's caller's voice from his head where it still seems to sing to him, as enticing as the passionate sound of a great tenor, like Carreras, say, when he was still young and unruined by disease.

Listening to Carreras's earliest recordings, Kevin waits all morning for the phone to ring, anticipating it with both dread and excitement, twice more mistaking other people's ringing phones for his and Joe's, and works no faster than a few pages an hour on a new book about gnosticism in the modern world he'd promised to finish by the weekend. A friend of his not long ago had praised phone sex because, he'd said, in the absence of any actual body for anyone to worry about all his desires and fantasies could be fulfilled more completely than they ever had been back in the always-disappointing old days of cruising the bars and baths. "Angel sex," he called it because it was unrestricted by flesh or matter, unlimited by anything except perhaps a deficient imagination. "Sex is all in your mind anyway, isn't it?" he'd taunted Kevin. "Who cares whether it's real or not?"

Kevin thought he cared very much, but for the third day in a row when the phone rings immediately after the noon siren retreats into silence he jumps up to answer it. "Why?" Kevin inquires. "Why always the same time?"

"I don't know. I like it. When the big hand meets the little hand. Whatever turns you on, right?"

"Do you know who I am? Do you know my name?"

"Questions, questions. It was great yesterday, wasn't it?"

"I don't like cheating. I feel guilty. Worse than guilty. My lover and I, we're really in love. But I don't suppose that would be something you . . ."

"How is this cheating? Relax. Forget the guilt trip. We're just having some fun. You can't have fun alone, can you? You start this time. Say, 'I like your voice.' That really turns me on."

The scent of the gardenias Joe planted in boxes across the deck wafts in with the breeze and engulfs Kevin like Joe's too-sweet cologne. "I like your voice. You've got a real sexy voice."

"You want to come with me, don't you?" the other man prompts him.

"You want to come with me, don't you?"

"Yes. I do. Very much. More than you can know yet. Try

it again now. Don't be so shy. Or nervous. I'm not going to hurt you."

"I like your voice," Kevin begins once more, trying hard not to fumble the words.

"What's wrong?" Kevin asks anxiously as Joe washes that night's dinner plates in the kitchen sink. "You seem upset. You've barely said a word since you got home. Work going OK?"

"I guess. I might have sold a van today. Who knows though? He could back out in the morning."

"You feeling all right?"

"Yup."

"What's wrong then?"

"You have that look." He flicks some soapy water onto Kevin's face. "I've seen it lots before, only never on you, not once in all these years."

Kevin wipes off his cheek with his shirtsleeve. "What look?"

"The it's-been-great-but-I've-got-to-be-going look."

"I'm not going anywhere, Joe. I love you."

"That's swell. I love you, too." He opens the drain to let the greasy water swirl out. "But you still have that look. I need to take a walk. Want to come with me?"

A nerve under Kevin's right eye twitches. He rubs his middle finger over the spot. "Sure, Joe. Of course."

Wet and bitterly cold, the western wind gradually subsides as the sky darkens from chalky gray to slate. Their jacket collars pulled high around their necks, Joe and Kevin circle the peak, pausing several times to admire the view over the trees to the churning bay. Two mutts frolic on a steep slope as their master, to keep from slipping, holds on to a pine trunk, shivering.

Joe rubs his sides. "Let's head home. I'm freezing."

As they wind down the hill, they pass the street whose backyards border theirs or their next door neighbors'. In his driveway, Jorge Rivera is attempting to unlock his car door on the passenger side while with his other arm he effortfully supports his lover, trying to keep him standing as straight as his strength allows.

"I'm not going," Jerry insists, his voice slurred like a sleepy child's.

"Oh yes, you are," Jorge says.

"Here," Kevin offers. "Let me hold him while you open the door. What's that in your hand, Jerry? Your whistle?"

"Yes." Jerry brings it to his lips and blows on it. "See?" He blows on it again, much harder than Kevin would have thought possible. Like a lone figure on a wide and empty beach, Jerry stands up to his full height and beckons to him as if he were far away and almost out of sight. When he starts to stumble, Kevin reaches for his hand.

"Come on, now," Jorge entreats him. "Put that back in your pocket. Let's go, Jer."

He crosses his arms defiantly. "Won't."

"Just for a few days, I promise. Until the docs decide what's messing up your brain again so bad."

"No."

Without warning, Joe sweeps Jerry off his feet and, once Jorge has opened the door, settles him on the seat. Startled and frightened, Jerry stares at Kevin. "Come with me," he pleads. "Come with me, come with me!" He sputters and coughs. "Come with me, Jorge!"

Kevin uneasily backs away. "I'm not Jorge. I'm Kevin O'Brien, remember? And that's Joe there. Joe Meier, your old neighbors. Think barbecue ribs and beers, Jer, just a couple of months ago, remember?"

"Sometimes he mixes people up just awful these days," Jorge says, tears welling up. "Even old familiar voices have started to scare him." He opens the door to his side and slides in. "We'll be there soon, Jer. They'll fix you up, better than last time, I promise you. We got to keep hoping, don't we?"

"Come with me!" Jerry shouts again to Kevin, his eyes bright with terror.

Kevin glances over at Joe. "Should I?"

"It'd be a big help," Jorge says.

In the hospital, while Jorge stays with Jerry, Kevin waits in a corridor that seems to him an echo chamber amplifying every noise to a sort of shriek, the lights overhead as bleakly bright as those in a bus-station rest room. He tries to shut his mind to its voices and ringing bells, the doctors' and nurses' names repeatedly called out over the intercom, but instead of the wished-for silence he hears only more repetitious voices inside him that he cannot still either. *It just goes on and on Kev we're living too long nowadays everything licked but old age the old deserve better a rest too you know the mind . . . how I loved your father the desert the thunderstorms the way rain settled the dust in summer I'm afraid of babbling that's why I'd like to be a dog or a cat they never complain do they but all I do is afraid of babbling sputtering nonsense I saw my poor old mother dead lo these years sitting in the rocker just this morning here's your hat what's your hurry remember that your father always so anxious to leave always so eager for guests to leave . . . play that again will you Kev the part with Melchior and Flagstad the love duet what lungs singers had in those days if I had a million zillion bucks I'd be a patron of the arts and buy paintings and hang them on all my walls and commission new music new musical compositions what lungs lungs like that don't exist anymore do they too many singers on diets . . . what madness it is to want to cling to life when there's so little life left no pleasure in anything at all anymore but the alternative is worse isn't it don't laugh you'll see I'm glad things worked out so well for you and Joe is his name isn't it really glad for you both so young still believe me I need to sleep dear I wish you could come with me but some things people are meant to do alone I guess trees I just wish there had been more trees . . . what do you say now wake up now Jerry?*

A few hours later, Kevin slips gratefully into bed. "Are you asleep?"

Joe shakes his head in the dark. "Rough time?"

"Yeah. Jerry started bawling like a baby because he couldn't hold his head up or control his bowels."

"Damn."

"Why does dying have to be so undignified?"

Joe scratches his whiskers. "You remember how I've told you when I was a teenager, Kev, I used to like working with cars more than anything. I thought the whole world was nothing but torques, revs, gear ratios, mills, bores and strokes, overhead cams, rockers, and tachs. Then, when I was in Nam one bright afternoon, I saw an armored personnel carrier back away from a mortar barrage and crush another marine who'd fallen in the road. Listen, when you've been taught how to stab someone in the lungs to sink them in a river and not make a sound, it makes you feel different about life, about dignity. Human beings break real easy, Kev. I used to love engines because you could fix them to a fine tuning. But all machines break down too, sooner or later. The human body just wears out a little faster for some people, that's all. Nobody can change that . . ." He rubs his face. "What if what's happening to Jorge and Jerry happens to us, Kev?"

"I don't know."

"Neither do I. If you could just turn off your brain . . . not have to think or talk or hear things."

"Then you might as well be dead, Joe."

Sometime during the night Kevin wakes out of a deep sleep to the phone's ringing, but when he reaches the hall he realizes he's only been dreaming. As he cracks open the door to the deck to get some air, the cold night wind slaps his face. Cloth, like a curtain blowing, flows across his arm. When he twists around, he thinks he sees a face like a mask of crumpled linen hovering just a few feet away, close enough so that something like drapery seems to slide to the floor. But all he finds when he turns on the lamp is a pile of dirty laundry Joe had left there for him to do in the morning. He opens the closet door and removes from his jacket the whistle that Jorge had asked him to take so that Jerry wouldn't try to blow it at the hospital where Jorge had decided to spend the night. Kevin blows it softly so as not to wake Joe. When no sound emerges, he tries harder, then harder still. He gives it one more blast, his full lung power behind it. He might have just blown a bugle. When he turns to look, Joe stands naked in the hallway by the phone.

"I still don't know how Jerry does it," Kevin apologizes.

The next morning, Kevin works even more sloppily, less attentively than he had the day before, his mind divided between thoughts of Jerry and irresistible hopes that his caller might phone again. Images as hot as those that used to flash across his brain before he left for the baths flicker through him, a new one every few seconds. After an hour at his desk, he concedes to himself that he cannot read anything, much less improve it. Instead he stares without attention at one talk show after another, the volume always turned off as he tries without much success to read lips. A little past noon, right on schedule, the phone rings just as the last dog finishes its howling.

"I've missed you," the voice says. "A lot. I need you, you know."

"I've missed you, too," Kevin admits. "Yesterday was a long day."

"But I'm here now. Do you want to come with me again? I know you do. It's what drew me to you. It's why I chose you. You're not really happy there, are you? Be honest. C'mon. Just say the word." Kevin can almost feel the man's breath nuzzling his ear. "C'mon."

"Where're we going?"

"Where else? To heaven, man. This time, I'm going to take you all the way to heaven."

"Bragger."

"You'll see. C'mon now. Let's go. I'm going to lift you

up beyond the clouds. Visit paradise with me. OK, then. Now . . . ," he begins.

Shaking afterward, trying hard not to cry from disappointment, Kevin lies on the floor, his stomach and chest covered with his sperm, the handset still propped between his jaw and shoulder. "Don't call anymore. Please."

"What're you scared of, man?"

"Just don't anymore, all right? Promise?"

"You don't get off that easy, man. I told you, I need you. You're the only one. There's no one else left. No one else who will even talk to me, see?"

"Promise," Kevin begs.

"Promise? Me? Haven't you heard what I was just telling you, guy? You belong to me now. Besides, dead men don't make promises. I'll do what I like." Kevin hears the line break. Only an odd squeaking, like that of bats, persists for a few seconds longer.

He soaks in a bath he's drawn full of cold water that reaches to his chin as he lies in it. Every once in a while he retracts his head under it like a turtle retreating inside its shell, away from noise and danger. As he pats himself dry, his skin, chilled by the water, is as pale white as a thin sheet of ice. *Dead men*, he repeats to himself, *don't make promises*. Suddenly dizzy, he grabs a towel rack to keep from falling. His thoughts are absurd. He knows that. But despite all the good reasons for denying them, he still cannot shake them. It seems almost obvious to him all of a sudden. The voice he'd been hearing for three days was a dead man's voice. The paradise it promised was some kind of hell. How could he escape? Or perhaps the better question was what was happening to his brain.

"I've had the number changed," Kevin informs Joe at dinner, handing him a piece of torn notepaper with the new one written on it. "It's unlisted now. Once you've memorized it, swallow it or burn it. Don't give it to anyone unless they re-

ally need to know it, like Jorge. I'm tired of phone solicita-
tions and crank calls."

Joe reads it and sticks it into his shirt pocket. "How many
times, Kev? How many times did he call back?"

"Who?"

"You know who."

Sighing, Kevin avoids Joe's gaze. "Three."

"Why didn't you just hang up?"

"It happened every day at the same time, right after noon,
just like that first call. I know I shouldn't have let him talk. I
know I should have hung up right away, just like you did."

"But you didn't."

"Maybe there is such a thing as a siren's call and rocks you
wreck on. While he was talking you and everything else real
almost vanished from my head. All I could hear was his
promising to take me to heaven. But it wasn't heaven, Joe. It
was just hot sex. I think I need a new line of work, something
without any words to fool me. Maybe I'll try carpentry. I was
a pretty good little carpenter as a kid. Maybe I could make a
decent living at it if I tried hard enough."

Out on the deck, Joe puts his arm around Kevin's shoulder. The sickle moon is bright as a pebble in sunlight. A cold
wind rushes through the trees. Two cats scrap noisily near the
fence. A phone rings up the hill where piano music dimly
plays. A light switches on in Jerry's room and Jorge slides the
window open. "Kevin? Joe?"

"Yes?" Joe answers.

"The docs tell me Jerry won't be coming home ever again.
I don't know what to do."

"You want us to come over?" Kevin offers.

"No. I'm returning to the hospital in just a few minutes.
Do you still have his whistle, Kevin? He thinks I stole it from
him to keep him from getting help. He wants it back so
bad." Kevin retrieves it from his jacket in the closet and
tosses it up to Jorge who catches it easily. "You'd think it an-

swered prayers." He slowly slides the window closed and turns off the light.

"He sounded very far away, Joe."

"Jorge?"

"The voice on the phone. Lonely, too, as if all the world that mattered were leaving him. I wonder if, when you die and your body's rotted, all the desire you ever felt lingers somewhere as frantic as some old geezer still cruising the johns. What if all that survives of us is our longing? Is that our phone ringing?"

"Calm down, Kev. It's Gary's. You're right. You've been reading too much California voodoo. Better lay off it for a while. Car repair booklets, that'd be the ticket. Computer instruction manuals."

"Forgive me?" Kevin whispers.

"Are you sure you're not tired of us, Kev? It's only going to get rougher. We've been lucky, you know, real lucky, you and I. We're overdue."

"Yes, I know. I do know." He flinches and reaches for Joe's hand. "Whose phone is that?"

"I don't know. Not ours."

"Stay home, tomorrow, will you, Joe? Indulge me for just one more day, all right? I know it's nonsense. But I don't want to be alone if I'm wrong."

"This is the goddamnest excuse I've ever had for taking a day off," Joe says as the siren sounds at noon, "waiting for a phone call that can't possibly come. What do I tell my boss? My lover believes he may have been cheating on me by having hot phone sex with a spook? I don't think Ed Hatcher will swallow that, Kev. There's only so much these straight guys can accept."

Kevin watches the clock as the dogs cease howling. "So far, so good. I guess." He takes a deep breath, holds it, and, having let the air rush out, breathes in again.

"Nothing," Joe observes.

"Not yet. Give him a few minutes more."

"Still nothing," Joe says as the minute hand indicates a quarter past.

"Maybe he knows you're here."

"Kevin!"

"I know, I know," he apologizes.

"Besides, my being here didn't stop him the first time."

When the minute hand reaches twenty after, the phone starts to ring. Kevin's eyes widen. "Shit. I thought changing the number might work. Or maybe I had the number changed just to test him, to test his powers, to see if he could get through to me again."

"It's still ringing, Kev."

"Don't answer it."

"Look, it's probably only Jorge. I gave him the number this morning at breakfast. Or the phone company testing the phone, to see if the new number works." He moves to pick it up.

"No, Joe. Don't."

"For heaven's sake, why not?"

"Because I think I need to believe that it could be him, even when I don't want it to be. I need to believe that this was some sort of sign, even when I know full well it couldn't have been, that I'm making it all up in my head, that it was all only a tasteless joke, a tease. If it is him, I know he won't try again. Not if I don't answer. He's got to be frightened too. He talked like a scared man, Joe. He didn't know anything more about heaven than the rest of us." He takes a deep breath again, even longer than the last. "Maybe it would be better if we didn't survive. It's stopped ringing. It's over now, I hope. All of it."

"I know I wouldn't want to linger," Joe says, "after my body's gone. It would be too much like the way Jerry is lingering now. I think I'd rather die fast, all at once."

"But who's ever been given a choice?"

"There's suicide."

"But how has that ever really been a choice?" Kevin grabs his lover's arm. "Will you again? I want to again, Joe, so bad. Like the old days," he whispers, "before we got afraid to. Now more than ever. You in me."

"Are you sure, Kev?"

They rush into the bedroom where they strip quickly. Joe rises to kneel between Kevin's legs. He bends over to kiss him. At the first thrusts, Kevin feels his body begin to shed like a snake on a rock. He coils around Joe until his skin splits and slithers out of his old dry scales to bask on the rock of him, as quiet as the legless dusteaters that when he was a kid were the most real living thing that dozed under the Texas sun. He opens his mouth to speak but all it emits is a kind of hiss. Laughing, a little frightened, he holds Joe tighter and tries again.

"Shshshsh," Joe hushes him gently.

"No more talk," Kevin finally manages to force out. "No more voices. No more fantasies of anyone else. Or of anywhere else either. Just this. Just us. It's enough. You've always been enough, Joe. More. More than enough."

"Sure, Kev. Sure, babe," Joe soothes him, his smile unironic, his eyes bright with patience, as peaceful as a child's.

Driven by the fog, the wind swirls through the adjacent yards as if down a back alley. A tin can bounces across a walkway. Sheets flap flaglike on a line. Two acacia, their branches tangled like lovers' arms, bend and creak. Leaves rustle like crumpled paper. Gary Adams orders his barking dog to be still. Luke Medlin turns a nearly twenty-year-old Donna Summers album up so loud that the distortion almost eliminates the music. Chimes hanging from a balcony clatter like lead pipes. Holding each other tightly underneath the heavy blankets that they've pulled over their heads, both Kevin and Joe at first mistake their phone's ringing for a neighbor's, far away. After it quits and starts again, Joe rolls out of bed to answer it.

Kevin watches him as Joe listens intently for several minutes. Then, beckoning Kevin to join him, he speaks quietly into the mouthpiece. "Yes, Jorge. I understand. Yes, I think you're right. I'm sure Kevin will. Of course he will." He claps his hand over the phone. "Jerry wants to talk to you. Be gentle, kid. Jorge says it's only a matter of hours."

"Why me?"

"Jorge says Jerry doesn't remember anyone else's name anymore. Just yours. Everything else is gone."

Kevin places the phone to his ear. "Jerry?"

At first Kevin thinks the connection is bad, so far away and nearly inaudible does Jerry's voice sound, as thin as a thread spun from a spider. "I don't think he can hear you," Jorge says somewhere close by the bed.

"I said, 'I'm not going unless you come with me, Kevin.' You're coming with me, right?"

Kevin fights to keep his voice steady. "Sure, Jer. Of course."

"I'm scared, Kevin."

"So am I, Jer."

"Everyone here wants me to go. Do you want me to go?"

"Yes, Jer. I do. So that the pain will be over."

"Do you think there's a heaven, Kev? Do you think there's a life after death? That's what I need to know. No one else will say."

"Why does it matter what I think, Jerry?"

"Please answer my question."

"Yes. I do, Jer. I do believe in an afterlife. I don't believe any of us really dies. Not in any way that counts. OK? Jerry? Jerry?" But the phone has gone dead, apparently hung up, probably by Jorge.

Kevin hands it back to Joe and grips his shoulder, looking

into his eyes to try to see there how seriously he has just lied, and, finding no reproach, he kisses him like a bashful new lover, as unsure as ever of what he believes or needs. He wipes his palm across his face. "You don't think it could have been Jerry, do you?"

"Who? Your mysterious caller?"

"It didn't sound like Jerry. But then Jerry hasn't sounded like Jerry for months."

"Stop it, Kev."

"Every spring my mother used to ask my father to plant another tree, even though the desert soil and climate had already killed more than he could count since he had married her and brought her there. You can't stop longing, Joe. It doesn't quit. I know it doesn't. So do you."

II

Self-Portrait with Cecil and Larry

WHEN I WAS YOUNG, I thought that if you could see the light in things you had seen everything there was to see. You didn't really need people or their bodies. A muskrat's fur glistening when it has just come out of the water or the deep dark green of magnolia leaves blackening in the noontime sun were enough. I'd drive over to Pierre Part to take a look or I'd find myself someplace in the Atchafalaya swamp awkwardly paddling a pirogue to see the moss, the fallen tupelos, and the hyacinths twining together over water that, like a thin sheet of glass laid on an amalgam of dark earth, caught the glaring sun and threw it back up into the sky where it burned all the hotter for having been drenched in light where it fell.

I spent a lot of time there in my early twenties, paddling and looking. The colors in my early paintings soaked up light like a sponge does water and then squeezed it out again, cleaning even the brightest colors until all you could see in them was whatever was darkest in yellow or orange or red. But as I grew older, light alone was no longer enough. I wanted more. I wanted earth. I wanted matter. I wanted bodies, boys' luminous, perfect bodies. Or nearly perfect. So I hired them and drew them, to share with others their carnal gleam and shine.

"Where do they all come from?" is still Cecil's recurrent, amazed question about the Quarter's hustlers, as if they all somehow had to have sprung up at once, fully armed with their beauty, from the same acres of fertile soil that he might plot out on a map. He thought it might be nice to take a trip to the source.

"Hattiesburg," I answered him once, because I was sick of the question and had just sketched a boy who claimed that as his hometown. By Cecil's logic, if it was true for one it must be true for all. It was simple. Each year some god obviously spills his seed over Hattiesburg.

Cecil nodded knowingly. "Oh? I thought so. But why Hattiesburg?" he pondered.

In fact of course, as Cecil knows better than I, they come from all over, though mostly from somewhere in the rural South, in my experience primarily from Arkansas and Mississippi, which offer them no place to go except New Orleans. But Louisiana, Texas, Alabama, Georgia, even South and North Carolina contribute their share. None of them stays long on the job, a season or two at most, although a few, a very few settle into the Quarter itself, having found another sort of work or someone to take care of them or perhaps, most rarely of all, both.

Every one I ever met behaves like an immortal on a spree, as if his own brave youth alone were powerful enough not only to survive but to conquer anything, even time itself. Youth is to them an inexhaustible resource with which they have been blessed and which they can pump week after week, month after month, year after year. They are the new oil barons of sex and strut with that cockiness of the recently very rich over that turf, those corners of the Quarter which they claim as theirs and theirs alone.

Sexy they certainly are. They fill the air with a pungent scent, a peculiar perfume all their own that clings to the skin and will not let you rest. You can smell it everywhere in the Quarter, even after it has just rained, the thick sweetness of it still hanging suspended in the air like honeysuckle or roses or gardenia. When it is hottest, they strip down to cutoffs or shorts, their sweat-drenched bodies sparkling like a spider's web seen along the roadside from a passing car; their tanned skin like dark gold beaten thin, smooth, and ductile and fashioned to the perfect symmetry of their frames.

I saw them once or twice or maybe three times at the most on the street or in a bar, I hired them, I painted them or drew them in my studio in a day or two, and then I always let them go. There was no time to make distinctions. Not one of them ever lingered long enough for me to have a specific memory of him. One beautiful body always blurs into all the others, as light vanishes into light. Yet there they all are everywhere anyway, haunting me still in my drawings and paintings, each boy's body isolate and glimmering in the night.

Cecil champions these pictures with as much enthusiasm as if he had made them himself, invariably capturing his somewhat skeptical audience with elaborate anecdotes about each boy that hold and amaze them all. How has he learned so much? How much is really true? When asked, Cecil merely grins back at each inquirer and keeps his own counsel. Of course, I should be troubled by his tales. Sometimes, I am, especially when they become too lurid or complex for anyone's, even the most gullible man's credulity. But mostly I don't mind. To me, he is merely engaged in an age-old Catholic practice, like a priest elaborating a saint's life with intricate verbal detail when what he really ought to be doing is pointing silently to the picture near the altar of the racked and burning heart. That is his own heart, and my heart, too.

"It's started," Cecil says and sighs. He's standing on his balcony and is slowly cleaning with a damp rag a just-assembled stack of dirty ashtrays from his last night's salon, examining each one carefully and then setting it down on a brilliant glass-top table to dry. Cecil owns thousands of ancient 78s, almost all of tenors. Once a month, certain of his friends like Bayard Reeves and Paisley Harrell gather to drink, to smoke, and to listen as Cecil projects relevant slides upon a bare wall. Yesterday, the salon had been an examination of the career of Giuseppe Anselmi.

"Blast!" he shouts as some hammering begins down Ursulines closer to the river. "There goes up another damned For Rent sign." He sighs again. "Each year it seems to be starting earlier. What on earth can be happening to our people? Where has all their fortitude gone? This is New Orleans, for Christ's sweet sake. It is supposed to be hot."

I flap my newspaper and peer over it. "What do you mean, 'It's started'? What's started?"

Silhouetted by the radiant morning sun, Cecil is so tall and thin he seems to dangle like a skeleton from a string attached to the doorway's lintel. He wipes his now-empty hands on his apron and enters the room, a shadow from the gallery's wrought-iron lacework following him and falling across the floor like a web of branches. Cecil puts his hands on his hips. "The flight, of course, the yearly pilgrimage to God knows where. Some place cool and dry one imagines," he says irritated. "The sissies are all fleeing the triumph of the sun."

"Oh," I say, taking a sip of my beer and going back to my paper. Or to Cecil's paper, actually. I wanted to see if my show had been reviewed yet.

He gropes my right bicep inquisitively, as a kid might grab Santa Claus's beard to see if it was real. "You'll do fine," he reassures me.

"But there's not been one word," I bitch. "There's been no notice at all."

"Really, Bo! That is not what I had in mind. There are far more important things!" Cecil sighs again. I've never known anyone to sigh so much or so convincingly as Cecil Carruthers. Not just when he's down or blue. When he's happiest too, he's still forever sighing, as if it's a sound his body can't help making. "I don't know why people choose to live here at all," he berates me, "if they don't enjoy the heat."

"Don't look at me," I protest. "I'm not going anywhere. I was born here too, remember? Or doesn't that ungenteel part of town count?"

Cecil employs an edge of his apron to wipe some drops of sweat off his forehead. "Isn't Bayard Reeves from St. Francisville?"

"It's possible. Why?"

He begins randomly dusting tabletops with another edge of the same apron. "I'm not sure. It's just all so strange. Yesterday afternoon at the bar where I was of course recuperating from a series of disastrous rinses, poor Mrs. Hand will never be able to reclaim her natural color I'm afraid, and readying myself for my splendid evening to come with a gimlet or two, I could have sworn I overheard him say something familiar about North Carolina. *North* Carolina." He shudders. "I mean, really. All those Protestants and their hideous visions of demons everywhere and harlots cursing little children in the streets. However could one bear it?"

"Cecil," I advise him, "if you don't pay more attention to what you're doing you're going to knock over that last ginger jar. And then you'll have none. Remember the other two?"

"Thank you, dear Bo." He carefully slides the jar back to the table's center, suspends all work, and stares wistfully out toward the balcony. "Of course, when my great great-grandpère died of the yellow fever in 1853 and his daughter, my great-grandmère's sister passed on of the cholera only a few years thereafter, rumor has it that there was actually some talk of the family's seeking at least temporary shelter in safer climes. And when my father's father slipped off one night so mysteriously during that truly terrible heat wave thirty years ago, well," he sighs, "mine hasn't been the healthiest of genealogies. Or the easiest either. Yet never once have we lost faith. Not once."

"You're such a snob, Cecil. Cecil Claibourne Carruthers is a snob," I tease, a schoolboy's taunt, and shake his paper at him.

"Am I?" He more or less collapses backward into the rigid Victorian couch whose maroon velvet plush had long ago worn down into an almost silklike shine. Cecil tried to hide the fact with mounds of pillows, and, though the ruse did not work, it made the monster a bit more comfortable. Not for Cecil, however, who is far too long-legged, thin, and bony for it. Lying down in it, even after he has jack-knifed his legs up and hung them over an arm, he still has to support his head on a pile of pillows and hold up his arms so that he looks like a zigzag ruler unfolding. "But don't you love the fact that you come from some place like this, Bo? Some place so real. Doesn't it make you feel all settled in and cozy?"

"No, actually. It doesn't. The politics for one thing," I begin.

"Stop. Not another word. You know how I loathe all politics," he declares firmly, settling himself further down into his impossible couch and sniffing a carnation he has removed from the coffee table as if to clear his nasal passages of a bad smell. "All politics," he reiterates, undaunted by my obvious disapproval. "Tell me," he says, interrupting himself, "is that really a living fly lodged on that chunk of cracking plaster up there, Bo? Isn't it huge? What a peculiar summer it's proving to be thus far. Everything's grown so prodigiously that even the flies have become monsters."

"Yes," I agree, trying to conceal my yawn with the beer can. "It's been quite a summer."

"Indeed. Perfect I would call it. And we who have taste, good taste, no matter what our birth or place of origin, must blithely believe in nothing at all except the inerrant accuracy of our own judgments. All one needs in life are taste and a lovely tan. I adore the sun."

"But you're a Catholic," I object.

"So are you," he smiles slyly.

"Was," I correct him. "Was a Catholic. I stopped believing

in God after my first trick, when I knew I'd found something better."

"'Was,' 'are.' It doesn't matter to me," Cecil says. "In religion one tense is as good as another. That's the sublime thing about religion. For the devout, it's impossible to make a mistake in the use of tenses." Cecil examines the nails on his hand carefully, attentively, like a manicurist at work. "You see, there's always another, better world to live in, if only one has the courage and perseverance. Not a political but an ideal world, a perfect world of taste and style that abolishes death and cancels out everything mean about existence. I first heard it calling to me as a wee child in the voices of certain immortal tenors. It was all in the style. A person can listen to a thousand performances of 'E lucevan le stelle,' but until he's heard Fleta or de Lucia he's just been listening to tenors singing Puccini. But once Fleta or de Lucia has sung to him, then he has heard the voice of a god beckoning him to paradise, summoning him to a blissful bower of pure art, as pure and holy as the mass itself, perhaps purer, more holy, more sacred."

Cecil stares at me, or rather into me, like a thief casing a house he's preparing to rob. "I've decided something about you, Bo. You're no Catholic. You think my lovely garden a sinner's fancy. You're really Protestant after all. Way back in time immemorial, there were probably rebels and heretics in your family, Huguenots undoubtedly, a not uncommon occurrence, after all, among some Cajuns. It's in your blood. For all Protestants of whatever allegiance confuse the two realms, the political and the religious, just as you do, wanting to change the messy real world into something as perfect as, say, a Fauré song or change the perfect Fauré song into something as nasty as the real world, depending upon whether they belong to the right or to the left. What they all refuse to do, however, is to leave things alone. They don't understand that the world will always be a shoddy mess, that Fauré's songs are eternally perfect and incorruptible. Whereas I, on the other hand, having to choose would always pick the songs, that perfect and unrealizable ideal that silences us all."

For some reason just then I notice how Cecil's hair is sticking out of his thin head in three clumps, like a fleur de lys on a finial.

"A new barber?" I conjecture.

"An old one gone mad and seeking vengeance on a supposed competitor," he corrects. "Oysters," he proclaims suddenly, "I must have oysters. Don't you think oysters would be ideal now. And a little champagne?"

"Cecil!" I holler at him impatiently.

His eyes dart birdlike around the room. "Someone calls?"

"Cecil. Forget oysters. Forget politics. Forget opera even for a minute. Do you really like my new pictures or don't you?"

He reaches over to pat my head. "But who in their right mind wouldn't, Bo dear? But I must confess that most of the time I try not to think about them. Those lovely boys simply break my heart. So fragile an organ the heart, don't you find, Bo?" He stretches, releasing a lion's roar of a yawn, and settles back down into the layers of pillows. "Like thin, thin porcelain or a delicate wineglass stem or a bubble floating idly down a stream. The heart's no stronger than that. Whoever conceived it as a muscle got it all wrong."

I crush the empty beer can in my hand.

Cecil regards me uneasily, cocking a disapproving eyebrow. "Really, Bo."

"What?"

"Such a vulgar display of brawn is quite unnecessary. If you don't mind a lit-tle bit of advice, I think you may be in some danger of overdoing the muscles. Like my poor father's last business so long ago, your body is now in considerable danger of overexpansion. I trust I needn't point out to you the consequences of such bad planning, fiduciary and otherwise. Someday it will all collapse at once, like a mismanaged trust. All those muscles you're currently so proud of will have deteriorated into so much fat and flab, which, as you know, is utterly worthless currency in this ungenerous world. Be warned. Thin, as I like to say, is beautiful."

"Working out makes me feel good. I enjoy it. So what?"

"You can't pump the soul, darling."

"Cecil, I know that."

"Then spirit yourself back to work immediately. Do something. Paint a pretty picture. But stop all this moaning and ululation about not being noticed. It's wearing me down, like listening to the squalling of these modern tenors who will not sing on pitch." He checks his watch. "Walk outside with me for a few minutes, onto the gallery. I want you to see something. Or rather someone. We may be lucky."

I follow him out, a new beer in my hand, and lean back against a colonette, Cecil nervously tracing one of the S-curves of the wrought iron over and over again in the air. The smell of onions and peppers and garlic spills over from the house next door. On the other side of the street on another balcony, three men stand like us poised gazing down towards Bourbon Street.

"It's almost noon," one of them shouts across to Cecil.

Cecil laughs. "It's been steady for six or seven days now," he whispers to me. "Every day at noon. Or nearly noon. It's made my little lunches most enjoyable, believe me."

"What's been six or seven days?"

"Not 'what.' 'Who.' Listen." As around the corner on Bourbon a second door slams shut, Cecil grabs my belt buckle, jerks me forward, and shoves me to the river side of the balcony. No more than a second or two later, like the central figure in a vast triumphal procession of which he is the only visible member, the boy passes down Bourbon across Ursulines towards St. Philip and disappears. "Perfection," Cecil breathes. Slouching, he folds his arms and crosses his legs, dandyish, the slight, sly smile on his face as he studies me like that of someone grown too wise, too refined, for passion himself but still amused by it in others. "I thought so," he says. "Bayard Reeves had a similar reaction just yesterday."

"Cecil," one of the men across the street hollers at him. "Who the hell is that?"

"How should I know?" Cecil yells back.

"Divine!" another exclaims. "Ravishing!"

"Let's follow him," the third suggests. "Let's see where he goes. Let's catch him and rip all his clothes off his body and . . ."

"But my brunch is practically on the table," the first protests.

"Tomorrow then," the second proposes.

"Right!" the other two agree.

"Cecil," I whisper. "What is all this? Who was that?"

"Shshshshsh. I'll tell you in a second, but only you." He drags me back into the living room and to heighten the effect draws the curtains closed. We face each other, his hands on my shoulder, digging in hard. "You mustn't tell a soul, not a living soul. I have a reputation to protect."

"Of course not, Cecil. But what is it I'm not supposed to tell?"

"His name is Shannon." Cecil swallows hard and stands very still, almost rigid, like someone about to confess a mortal sin. "Now guess how I know he's for hire."

So naturally it is to Cecil I first show my most recent work later that summer. I'd invited him and Shannon to lunch shortly after finishing the series of drawings, wanting right away to show them off to him, hanging my newest pictures everywhere, in all my old house's rooms including the bathrooms, down the halls, along the walls bordering the staircases, in the vestibule, on the one windowless wall of the enclosed portion of the back porch.

Though I notice immediately how the pictures unsettle Cecil, he waits, hesitating. "Bo?" he finally says to me as he munches quizzically on his salad.

I try to forestall him. "I know. You don't like nasturtiums in your salad. You don't think people should eat flowers."

Shannon wrinkles his nose, his fork scraping against his nearly empty plate. "Really? I've been eating flowers? Those yellow things were flowers?"

"Don't be silly," Cecil says. "I've been eating flowers since I was a mere slip of a thing and everyone knows how butch I am. Not one in my poor mother's garden was safe from me. No snail, no slug, no bug, no aphid, but I alone escaped her poisons. And, see, I haven't wilted yet. Perfectly pure are flowers. No, darling Bo," he glances up at the wall behind me, "it's something else I had in mind, something that's been bothering me since we sat down to this lovely repast, staring down upon me disapprovingly as it has all meal long. Tell me, Bo, sweet, isn't there something a lit-tle . . . well perhaps more than a lit-tle . . . 'off' about that new one there over the mantle? He looks terribly cross-eyed to me."

"He is cross-eyed," I say.

"Oh? Imagine," Cecil says. "What a novelty. A cross-eyed hustler. Still . . ."

"He isn't a hustler. Not this time. I tell you. I've changed."

"Oh? What does he do then with pecs like that?"

"Who isn't a hustler?" Shannon asks.

"Hadn't you heard? Lots of people," Cecil sighs. "Lots of people aren't hustlers."

"His name is Sergio," I say.

"Sergio who?" Cecil says. "From where?"

"Who knows? Somewhere. Bread?" I say to Shannon, passing him the basket. "Or more salad? You look still hungry, Shannon."

"Shannon is always hungry," Cecil brags. "He's got an enormous appetite, haven't you, Shannon?"

"Yep." Shannon mugs back and pounds his stomach. "There it is. The bottomless pit."

"How well I know," Cecil sighs lovingly. But he quickly returns his attention to me. "Then there's that other new one near the top of the front stairs, off the landing. Is he or is he not missing a leg?"

"He is."

"A cripple? Really, Bo."

"If you like."

"A crippled hustler?"

"In this case, yes."

"That's too bizarre. I've never seen a crippled hustler in all my born days."

"Wasn't there a one-armed hustler some place in Tennessee Williams?" Shannon counters.

"Thank you. That was to be my point to Bo exactly, Shannon," Cecil says. "But I think I would prefer it if you did not display so often that you are so very well read. It's utterly disruptive to my image of you as trade. You see, I prefer to think of you as a simple, innocent son of Alabama who has come to New Orleans to work on an offshore oil rig in the gulf and who has never ever looked at anything but women, television, and me. Certainly never at a book." He shudders.

"But I did work on an oil rig. And I am from Alabama."

"That's simply the truth of it. It's the image I care about, not the truth of things. For sex's sake, it is very, very important to keep one's image pure, do whatever you will. We are all already much too aware of what an awful, unsexy mess the truth is, though for reasons of his own Bo seems to have once more removed the lid from the pot of that unsavory stew. I intend no disparagement of this splendid lunch, Bo, it's only . . ."

"Yes?"

"The one at the bottom of the stairs. His face looks like

something that's been mauled by wolves. It's more than a tad kinky, wouldn't you say? It's worrisome, darling. You live in this big old spooky house all by your lonesome where the plaster's cracked and collapsing everywhere, cobwebs dangle from the ceiling, the garden is a dying brown jungle, the premises are permeated with an odor of must as foul as my Tante Marie's sickroom, an enormous ugly tabby cat large enough to have devoured a child stalks the corridors after God alone knows what sort of additional meal, its tongue darting in and out of its mouth like a lizard's and . . ."

"Lordy, Cecil," Shannon says.

"It's all right," I say. "Let him continue. He will anyway, you know. Nothing stops Cecil when he's on a roll."

"And now these new drawings." Cecil sucks in a long breath. "You've been hanging around that shabby bus station again, haven't you, Bo? I warned you what that sort of pro-longed mingling among the rabble might do to a sensibility as impressionable and ill-defined as yours. Tell me about your dreams. Have they been horrid? Processions of the dead car-rying the living down to the sea in coffins? Grinning skulls? That sort of thing? Poor Bo, are you really so frightened by death?"

Shannon lifts up his wine glass to play with it, swirling the little remaining wine in it around against the inside of the bowl. "What's it like?"

"What? Death?"

"No. Working the bus station. I thought it was kind of dangerous, the vice boys and all . . ."

"Dangerous? Sure, it's dangerous. That's part of the fun. Who would like dessert?" I ask them genially.

"He doesn't really," Cecil smirks.

"But then why did you say he did?" Shannon says, con-fused.

"Maybe I've changed, Cecil."

"Nonsense. Artists don't change. It's only your work that's so rapidly changed. It's become so . . . so . . . so . . ." Cecil stutters, frustrated at the word's failure to come.

"'Gothic'?" Shannon offers defiantly.

"Oh my God," Cecil groans. "He's done it again. I'm ruined. I'll never get it up for that boy again. But yes. Yes, thank you, Shannon. 'Gothic' is it." Cecil folds his napkin carefully, places it aside, and leans forward, resting his elbows on the table, his hands bent at the wrist, a praying mantis about to strike. "It's all so damned Southern Gothic, like this bizarre house you've chosen to live in, Bo. No one locks their crazy uncles up in attics anymore, honey pot. Mammies don't drown illegitimate babies in wells. Mammies don't even exist, alas. But fortunately neither do fey young men who shoot themselves for having been revealed in the midst of the terrible deed by an unsatisfied wife's peeking through the keyhole of some piney woods cabin. Shannon tells me it's the new South now, sweetheart. Skyscrapers are going up everywhere. Public housing abounds. You can air-condition almost anything. And you, I, and Shannon here are as good as legal. You don't have to hide behind those big black eyes and bushy beard of yours anymore or in all this ghoulish darkness. It's safe to come back outside. Look at me. See how Shannon's changed me? A lark sings on my roof and the sun shines every day."

"Whatever gave you that dumb idea, Cecil? I'm not hiding. What would I want to hide?"

He catches my expression. "Change the subject fast?"

"Please."

"Well, then, I will." He coughs nervously into his fist. "You have noticed many times without my having to point it out that Shannon over there, despite his insistence on forever displaying his brain, is nonetheless an exceptionally well-developed young man. His muscles, I can assure you, are veritable tempered Birmingham steel. His roommate, it turns out, is similarly accoutered, only about twice Shannon's weight. An astonishingly large lad, Dennis. Eheu, also a long-unemployed one who unlike Shannon refuses to ply the occupation you and I, Bo, both know so well from the opposite side of the street, so to speak. Patience, sweets. Don't fidget so, as my mother used to say, I'm getting to the point.

"It seems that just a couple of miles on the nether side of darkest Morgan City is this delightfully outré place called Guidry's Wrestling Palace, specializing, I'm told, in all sorts of wonderful curiosities. Salt-and-pepper mixed doubles. Midget tag teams. Man and beast. That sort of bread and circus thing. So I do take it all back. I must, I suppose. The Southern Gothic is alive and well and fighting it out on the outskirts of Morgan City. Make of it what you will, Bo. They are your people, aren't they?

"Now it seems that this Guidry's also offers a challenge match, a thousand-dollar challenge match that Dennis happened to read about in the paper. It takes place every Saturday night and is a complete fraud, of course, but frauds can sometimes work to one's profit. Dennis has decided in any case to try, with Shannon and me in tow for moral support. It will be grotesque, certainly, all those endomorphs flailing away at each other like game cocks lunging at one another's flapping combs, the auditorium filled with the sound of blood-crazed yahoos hooting. Quite horrible," he sighs, "but I'm going anyway. I can't wait to see Dennis in a bikini. How about you?"

Though it is Cecil's car, Shannon does the driving, Cecil seated next to him as our map-reader and guide and losing our way for us three times. We arrive at Guidry's forty-five minutes after the deadline for Dennis to register, two others having already signed on to challenge Junior Jordan, known also as Monster Mash, enough for that night's scheduled bouts.

"What should we do?" Shannon asks us as we huddle around the box office window. "Stay? Leave? What?"

Cecil contemplates the swarthy face of Junior Jordan on the poster. "Think of it, Dennis. It would have taken at least a week in the tub and a hundred dollars of the best bubble-bath to wash that from your skin, I'm sure. And you mightn't have won a dime." Dennis does not appear consoled.

"I still don't understand how you missed that last right turn, Cecil," Shannon complains.

"That's a boring topic, Shannon," he declares. "I wonder. What was this place before its conversion into a wrestling palace? A roller rink?"

"Looks like it," Dennis says grumpily.

"Oh, how I do love my native state!" Cecil exclaims. "How it satisfies all my aesthetic needs! We really must stay. My treat?" he offers. "Bo? Surely you'd like to. It must be superior to twenty bus stations for glamour."

"What do you say, Dennis?" Shannon asks. "It was supposed to be your night."

Dennis scratches his head. "We're here, aren't we? Might as well find out what I missed."

Cecil buys our tickets, hands them to the ticket taker, and dances us down to our seats, the four of them together ten rows back from the crude boxing ring that doubles as the wrestling arena. The hall is a little less than a third empty but full of smoke, a heavy, blue-gray smoke that hovers overhead like summer thunder clouds, threatening rain. But, if lightning had cracked right then and there, no one would have heard it over the yet louder thunder of their own voices, an ear-piercing rumble that only the amplified rants of those who are performing on the canvas can occasionally penetrate. A woman holding a squalling, crowd-maddened baby hurls herself up behind us and screeches something vile at the announcer, dropping back down into her seat just as someone behind her squeals some more terrible curse at her. Since the

floor isn't tiered, somebody is perpetually shrieking something obscene at someone else, usually directing them to sit
back down, enough obscenities being thrown around the hall
like the ball or towel in a game of keepaway to force one to
remain constantly on one's toes, alert and ready.

Cecil leans his lanky body across Shannon and grabs my
knee. "Isn't this wonderful? Exactly like your new imagery.
There's not an undamaged body here." I jerk my leg away
and refuse to answer. "What's wrong with Dennis?" Cecil
shouts. "He looks faint."

"Dennis?" I say, turning toward him and nudging him.
"What?"

"Are you OK? Cecil thinks . . ."

"Look!" he yells, growing even paler. Junior Jordan is
parading down the aisle, hands raised as if in victory, letting
the roaring crowd have its first good look that night at its
hero. "Oh, God! Cecil!" Dennis screams at the top of his
lungs across both me and Shannon. "Oh, thank you, Cecil!
Thank you, thank you. A million dollars wouldn't have been
enough! I owe you my life! It's yours!"

"You see!" Cecil hollers back to us all, vindicated.

The first challenge match lasts only minutes. Afterward,
two more or less regular matches pass in almost as quick succession, taking no more than ten minutes each. Shannon is
getting restless, so am I, since Junior Jordan, Monster Mash,
is scheduled to return only after the midget tag teams are
through and Alaska Wolf Joe has struggled with a bear. The
salt-and-pepper battle will be last, leaving the crowd in a
hateful mood. It's time to get out while the getting is good.

So I can't say when I first spot him walking, strutting, no,
more nearly prancing down that mean aisle, Slick Williams,
Short Stuff Slick his partner, ten respectful paces behind him
wearing a shiny black robe like his but without the rose
embroidery on its back. As he climbs into the ring under
the ropes, the woman behind me lifts her still bawling baby

up high into the air and bellows out, "See! It's Buster Pues! Ain't it a riot? And his partner there is tiny as duckweed, no bigger than you, honeybun. Go ahead and holler. Ain't it a scream?" The others are all laughing too. The hall is sick from laughter.

I know nothing about bravery. Nothing. That night, though, he is by far the bravest man I've ever seen as he struts down that aisle like a toreador circling bloodied sand, the crowd itself, snorting and puffing at him, scratching at the ground, waiting to charge, enraged without knowing why it was enraged by the red cape of his deformity—a grown man no bigger than a shrimp, a dog's turd, my old man's shriveled cock, my sister's nipple, my old lady's tit, a worm. All the while he is in the ring, he more than the other three manages to provoke them. He moves too well, too confidently, too bravely to be endured. He never cowers. When he and Slick having won are booed, he holds his ground like a champion and dares them again with his eyes, as if he knew the exact spot he could plunge the sword that would kill their surging animal pride.

At that I shout, "Let's go!" and like one we shoot out of there.

"*Barbare!*" Cecil exhales, collapsing into the backseat of the car, it being decided by a swift voice vote that Shannon would drive back and Dennis would direct us. The lights in the parking lot are a strange, dim, eerie yellow, like the light emitted from a halloween pumpkin as the candle dies. "Is something wrong, Bo? You're pale."

"Am I?"

"Quite." Cecil feels my forehead. "Well there's no fever at least. Still, you're clearly overheated."

"I wish you wouldn't pay so much attention to my body all the time, Cecil," I grumble. "It makes me feel like a freak."

Steering the car over a bump on the side of the road, Shannon turns onto the narrow country highway. With a pocket flashlight, Dennis reads the map. "We can pick up 90 at the first light," he directs. "That's where we turn left."

"I never would have guessed it was so easy," Cecil says ambiguously—I couldn't tell whether to me or to Dennis—and falls right off to easy sleep.

The next day, claiming I am a promoter from Jackson looking for novelty acts, I get his address without any questions asked because, the voice on the phone at Guidry's says, he reckons it's about time he and Slick were moving on. "They're not quite right, those two," he warns me.

A mile and a half up the road from Guidry's, shortly past the picture of Albert LeBlanc wearing the tilted crown on his head and the sign that proclaims him the King of Mobile Homes, I find the trailer park. As I drive in, Slick is heading out, so I park on the gravel patch he's vacated.

Nervous, I knock too hard on his door. "Who's there?" he pipes. The high, sweet voice surprises me.

"A friend," I say.

"Sure."

"No, really," I say louder.

He cracks the door open. "What kind of friend?"

"A friend with work. Can I come in?"

His face is as brightly smooth as silk. I hadn't realized he was so young. "I don't think so. What kind of work?"

"I'm an artist," I force out. "A painter."

"So?"

I back down three steps onto the ground to make our eyes meet more nearly level. "I saw you fight last night at Guidry's. You were great. I'd like to paint you."

"Why?"

"I don't know."

Utter immobility except in his brain, the part that weighs and balances, calculating. "For money?"

"Uh-huh."

"What for?"

"For posing."

"Posing, huh? How much?"

"Twenty dollars an hour, plus room and board while you're working."

He whistles like a kid. "Not bad."

I stretch out my hand. "Bo. Bo Naquin." We shake. "How about it, Buster?"

"You better call me 'Larry.'"

"Larry, then. What do you say?"

"The gimmick. Slick says always wait for the gimmick. I'm waiting."

"Gimmick?"

"Yeah, there's always one for little guys like me. A catch of some kind. A trick. Something weird. You know. What is it?"

I breathe in deep. "All my work's of nudes."

"Christ!"

"It's not like that, Larry. I promise you. Can't we talk?"

He drums on the door with his thumbs. "Well, not here for sure. It's Slick's place. He wouldn't like it. How about over there? A path cuts through those pecans. We can walk to the bayou. It ain't far. It's pretty there and quiet too. I'll have to get some shoes."

We hike in silence. Just where the mangrove shrubs end near an expanse of green-brown earth grass, though, leaning out over the water and gingerly picking up a crawfish by its back with his fingers, he says, "This one's in berry," as if surprised, handing it to me to see. I drop it, but he doesn't seem to mind. We stomp some more aimlessly about the marshland. Once, when I start to slip into the flow—I'm wearing the wrong kind of shoes for this country and have been sliding more than walking where the ground turns slickest—he grabs my belt and pulls me back to safety and a firmer turf.

"When I was littler," he says laughing, "and fished the Trestles with my dad he was almost falling into Pontchartrain all the time. He was near as burly as you and twice as big. Good thing I got strong. I had to rescue him plenty. I could do it, too."

"Where's he now, your dad?"

"Dead. They're almost all dead. It happens early when you're poor. I got a sister somewheres in Slidell married to a jerk who wouldn't give me the time of day."

"And Slick Williams? He's family?"

"Slick? Heck no. Slick's just another guy like me I met in Memphis at a match last year when I was snooping around for a job. He's bad to go to the bottle. But lots of the time it ain't so rough. You got to stick to something's the way I see it or else they'll really keep you down for good. But I don't know about Slick anymore. He's smaller than me even, but, boy, can he get tough."

I bend over to twist off some grass to chew. He throws a heavy stick he's been carrying up at a bird, a missile thrust ten times his height and more up into the spare, gray sky. It splashes into the bayou. "I hate to wrestle. I hate it. Let's go."

"Where to?"

"To New Orleans! Why not? That's where you live, isn't it?"

Inside the trailer, he tosses his clothes and things into two cardboard boxes from the grocery store, pausing only when the second is near full. "You want a beer? I think I want to drink a beer." He opens two. I drink quickly, belch once, then belch again. He squats on his stool and ponders. "I better leave a note for Slick. He'll be awful pissed to find me gone, not that he didn't expect it to happen one of these days. But we got some new bookings in Texas next month. Slick thinks that's where the big bucks are. Crowds and dough. Texas. He's all the time talking about Texas like it was heaven or some place almost as good. You know what's funny?"

"What?"

"He thinks I'm too conceited so he's always putting me

down." He locates a pad and pencil, writes, and leaves the folded sheet of paper on the table.

"Ready?"

I take one box, he grabs the other. "Sure. Why not?"

On the trip back to the city, he turns sulky, staring out the car's window as it rains. "Gray skies, gray metal roofs everywhere, gray cypress shingles on all the houses, gray people, even the moss is gray. I hate this country. It's mean."

"It's mean everywhere, Larry." Suddenly scared, without meaning to, I blurt out, "What am I doing?"

"Beats me," he says. "You want to take me back?'

"No," I say, wiping the sweat off my face with the back of my hand. He settles back into the seat, his feet sticking out over the edge, and smiles.

Using only the porch light, we carry his stuff into the living room. I have him stand in the middle of it, click the porch light off, wait, turn the living room's on, wanting the full effect of my work to come all at once. He whistles his kid's whistle. "You drew all these?"

"Surprised?"

"I sure am. You weren't lying. They look real lifelike. You're really good."

"Thanks."

Silence, followed by a frown. "Where have you been hanging out? Hollywood?"

"No. Here. Just here."

"Nobody really looks that good, except maybe in the movies."

"Some do. A few."

He zeroes in on the one that hangs at the bottom of the stairs. "Whoa. Wait a second. What happened to him?"

"A wreck. A motorcycle crash. He wasn't wearing a helmet. The surgeons didn't bother to fix him right."

He looks apprehensively up into the dark. "There's more like him upstairs?"

"One or two, I forget. His name is Carl. I liked his pride."

He says, "I like the others better."

That night, he sleeps in the room way at the end of the hall in a brass bed he needs a chair to reach. I had to find one in another room. It was awkward. In the morning, he refuses to pose.

"Why?"

"Let me wear my shorts," he pleads. "Let me pretend I'm in the ring. Maybe I can do it that way."

"Larry!"

"Why not? Why can't I be dressed? Why do I have to be naked?"

"It's what I do, that's all. You've seen."

"Boy, have I! Why can't you do something different for a change?"

"I am doing something different. I'm drawing you."

"What's that mean?"

"It means 'I'm drawing you.' That's all. What should it mean?"

"Please?"

"I don't understand."

"I don't either. But I can't. I don't want to take my clothes off in front of you. Let's do it different. What do you say? Please?"

"You mean you simply went down there and hauled him back," Cecil says in amazement late that afternoon, "like an order of carryout barbecue? Really, Bo. No wonder he's frightened." He's busily rearranging his favorite records in a back room, a semimonthly task. A gentle, cloud-softened light seeps in between the bamboo slats, covers the windows on the walls, and delicately crosshatches the shelves like an old etching. Cecil shades his eyes. "Hand me that stack of Pertiles, will you, Bo? Careful now. That's it, fingers touching only the edges." He slips them into their new inner sleeves.

"Yes. Aureliano Pertile. Toscanini's favorite singer, you know, often crowned with laurel. A bounteous, magnanimous tenor. But his expressiveness would bloat and come to mark the end of true style," he sighs. "Psychological acuity, after all, is not style, though no one seems to understand that important truth these days."

I pass him over the last two. "What am I going to do, Cecil?"

"Sorry? Do? About what?"

"What do you mean, 'About what?' About Larry, of course. What else have I been talking about for the last hour?"

"Were you? I hadn't noticed amidst the groans. Let me ask you one question, though, darling. Don't you find the whole situation, ah, peculiar? Or if not peculiar then a trifle strange at least?" He carefully counts the number of record jackets and squeezes them into position on the shelf.

"Mind you, I'm not judging. How could one judge what is so anomalous? But surely the, ah, situation must make him much more uncomfortable than it does you. After all, this is your home, in a manner of speaking. He, on the other hand, is in a kind of perpetual exile wherever he goes. And that's the root of it as far as I'm concerned, although one must never discount the practical significance of your difference in size. Surely you have thought about what that difference might mean? It leaves me quite unnaturally curious for a sister and a little breathless with wonder." He pauses to count more jackets. "Now the Lauri-Volpis, if you don't mind. No, those others with the pink labels. Have I ever played any of them for you?" I shake my head while swallowing more of my beer. "Really? I haven't? Well, then, I must. And soon. 'A te, o cara . . .' Wonderful!"

"Not now, Cecil. I wish you'd stick to the subject."

"I didn't know there was a subject, hon, not a real one. I thought you merely wanted to talk, exposing the anguish of your *maladie de coeur.* By the way, what's the little fellow doing now?" He shoves himself up off the floor and brushes off his pants.

"Looking around, walking, getting his bearings. I don't know. He simply took off all of a sudden. He didn't tell me where to."

"Oh, dear."

"What do you mean, 'Oh, dear'?"

"Well, there is apt to be rather a lot of gawking, especially in the Quarter, as accustomed as tourists are to staring at freaks. But I suppose he's gotten used to all that by now," Cecil sighs, as if at some memory all his own. "One must, mustn't one? Eventually." He takes three of what I know to be his most prized records and fits them carefully one by one on the highest shelf, which none but Cecil himself can easily reach. "Well, that's done at least," he says, rubbing his hands together. He walks over to the corner, pulls up the shades, and twists their cords around a hook. "It's started to rain, quite hard in fact. That should chase him somewhere." He turns to face me. "Oh, darling Bo, poor friend. I fear it just isn't going to work out."

"Why not?"

"People" is his simple answer. "Take Bayard and Paisley, for example."

"I'd rather not."

"But that's just it. Tomorrow they're coming for luncheon. Now suppose I invited you and the runt."

"Cecil!"

"Please. I want to make my point." He pretends to be seating his guests. "All right. You're here, you and Larry. We're all now sitting around my table, you two, me, Bayard, Paisley, and the sixth some gorgeous hunk I'll pluck from that nettle danger tonight . . ."

"Not Shannon?"

"Only once he's promised me never to read a book again.

And he did look ever so ill-informed. Well, Shannon then, for consistency's sake, though I'm afraid I may be falling in love with him after all, Bo. Isn't that sad? And it's all so damned expensive. Anyway, my point is that all during the meal neither Bayard nor Paisley can keep their eyes off little Buster Pues. I won't speak for Shannon or for myself, only for Bayard and Paisley who are, let me remind you, lovely men in many ways. But my Lord how they will stare. Like most royalists, they believe that people formed like that were sent to Earth by God to fulfill one purpose and one purpose only, to amuse them. To be fools and jesters to the court. They simply will not accept them . . . or perhaps I should say 'us' . . . in any other role and in this way, of course, they prove identical to the rabble they detest.

"As you are aware, Bayard in particular has an aversion to anything the least bit irregular. You've surely noticed how he regards all those who exhibit even the slightest physical eccentricities as if they were hideous mutants, inexplicable and abhorrent errors in an evolutionary scheme that otherwise has led so soundly, so happily to himself and his equally perfect lover. Poor Bayard. I once heard him shriek in outraged horror at the sight of a foreskin. So unclean, so unnecessary, don't you know? He's quite convinced he was born without one, in some advanced stage of natural development as if without tonsils or an appendix."

"I don't like them, neither one of them," I say. "But you're exaggerating, Cec. They're not that bad."

"Aren't they? Unlike you, I do, I do like them. Or rather I enjoy them," Cecil says, "quite a lot, even if I am myself too tall and gangling for their complete approval and flap around far too much as well. But they are bright, they are often generous in ways that might surprise you, Bo, and they exhibit nearly perfect taste in certain areas I care about greatly. And if you and Larry were to join us tomorrow for this luncheon I am now imagining us all attending they would be the souls of tact and discretion. Too tactful, too discreet. For you more than most should know that no man can control the destiny of his eyes. And their eyes, the look in them, despite their best intentions would be cruel and withering. So it will often be with others. They can't help it." Cecil lays a cold, pastoral hand upon my shoulder. "You have not made a convenient choice, Bo. Are you sure you want your life to become more controversial than it already is?"

"I'm not altogether a heathen, Cecil," I respond. "I pray too, you know."

"Like for Larry now? And what do you ask for in these prayers of yours?"

"I've got to have some secrets, Cecil."

"Do you?" he smirks. "I thought secrets were what artists of all people were least good at keeping. I thought an artist was the sort of man who would spend his whole life in a confessional if he could, sneaking out occasionally only to commit a few new sins in order to have fresh material to talk about and not bore the priest. Now you want to make this peculiar change in your life, you've been hinting at it for months with these scary new drawings of yours, you who have known so many beautiful men so much more intimately than most. I don't understand it, Bo. Why are you deliberately trying to make life, in this unnecessary way, ugly? Why Larry?"

"That's a question I won't even attempt to answer, Cecil. I couldn't," is all I say. "I've got to go."

I leave his house quickly, not so much angry at Cecil, though, as distraught at my own inability to tell him what I also want to hear. I have no response to a question I need answered myself. Despite the rain, I can't go home. What if he isn't there? Instead, I wander down to the river, to that open stretch of the embankment across from Jackson Square that looks out toward Algiers. A freighter is pushing its way upstream. Behind it, a ferry bisects its wake. In the pause between storms, tourists stroll idly around me, eating, drinking, smoking, playfully snapping photographs of one another until the first heavy drops begin to fall again and drive them all away. None of them has seemed to notice the barge reinforcing the levee. I wonder why. They leave unworried, though the river has been steadily rising for the last two weeks, swelling from the heavy runoff from the late summer rains hundreds, even thousands, of miles away, threatening floods. I don't care either, but for a different reason. The Mississippi doesn't belong here any longer. If men had not intervened and stopped it, it would have long ago altered its course one fine day and flowed into the Atchafalaya. We should have let it go, because if the river cannot change, if it is not free to shift its channels as it likes according to the whims of its power, it cannot be said still to live. It is no longer the Mississippi. It is something else that we have made, false and dead.

So what? All nature is not true either. That is what Cecil believes. Thomas Cole had expressed the same thought nearly a century and a half ago. All nature is not true. My first teacher in landscape, Caleb Moore—a wonderful visionary artist who three years ago destroyed all his paintings and took off for Honduras to start over from scratch—agreed with Cole, whose work had so strongly influenced his, and wrote Cole's words up on the board for us all to read and commit to memory on our first day of class. "All nature is not true. The stunted pine, the withered fig-tree, the flowers whose petals are imperfect are not true." Nor was the river true to Caleb, its path too arbitrary for perfection. Hence, he argued, we must bend it to our will and save ourselves. Hence, others argue, we might bend all things of nature to our will. Strip the jungles of Asia, melt the icecaps, burrow deep into the sea as long as we have our way. But if reality succeeds—I mean, if we are lucky—the river and the jungle, all aberrant imperfect wild things, will always defeat our folly in the end.

The stunted pine, the withered fig-tree, the flower whose petals are imperfect, not true? How strange to admit only perfection to God's paradise of truth, His light without His darkness. Perfection is imperfect too. That's what realism means. Those hustlers whom I drew, desired, and always failed to love enough were in their perfect way as imperfect as myself or Larry, if only because I could not bear to love such perfect things until I'd learned to love imperfect ones much more.

The hot rain streams off my hair and beard and rises off my skin like steam. I seek no spirit's intervention, I wish for no different world, I hope for no greater understanding because I know it will never come. I simply pray, water flowing off me and my outstretched arms as if off a bush, a thin rivulet of it pouring away from my rooted feet and down into the mounting river. After a few minutes, I bolt and head for home.

Though it is almost dark, he sees me coming from an upstairs window and rushes down to the porch to greet me at the top of the stoop with two bath towels and a blanket pulled off the bed. "What's that?" I say, wiping my face with one of the towels.

"This?" He touches the lanyard hanging around his neck. "I bought it in a store on Royal Street. See?" He yanks out the whistle and the key from under his shirt. "I didn't want to lose it."

"You're staying then?"

"Staying? Sure I'm staying."

"You don't mind?"

"Mind? What is this, Bo?"

"There's no mistaking, is there, what I am? What I want? That I lied to you back at the trailer park?"

"Jesus," he says, "give me that towel. You're soaked clear through. Where were you?"

"Down by the river. Praying."

"Oh, yeah? That's weird." He wrings the towel out. It's as wet as a just-used wash cloth. "My mother used to pray. So did my father when he thought I wasn't watching. It never did no good from what I could tell. Let's go in."

I follow him, almost tripping on the blanket I'm dragging. "Christ."

"Here, give me those," he orders. "And take off all your clothes. This floor's already as wet as that sidewalk out yonder."

I start to unbutton my shirt as directed. But I can't. I can't get any further than the third button, not with him standing there, eyes glued, too curious. "Stop looking at me like that."

"See?" he says, grinning like a cat.

I blink. "That's all it was?"

"Pretty much."

"I thought . . ."

"Don't tell me what you thought, Bo. It doesn't matter."

"You're shy?"

"Don't look so surprised. Just show me where the mop is. You go take a shower."

I am out and nearly dressed again when he taps lightly on the door. "It's open," I say.

He peers around, hesitant. "I made some good green gumbo while you were gone, if you want some. It'll revive your innards."

I thump the bed next to where I sit. "Larry."

Two steps forward, bolder. "I pushed these two chairs from cabinet to cabinet in the kitchen, looking for stuff. I found it all, except the sugar. You keep a well-stocked house."

"We'll have to change some things. Cut some down to size. Build others up."

"Aw, you don't have to."

"Sure we do."

A few steps closer, his face scrunched up like a doll's squeezed between a child's rough hands. "How did you know, Bo? How did you know to find me? How did you know what I wanted?"

My heart is beating noisily. "How does anyone ever know? Yet you do sometimes. I don't mean you guess. You know."

"It's that easy?"

"Easy? Are you kidding?"

"I've never known. Not about anything."

"Not about Slick?"

"That was an accident. Everything in my life's been more like an accident than you can imagine. We were just about to reach Gulfport for our first match together, Slick trying to teach me all he knew as we went. His trailer hitched behind us started riding strange. I turned around to take a look. He laid his hand on my knee and started bawling about all he'd never had. And that was it. The rest was only talk when he got bad drunk. He didn't want much more. He'd given up."

"You're worried about him?"

"Sure. He's all alone now, again. It's got to be tough."

"You want to phone him?"

"Naw. How could I? Besides, he knew it couldn't last. Sure, he helped me out. I'm grateful, but it wasn't a piece of cake. This is different."

"Different?" He yawns and stretches as if embarrassed. "What let you come with me, Larry, yesterday?"

"I don't know. Your eyes, I think. They weren't curious, just interested, you know? Most people look at me like they do when they're in a room with a television on. No matter how involved they might be in whatever else it is they're doing, ironing or eating breakfast or yelling at their kids, their eyes keep fixing on that tube, waiting to be shocked or something, looking for something different that'll tell them their lives ain't so bad. My mother used to look at me like that all the time. You didn't. Not once. Not really."

"It was bad at home?"

"It was OK. It was when they wanted to baptize me I ran. They'd been waiting, you understand, hoping that I'd grow."

"How old?"

"Maybe fifteen."

"That's young to run."

"Sure it is. They didn't bother to hunt for me. They were too poor. I just jumped in and came up swimming like a dog." He spreads his legs out wide and hooks his thumbs into his shorts, noble and defiant. "When can I start posing?"

"Tomorrow?"

"I was hoping you'd say tonight."

"It's been a long day. It's hard work, Larry."

"So you've said. You think wrestling ain't?"

"That's all movement. For me, you'll have to be very still, quiet and still."

"I'll learn," he says. "But one thing I'll never learn as long as I live. I'll never learn to look like that," he laughs, pointing over to a drawing of Shannon hanging above the dresser. "No way."

"So? I wouldn't want you to. He's beautiful all right. But you're beautiful too, Larry. A different sort of beauty, I admit. Why not? But it's as real as Shannon's there. In some ways, what I've wanted has always been the same. No phoney plaster cast and wire mesh studio Apollo for me. The beauty of the flesh alone concerns me."

A serious frown, too sensible. He stiffens, as if offended. "Beauty? Damn, Bo. Beauty? Me? You must be cracked in the head."

"Something like that," I say and gather him up under my arms, lifting him gently into our bed, feeling as strong as Praxiteles must have felt when he rescued his marble faun first of all his endangered pieces from the fire. Not that I am saving him from anything. More likely it is he who is saving me. And there is no fire threatening us, though something burned. There is only this choice to be made of what one loves the most among so much that is real and beautiful without ever knowing why you've chosen it.

"What should I do?" Cecil asks me one fall morning in his kitchen. Larry is scrambling eggs on his stove, ours having broken, standing on his favorite stool.

"He's trouble, Cec," I say. "Beautiful trouble is the worst kind, I'm told. I'm not sure I believe it, though."

"He wants to stay. He wants to move in with me. At least that's what he says. He says he has to change his life. No more hustling."

"He's looking for father, brother, lover, keeper, protector, backer, savior, nurse, counselor, rescuer, therapist. What else?" I say. "Sister of Charity?"

"Where's he now?" Larry asks, stirring.

"Oh, out for a stroll to get his bearings, he claims. Dennis threw him out, you know. I wonder what that means. Something ominous, I suspect." Cecil glides into the living room where I quickly follow him, leaving Larry with a wink and the work. Cecil fidgets with his turntable, opens a record box, and sets a disc carefully on the platter as if playing it could resolve his dilemma. "Georges Thill," he announces loudly enough for Larry to hear in the kitchen. "In this selection, he will be singing the role of that cad Aeneas. Please note the true heroic ring and appropriately metallic edge in the voice. In our century, the French alone have understood the essence of tragedy to be classicism, symmetry, proportion, detachment, elegance, and passion mixed in roughly equal measure, so that tragedy in opera means, like Aeneas, always doing the wrong thing for exactly the right reason and singing your fool head off about it, carefully never mispronouncing a syllable or missing a beat." He hesitates a moment, a figure of authority about to hand down an important decision. "I think it's too risky, Bo."

"You may be right, Cec," I say.

He declines backward onto his only recently reupholstered couch, not a pillow any longer in sight on it, and sits bolt upright, as erectly uncomfortable looking as a boy being disciplined to sit straight in a straight-backed chair. "And then I think about you and Larry," Cecil says just as Larry enters the room bearing two plates with scrambled eggs and toast on them. "Shouldn't I take you two as a kind of sign? I mean, who would have guessed that so bizarre a relationship could have turned out so well?"

"'Bizarre,' Cecil?" Larry questions, setting his dish down in front of him with a clatter.

"It is bizarre, Larry," Cecil insists. "You might as well face it today if you haven't months ago."

"I agree," I say, hoping to cool Larry down some. "I'm overbuilt, he's too small, everything's extreme in our house. Bizarre. You're right, Cecil. As for you, you're bizarrely thin and tall. Shannon's bizarrely attractive. Should I go on?"

"I still don't like the word," Larry says, heading out toward the kitchen to fetch the third plate.

"I only meant that it gives us all hope." Cecil stares at me plaintively. "I only meant that it's turned out so admirably."

"Don't worry, doll," I say. "When Larry gets back, I'll tell him that 'bizarre' once meant 'handsome.'"

"I heard that!" Larry shouts in.

"It did?" Cecil says, surprised. He cocks his head, forcing himself to concentrate on the music, hushing us both with a display of his hands. "Hear that? *Encor ces voix! Je suis barbare, ingrat! Vous l'ordonnez, grands dieux!* Those words are meant for me. A message sent from the gods. They're saying I mustn't play Aeneas and abandon the one I love for some higher destiny. What can I do? Of course I'll take the poor abandoned child in."

A few weeks later, I work to finish a new painting, a more than life-sized portrait of us three, Larry in the foreground wearing only tight red briefs, arms folded, staring out defiantly at the viewer; Cecil standing impossibly tall behind him, thinner than ever but impeccably dressed and gazing skyward, one pencil-sharp finger pointing like a marker towards heaven; me behind them both, naked, partially erect, leaning back against the trunk of a stunted pine, taller than Larry, shorter than Cecil, balancing the whole perfectly on the right, upsetting the balance wildly on the left, my muscle-bound, overdeveloped body the only umber patch in a composition otherwise dominated by oranges, yellows, cerise, gaudy pinks and flesh tones, chartreuse and brilliant darker greens, the whole as flat as a late Matisse and twice as bright as the fauvist ones, utterly true to life. When I look out the window, I see Larry down there leaning against that mimosa whose roots, like the spindly oak's next to it, crack the sidewalk more each year and lift it higher until soon a slab of it may stand almost as tall as him, short stuff, mighty mite, tag team terror, tiny tongue in twister, Larry, little Larry, my Larry, Larry Buster Pues.

How my heart rushes as I watch the swag, the brag of him as he saunters up Esplanade, his muscles stretching his baby blue tank top as if it is made of thin rubber, as if it is a balloon blown almost to bursting each time his lungs expand, his bright red shorts clinging even tighter to his sweating crotch, his lithe tongue from time to time licking off his ice-cream-stained lips with a motion as lazily casual as a horse's tail swatting at flies.

If I could stop what I'm doing on the picture, I'd yell down right this second, "Come on up now!" because I'd like nothing better than to hear the click of his feet crossing the

stoop and climbing those stairs to up here where this morning in bed we danced to no god, worshiped no perfect hero,
sang no hymns of praise to anyone except our imperfect
selves. Oh, how I'd like to shout out right now, "Come on up
here, Larry. Come on, Buster. The world is wonderful. The
day is racing. Hurry."

III

Buddy Loves Jo Ann

SWAGGERING, the cook leaned into his news-paper like a man eager to start an argument. His chef's hat was greasy and torn where it had been pulled too tight around the back of his head. Every time he flipped a page, he shifted his weight from one leg to the other. As he read, he sang along with the radio:

> *Sad bird,*
> *Perching in a cage,*
> *Sings to me*
> *A tune so strange,*
>
> *Sings a song*
> *No wild bird sings:*
> *Unkind love*
> *Has clipped its wings.*

After having observed him closely for the past several hours, Buddy was increasingly astonished at how the cook was always moving even when the man seemed to have nothing to do.

Though all four booths had been empty when he entered, Buddy Birnam had chosen to sit at the diner's counter with his back to the door and to the large wall clock above it, most of whose face, when he strained his neck, he could see in the mirror, its numbers reversed and its second hand ticking backward. The summer before Jo Ann entered first grade, the two of them had played every day, even the cozy rainy ones, in the bushes by the creek behind the toppled fence that marked the divide between the Turner and Birnam properties. From fallen branches, torn vines, and broad leaves, they had built their playhouse. Jo Ann had predicted often that it wouldn't survive the first big storm, but because they enjoyed repairing whatever damage weather and time inflicted upon it, it lasted almost until Buddy's eighth birthday. When Jo Ann determined it was finally beyond any more restoration, they strewed its remains over the woods' floor. Only in recent months had Buddy begun to understand why Jo Ann had insisted they be so meticulous in their work of obliteration.

The fluorescent lights in the diner were as harsh as those in the bus station where sixteen hours ago, in flight from Jo Ann's request for him to do what she had called "one last kindness" for her, he waited to leave for good the town where they had both lived all their lives. Was it wrong for him to refuse her wish? He was certain that it was worse than wrong, that it was damnable, but such conviction had not kept him from running away.

He sipped his coffee, now cooled to a barely palatable lukewarm. When they were children, he and Jo Ann vowed to spend their lives together until death, and they had kept their promise to each other in their own private way. Jo Ann was born on Dogwood Street, Buddy two years later fifty yards around the corner on Stuart Way. Neither of them ever slept a night of their lives farther apart than their two houses or under a roof different from the one under which they took their first breaths.

Buddy glanced at himself in the mirror. How had it happened that a man as seriously old as he was had never spent a night away from home in an unfamiliar bed? Did his asking the question to himself mean he felt regret? Most of his life he had lived, like Jo Ann, alone. Both of Jo Ann's younger sis-

ters had married so long ago he could barely remember either
of them. They'd each moved with their husbands to regions
of the country from which it seemed not even mail bothered
to travel the great distance back home. Neither returned for
the funeral after their mother died from a tumor that had
grown to the size of a child in her womb. Less than a year
later, Miles Turner was diagnosed with cancer in both lungs.
Jo Ann nursed her father for seven months, watching him
shrivel and shrink into a voodoo doll's mockery of his former
self. Was her own dying more accurately prophesied in his
death or her mother's? The truth lay in both, Buddy thought.

The day Miles Turner died, Grover Birnam's bayonet
wound from the Great War ripped open again as savagely
as if he had run naked into the full swing of an ax. Buddy
buried his father less than a month after Jo Ann began wearing black to mourn hers. Complaining about an itch that
wouldn't quit, Rosemary Birnam, Buddy's mother, took to
scratching her skin all over her body so vigorously with her
long, unpainted nails that it bled. After a while, the wounds
wouldn't heal. Six months later, he and Jo Ann watched the
last of their parents laid to rest beneath a sky as hurtful to
the eye as his mother's brightly lit hospital room had been.
The row of pine that bordered the town cemetery looked as
phoney beneath an ash white sun as a dime-store display of
plastic Christmas trees. After experiencing so much loss in so
short a time, they found in each other not comfort, which
neither had ever anticipated, but rest and a little peace.

Each now owned a house, though not one they would attempt to share as they had the make-believe house in the
woods by the creek. Until she retired, Jo Ann was a secretary
at an old, respectable, but unprosperous law firm downtown,
housed in a mid-nineteenth-century brick building. Only
half a block away stood another brick building, nearly as antique, which after the Great War had been converted into a
discount clothing store catering mostly to mill workers and

tobacco farmers who couldn't afford anything better. Since the month he graduated from high school, Buddy had sold cheap boots, shoes, and hats to these men and their wives and children, earning even less at his job than many of them did at theirs.

Early in his and Jo Ann's working lives, people somewhat better off than they but possessing what they both regarded as much less dignity started to buy up small parcels of the abandoned sheep-grazing land around them and to build on it houses that Jo Ann said resembled trucks or trailers or temporary roadside Dumpsters more than real homes. They couldn't last, she said. When, on a western curve of the creek that flowed eastward between his place and Jo Ann's, colored people began to move in, neither of them knew what to think. But, when pressed, they refused to join the protests organized by their angry neighbors. Thereafter they were frequently shunned, even at the New Hope Methodist Church they attended, as if the wings of virtue they were believed to have worn previously had suddenly dropped off and exposed them as rebellious angels. They acknowledged their ostracism to each other, but claimed not to mind. That the two of them had been correct to shun such rabble-rousing mischief was sufficient justification.

No day would end without their having enjoyed at least one meal together and a game of cards—gin and honeymoon bridge were their favorites. After Buddy relented and bought a TV so they could watch Kennedy debate Nixon, they would sometimes watch it for less high-minded reasons, but for entertainment still preferred the older music on the radio at Jo Ann's. Every other Saturday, rain or shine, they went to a movie downtown at the Grand, usually after the children had left their matinee and before the teenagers and younger adults on dates arrived for the evening show. The film over, they ate dinner at the Willow Cafeteria. Buddy invariably selected fried chicken, spoon bread, greens, and either apple pie or, if either was in season, cold watermelon or fresh peaches with syrup. Jo Ann varied her selections more, but preferred salads and seldom requested a dessert unless it was cubes of red and yellow Jell-O with a dollop of real whipped cream.

As Jo Ann aged, her buckteeth, bushy eyebrows, and pointed English chin all became more pronounced, as did the translucent clarity of her glass-bottle blue eyes. She started to speak to almost everyone with a frankness she had previously reserved for Buddy, but he knew better than to waste words trying to caution her. For seventy years she had deeply touched his soul. He couldn't tell you why because he didn't understand the reason himself, though he believed her without question when she said he had touched hers as deeply for as long. No one who knew them presumed to ask why they had never married.

How had so many years passed? What had they really done with seven decades, living their lives without event or incident into what astonishingly was now old age? But old age, the always uncanny passage of time, amazed them less than how simple, how easy it had been for them to have been happy for so long. And they had been happy, truly happy, hadn't they? Buddy was sure of it, in part because, unlike their poor parents, not one of whom had ever been blessed with sustained good health, they had been rarely ill or less than sound in mind and body.

Then the winter of his seventieth year, quite by accident it appeared, they both began complaining incessantly about this pain or that. One day, Buddy's joints ached worse than his teeth, the next his back hurt worse than his joints, and Jo Ann couldn't seem to stop coughing. Six months ago, on a Sunday evening while they were slicing peaches ripe from Buddy's tree, Jo Ann started to cough so badly she had to excuse herself. When she returned, her face was as white as her handkerchief where it had not been soaked with blood.

The cook refilled his cup. How much coffee had Buddy

drunk during the last several hours? When he sipped it, it was hot enough, but sour. Sitting on his stool while he waited for midnight, he had counted only four other customers entering the diner—two women wearing skimpy waitress uniforms, a young mechanic in his greasy coveralls, a check-out clerk from the Winn Dixie up the coast near the bus station, all of whom knew the cook Leo by name. Not one of them seemed to notice the old man, but Buddy was relieved that he was invisible to them. He had always wanted to feel invisible to everyone except Jo Ann. We are both, she had remarked years ago, an enigma too uninteresting to try to solve, as boring, thank heaven, as a story without a plot or a point.

For well over forty years he had been called "Mr. Birnam" by everyone who spoke to him. Only Jo Ann still used the little boy's name with which he had been christened. "Buddy," she appealed to him just a few nights ago, speaking with so unfamiliar an emotion that he almost didn't recognize the name as his own. "I know who you really are, Buddy. You're a poet. You see things with a poet's eyes. You experience life with a poet's soul. You're my favorite poet, Buddy." Embarrassed, he demurred politely, reminding her of how little poetry he had read in his life and of how much less he had understood. But with a wicked twinkle in her eye, she refused to withdraw her remark, instead adding, "True poets never deign to write a word."

To his eyes, the lights in the diner seemed to expose the thin bones under his fish-belly white skin. He rolled down his shirtsleeves and put his suit coat back on. Watching the cook as he worked, he felt his own body shrink into something even smaller than the gawky boy's body into which old age had returned him. Hadn't one adolescence been hardship enough for a lifetime? Burly, big-boned, swarthy yet ruddy-cheeked, the cook was as vibrant as the fire over which he worked. Reluctantly, Buddy glanced at the reflection of the clock as he spooned sugar into his cup. Quarter after eleven.

Why he had chosen midnight, so banal a time for such an act, he could not say, but once he had chosen it he knew he could not change it or back out. He had taken enough money from home for the bus trip southeast. No bills were left in his wallet. In his right pocket jiggled some change he would use to pay for the coffee and the tip. On principle, he had never carried a charge card of any kind. Again he checked the clock in the mirror. Was it running fast? "Death before dishonor," his father had declared to him one unforgettable night shortly before his graduation from high school. Buddy listened intently, deeply affected by his father's conviction. Nobody else, not his teachers at school or the preacher at church, had offered him words he could really live by. "Death before dishonor. That's the best and most difficult code a man can accept as his challenge in life. Never dishonor yourself, son." Had he ever really understood what his father meant? Buddy took as deep a breath as his lungs would allow. Amidst all the diner's unpleasant odors, was it also the ocean he smelled?

Neither he nor Jo Ann had ever crossed their county's borders; though, especially when he was a boy, he had often yearned to see the beach and ocean. One long weekend each spring, the boys and girls of his town would drive the three hundred and fifty-seven miles to the coast to party, reckless and free and, he was certain, nearly naked most of the time. Year after year, he had spied them leaving in their cars, returning only a few days later so inalterably changed, their bodies having blossomed as swiftly and beautifully as lilac in the sun, that he could not understand why any rational parent would let them go. Their transformation stunned him. During his own high school years, he hadn't bothered to ask permission from his parents. He understood they were too poor to allow him to indulge in such a folly, and in any case Jo Ann would never have gone with him. To her, girls who wanted such lives were silly. But, especially in the springtime when the pear and cherry trees blossomed, Buddy lamented not having seen the strand alive with young people frisking and basking in the sun while he was also young.

At 11:32, the last customer left the diner. Except of course for himself, the man whom Jo Ann Turner had called over the years the kindest, sweetest, just plain nicest person she had ever known. She had repeated those very words just a little more than twenty-four hours ago. What people did Jo Ann know with whom to compare him? Perhaps enough, he allowed, for him to accept the praise without really knowing what any of it meant.

The cook was scraping the flat grill, his body swaying to the steady rhythm of another rock song on the radio that sat on a corner of the counter. Every time he walked past it, he had to duck under the taut cord that just reached the wall socket over the last booth. Would Jo Ann have called him kind for having let Buddy linger over one cup of coffee, repeatedly refilled, for nearly three hours? Or would she have been repelled, as she often said she had been when she'd observed it in others, by such obvious brawn, grit, and brashness? Even how he flipped a burger was abrupt, almost sullen in that way that never ceased to shock her. "How different you are, Buddy," she would say, grasping his hand in hers.

An announcer on the radio was warning of a big storm. Over the last quarter of a century, hurricanes had washed much of that part of the coast into the sea, but the town of Crescent Beach had vowed not to die. When ruin was irreversible, was it better to accept one's fate or resist? As Buddy strolled the town's remaining boardwalk earlier that evening, the cold dense fog obliterated the sky, and the beach seemed to be vanishing before him like snow under a strong sun, melting back into water. Had that vision frightened or comforted him?

Before he could decide, he thought of Jo Ann lying helpless in her bed, alone. Was she accepting her fate or resisting it? Even if he could determine which was the right answer, how could that knowledge advise him? Shivering, he had walked into the diner only because it was the lone building along that strip of the shore with its lights on. Without waiting to be asked, the cook poured him a cup of coffee, piping hot. Soon Buddy felt warm enough to remove his coat and, uncharacteristically, roll up his sleeves.

The cook clicked off the fan over the grill. Had Buddy noticed its whirring before it had been turned off, or how close the surf sounded? In the summers when he was still little, or littler as his mother would later say, his father used to call him home for dinner from the porch. Buddy was certain he never heard his voice at all until his father, still crying out his name, approached the bank of the creek, just a few feet away from the green playhouse where Jo Ann's giggling gave them away. How much else during his lifetime had he failed to hear because he didn't want to hear it? "Listen to me," Jo Ann had said to him just before she told him the news he had dreaded for weeks. Had she expected him to put his fingers in his ears? In his own estimation, he'd already heard enough and seen enough of life. Why should he fear more? "Listen to me," Jo Ann repeated, her voice almost savage with insistence.

Wiping his hands on his grease-spattered apron, the cook rested on a stool he'd slid from the other side of the counter, a taller man sitting than Buddy was standing. He scratched behind his ear where patches of his hair were as gray as Buddy's had been twenty years or so ago before it had all turned dirty white and frizzy, like cotton in the boll. "Time to close," he announced. Without risking another glance at the clock, Buddy nodded. "Don't mean to insult you by asking, friend," the cook added, "but you got that look. I've seen it plenty. You found yourself a place to sleep?"

Buddy tried to recall the name of the motel whose sign he'd read as he stepped off the bus, luggageless. "The Seaside Inn," he said, with more of a question in his words than he had intended. "It's very comfortable."

But hadn't the Seaside Inn been boarded up like the two other motels he half-remembered seeing? He decided not to try to correct his mistake since it was his experience that most people expected the old to be confused. Even Jo Ann occasionally expected a certain dottiness from him, excusing his errors to his face as symptoms of his increasing years, though she was his senior by almost twenty-three months. Yet his failure to notice some things, especially important things, had made him increasingly uneasy. "You've been kind to let me linger," he said.

"No problem. Taking a little time away from home, are you?"

"Yes."

"Pretty deserted around here these days. Just a few people on their way elsewhere, like me. Not just because it's off-season. Mother Nature's done her worst. Devastation all up and down this coast for miles."

"It's a shame."

"I like a livelier place myself. Found this joint on my way to sunny Florida." He rubbed the same spot behind his ear. "Stopped here for a meal. I know what a goddamned bowl of chili is supposed to taste like. You know what I'm saying? Cook got so mad he quit right there and then. I accepted his challenge. Listen, a man complains to me and he's right, I'll try to fix it for him, make it good, you understand? No one's requiring you to pay rent for that stool, are they? You could sit there all night as far as I'm concerned. We all got worries and heartache, am I right? You bet I am."

"Certainly," Buddy acknowledged, slowly backing away and almost stumbling on an empty gum-ball machine on his way to the door. What had the man been implying? How had his legs gotten so tangled together? He prayed the cook would not think he was a drunk, or worse, infirm. "Good night," he said, waving cheerily. "Thank you so much."

As he left, Buddy opened and closed the door carefully,

making certain that he did not trip on one of the steps that led down from the diner to the gravel walkway. In contrast to the warm air of the diner, the outside air was chilly, though nowhere near as cold as the snowstorm he and Jo Ann had played in when they were still in elementary school. Wandering far from their house in delight at the strangeness of it, they had lost their way and almost froze in the unfamiliar woods before their fathers and two neighbor men found them, huddled together beneath the skirt of an old magnolia. Inside the diner, the cook flipped the window sign to "Closed" and pulled down the shades. A few seconds later, the lights inside and above the building went dark.

As Buddy walked north on the sidewalk parallel to the highway, the air smelled brackish and the cloudy night was a spotted greenish gray, like the throat of a frog. Almost every streetlight's globe was broken or lacked a bulb. At one motel, whose road sign optimistically proclaimed "Closed for the Season," grass had pierced the cracked cement drive. So much trash had littered its parking lot that the waste had formed along the motel's south wall an imposing half-pyramid of crumbling debris.

Moving much too fast, a car passed him on the left. As he stopped to watch it zoom through a flashing red light and out of sight, he heard as if for the first time in his life the sound of waves swelling and crashing onto land, a music more compelling to his ears than a church organ's. A few feet farther north, he turned east onto a rickety wooden walkway that zigzagged through the dunes to the ocean. Had the duckboards under his feet felt this way to his father as, crouching, he waited his turn to go over the top? The comparison, though his own, struck him as embarrassing and grandiose.

The wind soughed through the sea oats as it used to through the cane at home before the new people came and cut it down, planting in its place, if anything, clumps of scrub

trees and rugged shrubs through which the wind blew silently. The damp cold and wind-carried grit pricked his skin.
A sandpiper, foraging late, scurried past. Mournfully Buddy
gazed out toward the barely visible horizon where the mot-
tled cloudy sky darkened into the sea. Since rushing, frightened, out of Jo Ann's bedroom the previous night, he had
accomplished nothing that did not add to his already great
store of self-delusion and folly. Long ago, despite his mother's
shrieking protests, he had climbed the same tall pine from
which Jo Ann had fallen the day before and broken her arm
in two places. He had not broken his arm, of course. He was
only showing off, just as his mother, after scolding him once
he had been carried back down, had patiently explained.

Was it high tide? With effort, he slid one foot, then the
other into the frigid water. Was this gesture, too, only more
showing off? But before he decided to stop himself, he was
knee deep, the water creeping up his pants' legs and long
johns to his thighs. Death before dishonor, he reminded himself. Duty, honor, the code. His father had said it did not matter what you called it so long as you understood that the poor
and unimportant man must obey it as much as the rich and
great. But obedience to the moral law, he had warned, was
not the same thing as seeking to satisfy the opinions of others. The sole victory anyone ever wins is the battle against
himself. That is the meaning of honor, he said, the victory
over yourself.

So Buddy had lived honorably. He neither cursed nor
swore. He had never cheated anyone out of anything. He had
tithed every month of his life. He had kept his body, like his
house, spotlessly neat and clean. He neither ate to excess nor
drank at all, trying to keep as healthy as he could. Though he
did not really care for them, he went out of his way to be po-
lite to children and kind to animals. He made an effort to be
always courteous, however sorely he was tried, especially at
work. He had hidden from the world only what it required

him to hide, had lied to it only when it had insisted that he lie. Since their infancies, he had been faithful to Jo Ann. Above all, he had been faithful to Jo Ann.

Was he being faithful to her still? But what she had asked of him was impossible, dishonorable, wrong. "It would be a kindness," she had said. "Help me end my suffering, please. Please, Buddy. You have always been so kind to me. Be kind again once more, now. Tonight. This pain is more than my soul can stand." But to break the old injunction Thou Shalt Not Kill, above all to break it with Jo Ann, was a horror he could not bear. Death before dishonor, his father had proclaimed. If someone had to be killed, Buddy thought, surely it was better that he kill himself.

The water had reached up to his waist. Was he getting faint? How quickly his lower body had become numb. Waves were beginning to break closer, in swells twice their former size. As irresolute as he was frightened, he slowly began to back out, but as his left foot tested the bottom it found not sand but a hole into which it slipped. Losing his balance, Buddy tumbled backward, sucked beneath the water by an undertow that pushed his face down into the sand and scraped his right cheek across the spines of a shell. A counter-current dragged him deeper into the ocean. Some force, too huge to be only a wave, broke over him and shoved him across the ocean's floor over which he rolled like a terrified child somersaulting too fast down a steep, slick hill. If he had no time to ask himself, "Buddy, are you afraid to die?", his flailing body answered for him, fighting against its destruction, though his water-soaked clothes and old man's shoes, even as the current momentarily subsided, held him under like ten-pound weights. Had he blacked out before or after his body went limp, as if in acceptance of its death?

He couldn't remember. Nor could he quite remember being grabbed and dragged back to shore or carried in strong arms the quarter of a mile to Leo's apartment. When he woke up, he found himself in a tiny room, too small to swing a cat in, as Jo Ann would say. It seemed to his watery eyes as bright as the diner, though lit by incandescent bulbs he at first mistook for candles. He was lying naked and swaddled in bedclothes on a couch that hurt every inch of his body the way a monk's bed of rough planks would hurt. Across from him, Leo sat wearing a terrycloth robe and a beach towel wrapped around his neck. He offered Buddy something steaming from a mug. "Here. Drink it," he commanded.

"I can't. I hurt," Buddy mumbled petulantly. "My stomach hurts."

"Drink it anyway."

"I think I'm going to be sick."

"There's a pan on the floor next to you. Use it if you have to."

Against his better judgment, Buddy accepted the mug and sipped from it. "Chicken broth? Jo Ann always fixes me chicken broth when I'm under the weather. Or egg drop soup. She prefers fresh orange juice herself."

"Good for her. Finish it off now."

Buddy did as he was told. "I really don't feel so good. Awful in fact."

"Who wouldn't when they've just been dragged out of the Atlantic? But you'll be OK. It's just that I waited on that damn dune too long. I should've hooked you before that big wave threw you under. But the next one did us both a favor. Belched you up onto shore like that big fish did Jonah. You sure were heavy to carry for a skinny little old man. Your pulse was so slow and your face so white I thought we might lose you. But you were breathing good, only a little slow and shallow. You didn't take on much water. Battered and bruised is all. I've seen worse. You'll live."

"You followed me?"

"You were showing all the signs, old man."

Buddy tugged the musty comforter up to his chin. Something in it smelled faintly like hot metal. Or was the odor his own body? Since shame had forced him to quit high school gym, no one had ever looked at him naked. "Where are my clothes?"

"In the tub. I'll take them to the laundry tomorrow." Buddy touched the bandage on his forehead and scalp. "You were bleeding bad. What's your name?"

"Mr. Birnam. Buddy Birnam. I'm sorry, but I really am going to be sick." He rolled onto his side and aimed over the edge of the cushion for the pan.

"That wasn't anything," the man said afterward. "Hardly anything. Just a piddle. Feel better?"

"No." Buddy sighed as sincerely as he had ever sighed in his life. "My manners dictate that I say, 'Thank you.'"

"Don't mention it." Leo carried the pan into the bathroom, poured the contents into the toilet, flushed, closed the door behind him, and turned out all the lights with the click of two switches. "If you need anything, holler. There's no doctor within thirty miles of this town this time of year, but there's a county hospital half an hour down the road by car. The only thing is that I don't own a car."

Buddy wanted to blow his nose, but was embarrassed to have to ask for a tissue. He snuffled and shook his head. "They'd ask questions. All doctors ever do is ask questions."

"Maybe so. Sleep well, old man. I'll be bunking right behind you. We'll talk later about getting you home."

Was he already half asleep the second time Leo, lying on the floor, said "Good night" to him? Had he already fallen completely asleep when he heard the thundercrack of a storm and the rattle and dried gourd sound of rain against the room's one window pane? He couldn't tell but surely he was dreaming when he sensed the building sway as if the ocean had reached its foundations and begun to dig beneath them. He felt himself falling.

But nearly all his life, certainly since he was a little boy, he had sensed himself falling as he slept, a continuous plummeting through a dark rabbit hole like Alice's, though his burrow had no bottom to it and no door through which to enter Wonderland on the other side. He'd just keep falling until he woke when he would discover to his shame that, because his body had grown too warm under its covers, he'd thrown them off and exposed himself. Had he actually, as he fell this time, called out the cook's name?

He had dreamed many other dreams, of course, some more frightening, a few more pleasant. But of all his dreams the one where he plunged down an endless silent hole was the most recurrent. His dream, he called it. Had he been dreaming it again that night as he heard the rain still falling, as loud and close as if someone were showering in a room next to him? He clung to the comforter to keep himself covered.

Lumps and buttons from the couch's cushions pressed against his body. Was he awake then, both the noise of truck tires rolling fast over wet pavement and that of furniture being moved on the floor over his head real? He could taste the metallic cold of ice on his lips, then something warm and salty in the back of his throat. Children were playing, shouting and laughing and throwing leaves, in a yard close by. Trees shimmered in a summer breeze. The dark turned light, then dark again. All his body ached, more than it had ever hurt before, and his right cheek burned hot as steam. Jo Ann lay next to him, her arms crossed over her bosom in that attitude of fake repose that undertakers impose upon the dead. Beneath the odor of talc and rosewater, he could smell flesh as ripe as chicken left too long in the fridge. "Buddy," he heard her complain, "don't you ever throw anything away? But you're usually so tidy, Buddy."

Since he was two years, seven months, and eleven days old, they had never been separated by more than twenty four hours, not even when either or both of them were sick. As they played in the woods, erecting or improving their various playhouses, other children would sometimes hide in the trees and taunt, "Buddy loves Jo Ann, Buddy loves Jo Ann. Jo Ann and Buddy sitting in a tree, k-i-s-s-i-n-g."

Only Miss Adele Butterfield dared to try to separate them. Because Jo Ann had broken the rules, she'd said, and crossed the line that separated the boys' playground from the girls' at recess. Buddy was in the third grade, Jo Ann in the fifth. He overheard his mother repeating Miss Butterfield's hateful recommendation to his father. "Where's the harm, Rosemary?" he responded. "They're just children. For heaven's sake, where's the harm?" Yet when Buddy was a senior and Jo Ann, her year at business college completed, already working full-time at her job, his father advised him to try dating someone else. "Play the field, Buddy. You're still young. There are plenty of fish in the sea, some lots prettier than Jo Ann Turner." What sense did that make? The two of them had never dated.

"We'll have something finer than a marriage," Jo Ann had asserted when they were still children. And they had had something better, hadn't they? A life chaste and pure, free of anger and rage and jealousy and hatred. Oh, they occasionally bickered or disagreed about trivial things. They'd quarreled. Neither was perfect. Humankind, he had been taught to believe, was not capable of being free of sin. But Buddy loved Jo Ann, Jo Ann loved Buddy. If anyone sought proof, let them examine the path their feet had worn between their two houses, more solid and permanent than any the town or county had built from cement.

He heard Jo Ann's collie Mimi barking furiously in the backyard. Jo Ann had named the dog after her favorite character in opera, one she especially loved to listen to on the radio during wintry Saturday afternoons. When the dog Mimi died, put to sleep because she was blind and tormented with pain from old age, Jo Ann refused to listen ever again to Puccini's opera, unable to bear the tears she shed at the poor helpless flowermaker's death. Buddy called again to the dog that was yelping as if at an intruder, but his appeal went as always unanswered.

He opened his eyes. In an alcove, hardly a kitchen, the man stood cooking over a hot plate. Daylight exposed the room's shabby plainness. Years ago, the walls had been painted a glossy pink, now faded into calico patches. Curling squares of brown and rust linoleum covered the rugless floor. On the seat of a straight-backed chair sat a black-and-white television, turned on, but soundless. He wanted to signal to Leo that he was awake, but his consciousness of his nakedness delayed his doing so until he had carefully rearranged the covers over his body.

Leo poured a honey-colored liquid from the pot into a beer mug. "Here," he said. "Drink some more of my miracle brew."

Before he accepted it, Buddy tugged on the covers, drawing them back up to his chin, but in the process exposing his feet and legs, white and shiny as soapstone or a freshly stripped hog bone. "I'm not dressed," he protested.

On the outside of the closet door, an olive drab slicker hung on a hook. When Leo removed the slicker, Buddy saw his clothes, cleaned and placed on hangers, even his long johns neatly folded. "You've been sleeping for," Leo checked his wristwatch, "just about thirty-five hours."

"That's impossible," Buddy responded testily. "I've always been an early riser. I'll want to recompense you for the cleaning of my clothes, of course."

"With what? I checked your wallet. Not much in there, old man. Not even a driver's license."

"I never learned to drive."

Leo brought the four wire hangers draped with clothes to him and lay them across the back of the couch. "Your shoes are there, by the window. Ugliest damn shoes I ever seen. I got them dry pretty good, but they're cracked bad. Wearable. Well, what you waiting for? Me to dress you?"

Buddy grimaced. "Goodness no. Do you think I might have a little privacy?"

"I don't believe you, old man. You're too proud for me," Leo said before he closed the bathroom door behind him. "Holler when you're decent."

His body ached so bad, so much worse than it ordinarily did these days, that it took Buddy even longer than usual to dress, at least twenty minutes, not counting his shoes that required five more minutes to shove and somehow squeeze on. His back felt as if a knife had slit it from his neck to the crack in his bottom. Had his thighs ever been so sore? But the sweat he was shedding came from neither pain nor fever but shame. What was he going to do now? He hobbled to the john door and tapped on it, then settled into a chintz chair whose faded bluebirds perched on twigs as gnarled as his fingers.

Back in the room, Leo folded the bedclothes that lay piled on the couch, sat them on the floor, and stretched out on the cushions where Buddy still could not believe he had spent the last day and a half. He wished he could see a newspaper to confirm the date. What must Jo Ann be imagining about him and his absence? Was it true, as she once maintained, that there was a natural border between two people, like a river or a mountain range, that neither could cross at death? Then what was the reason for faith? As Leo maneuvered his body to find a comfortable position, the springs squeaked like a swing's chain, yet Buddy had not heard them protest once under his own weight. Leo sat back up. "So, old man," he said. "Tell me. What you want to snuff yourself for?"

"I didn't."

"The truth is powerful."

"Is it?" He had wanted to say "Leo," but couldn't. Why

was the man's name so difficult for him to say? He tried it
again in his head where it sounded less intimate. "Leo," he
said. "I'm not clever, Leo. That's what a teacher once told my
parents. Can you imagine? 'Buddy's a very sweet little boy,
but we're afraid he's not very clever with the others.' Jo Ann
says I'm intelligent. She's even flattered me into thinking I'm
quite bright. She said just a few nights ago that I was a poet.
I didn't understand. All my life I've had to let Jo Ann be
clever for the both of us."

Buddy twisted a loose button on his vest. How had it
survived the turbulence at sea when it came off so easily in
his fingers? He tucked it into the vest's watch pocket. Out
the window, he spotted a section of the boardwalk, a short
stretch spared some hurricane's destruction. How slight, how
shrunken, how terribly diminished the strand looked when
compared with the pictures he had seen of it during its
youthful glory days. For the first time Buddy noticed, to his
surprise, the ugly pattern of umber scars which crisscrossed
Leo's raw face. Once leaving church, Jo Ann had whispered
to him that no man's face, not even a preacher's, was as
truthful under artificial light as it was under the sun's. He
should stop fidgeting with the upholstery. He had always
been tempted to fidget when he was upset or nervous, giving
himself away.

"Did you ever live in a small town, Leo? Small towns can
be very . . . harsh." Buddy took as deep a breath as his sore
old dry lungs admitted. "For years now the town's gossips
have been saying that Jo Ann and I are really only children
who grew old without ever having grown up."

"Jo Ann?"

"How strange. Here I am assuming you know all about it
when, of course, you don't know a thing. Jo Ann's my friend,
my best and only friend. She's dying, very painfully and
slowly. She's been hiding pills so no one would notice beneath
silk scarves in a bedside drawer. She's certain that they will

work, but she's just as certain that she can't swallow them alone. She'd choke. 'So I need your help, Buddy,' she said. 'I need you to be brave. Just hold my hand. That's all you have to do. Just hold my hand.'" Buddy knew he ought not to cry. It would be weak in front of a strong man like Leo. Yet he wept despite himself, more copiously than he had in weeks.

Leo yanked a handkerchief out of his jeans' pocket and gently patted Buddy's cheek dry, taking particular care around the bandages. "You love her a lot."

"Yes."

"I understand."

"I'm sure you don't. No one ever has. I don't myself, not completely, not anymore."

Leo stood up, then half sat, half leaned against the sofa's broad back. "You sure are a proud old man." He crossed his brawny arms. Why hadn't Buddy noticed the tattoos before, especially the one with the lion? He wished he could read all the letters to see if they spelled a name. "My shift starts soon," Leo said. "You want to stay here for a little while longer or come to work with me?"

"Go with you, I think. I'm afraid of being alone."

"You must be hungry. I'll fix you a real meal."

It started raining again as they walked back to the diner, a cold, deliberate winter's rain without wind. Along one strip of surviving boardwalk, Buddy stumbled and grabbed onto Leo's left arm, holding it for support. Leo slowed the pace, and, as they passed a dune alive with sea oats, Buddy began to tell him the story of his life. Was Leo surprised at its uneventfulness or how quickly it could all be narrated? Never having spoken in this way to anyone before, not even to Jo Ann who knew it so well already, Buddy had nothing with which to compare Leo's reactions. Was he boring him?

The man had saved his life. But did he want it saved? And did that fact mean he owed Leo some knowledge about the life that he had rescued? What compelled him to continue speaking when clearly there was nothing more to say? Yet he did not stop talking until they reached the sidewalk along the highway, when Leo informed him of how he had bathed him with warm water and a washcloth earlier that morning while Buddy slept. Buddy blushed, his skin hot despite the air's chill, his fingers still clutching Leo's coat.

As they entered the diner, the day cook was already untying his apron. "One lousy customer all morning," he complained, "and all she wanted was coffee and half a Danish. Half a Danish. Why you took this job is beyond me, Leo. If it'd been me in your shoes, I'd have kept hitching down to Florida. Hightail it to where it's sunny and warm all year. But me, I got a wife and a kid and a second job I'm late for now."

"Frank, meet Mr. Buddy Birnam," Leo said. "Mr. Birnam's passing through town on his way back home. Had a little accident a couple of nights ago that slowed him down a little, but he's fine now. Isn't that right, Mr. Birnam?"

"Wish I could go home now," Frank said.

"Give my best to Dorothy and Marlene," Leo said.

"Sure. When I see them," Frank said, slamming the door behind him.

Buddy's head felt hummingbird light in the diner's warm, steam-filled air. At Leo's direction, he slid into a booth where Leo poured them both a cup of coffee. After their second cup, Leo returned from the grill with two bowls of tomato rice soup and two cheeseburgers with bacon. Buddy ate his burger with the relish of a small boy on his first outing. Between bites, to slow himself down, he found himself talking too much again. "I own a small house. Not so much a house as a cottage, really. Cozy. But it has two bedrooms, and the yard is lovely, with several fruit trees that still bear the sweetest fruit and a pleasant pond with a little gazebo my father built next to it for shade in the summer. Only the squirrels and the crickets and the frogs make any noise at all. It's where Jo Ann most enjoys reading. I should call Jo Ann. She must be very worried. I have failed her in so many ways. This is excellent soup, Leo. Did you make it yourself? Where did you learn to cook?"

"In the army."

"I was drafted during the Second World War, but to no one's surprise, least of all mine, they refused me. I couldn't have been more grateful."

"I was stationed in Deutschland. Not a bad place, Deutschland, once you get used to all the Krauts. I stayed in six years, then quit. Knocked about for a while over there in Europe, caught a freighter back to the U.S.A., did some short-order cooking in the Big Apple, but New York got stale fast. Tried K.C. and Denver and L.A., then shipped out on the high seas. I've set foot on every continent except Antarctica," he boasted, "I've watched Indian holy men transform straw into spun gold just by capturing the sun's fire in a glass, tasted berries that ripen in the snow, smelled flowers whose perfume was too seductive for any man ever to capture in a bottle, seen birds and beasts no man has ever caged in a zoo. I could write down hundreds of true stories that no one would publish out of disbelief. This here," he said, waving his arm in a dismissive arc, "this crummy joint is just a stopover on my way to the Keys where they say the sea is like flakes of sapphire and the sunsets are red as rubies. Yes sir, Mr. Birnam. I'll be on my way soon, back on the road, free and happy."

Buddy twisted his head to look at the clock. Who was giving Jo Ann her five o'clock medication? Or was she, as she had threatened to do, already refusing it? He set his soup-spoon in the empty bowl. "Please lend me one hundred and eight dollars and forty-two cents. I promise to mail you it back with all the rest I owe you as soon as I return home. You have my word."

Leo whistled. "That's a lot of dough, old man. I wish I had that kind of money."

"You don't?"

"I don't. You think I'd be hanging around this dump so long if I did?"

"Couldn't you get it?" Buddy persisted.

"Who from?"

"That man Frank?"

"He's worse off than I am. You heard the man. You never look at me when I'm talking to you, old timer. Why is that?"

"Don't I? I suppose I don't. Please accept my apologies. I imagine I discovered a long time ago that if you really look at someone, even if they are a stranger, they almost always say something to you you don't want to hear. Do you think you might call me 'old' less often, Leo? It's my impression that you're not so young yourself."

"Young as I have to be, Bud. But here's what I'm going to do." He disappeared behind the grill into a small room that might have been a closet. When he returned, he stood next to the table and counted out one hundred and twenty-five dollars. "From the safe," he explained. "But it'll be more than my ass if it's not back in there before the owner checks it next, whenever that is. He's a drunk, but he knows how to count his cash. Do you understand, Buddy? You know what I'm saying? I'm putting my faith in you, old man. I got a record." He pushed the money toward him. "Look at me."

Buddy did as he was told. "But this is theft."

"Damn right."

"I'd be breaking the law."

"There's a higher law here. We have to get you home to your Jo Ann."

"I've never broken the law before. I've never done anything illegal."

"What's taken you so long? Besides, didn't you know that offing yourself was a no-no?"

"Yes. I knew." Buddy stared down at the pile of bills. "Do you suppose you might change that five into coins so I could call Jo Ann?"

When he returned from the corner phone booth, he was hobbling slightly. Wearing a cook's hat, Leo was slicing potatoes behind the counter. "The trick in life is always to keep busy, even when it doesn't make any sense. Who's going to eat these fries? Me, myself, and I, that's who. What did she say?"

"I woke her. But she didn't seem surprised it was me. She had been waiting for my call, she said. She said, 'Don't delay much longer, dear heart, or I'm afraid I'll die cursing God.' Would you like an I.O.U. for the money, Leo?"

"Nope. Never been able to redeem one in my life. Besides, it's not my money, old man. Please don't forget that."

"My bus is due to leave in forty-five minutes."

"You going to be OK?" Leo tossed some potato slices into a wire basket and lowered it into the hot fat. "Look, old man. Buddy. You want me to go with you? All it would take is a nod from you, my hand in that cookie jar again, and the closed sign on the door. Nobody'd ever find me. I leave memories," he bragged, "but not traces."

Buddy gazed at him, dumfounded. "Why would you want to do that?"

"Maybe I like you. Maybe I've got a soft spot for sad, sorry old men. Or maybe it's just because that sounds like a cute little place you have there and I could use a rest. You know what I mean? I never spent any time in a hick backwoods town. Maybe I'd like it. A new experience, worth the try. Whatever. You need some looking after for a while. It's the old story. I help you out, you help me out. A deal?"

Buddy shook his head. "How could I explain it to Jo Ann?"

"Jo Ann, Jo Ann. Jesus, Buddy, she's going to be dead soon."

"You think I'm not fully aware of that fact? How could you say such a hurtful thing to me?"

"You got to face facts. You ever face facts? The truth?"

"I should be leaving, Leo. I'm a slow walker at best, but ever since my . . . accident . . ." He turned toward the door, then shifted his body back so that he could face the counter one last time. "You've been very kind, kinder than I had any reason to expect from anyone. Pray for me, Leo."

"What for? I don't believe in God."

"Don't be ridiculous. Everyone believes in God, even when they don't particularly want to. I've tried very hard not to believe in Him lately. But it seems I have no choice."

"You're a strange old bird, Buddy Birnam. It's starting to rain hard again," Leo observed. "There's a spare umbrella leaning over in that corner, left by some dude in a beamer on his way to Savannah. It's yours."

"I accept," Buddy said, picking it up off the floor and waving good-bye.

"Wait a second. Don't leave yet," Leo said. "Just one thing more." He wiped his hands on a towel, put his hat down on the counter, walked over to Buddy, wrapped his arms around him, and kissed him hard on the lips. "There," he said, stepping back.

Buddy wiped the back of his hand across his mouth. "Are you out of your mind?"

"Sure. Give my best to Jo Ann." Leo glanced up at the sky. "Jesus, what crummy weather. Don't forget that dough you owe me," he shouted after Buddy who was halfway down the walk. "You sure as hell aren't going to forget me. Nobody ever does."

As he waited in the tiny, unattended bus station, Buddy watched the door or gazed up at the clock, afraid that Leo would appear at any moment. Could a man take such liberties, should he be allowed to, just because he saved your life? How little he understood the younger generations. What did Leo mean by kissing him, a man who had never been kissed like that in his life? How could he bear such effrontery and presumption along with all else that was horrid in his life, which he was just beginning to admit to himself that he had no choice except to bear?

When, almost an hour late, the bus pulled into the station, Buddy was frantic with worry. What could he tell Jo Ann? She would expect the truth, all of it. She'd intimated as much on the phone. But hadn't they always accepted the necessity of a few secrets between them? Didn't some secrets hold you in their arms and keep you safe and good? He found a seat in an empty section of the bus near the back.

As the bus drove away, he could barely see out because of the condensation that covered the window like frost. He tried to wipe it clean with his coat sleeve before the bus reached the diner, but the driver sped up just as it passed it. Was that Leo's broad back he saw stretching as it bent over the table in the first booth? Was he serving customers?

"Oh, no!" Buddy cried out. "Driver! Driver! Please stop this bus. I must get off. Immediately!" But the bus moved only faster, the driver ignoring him.

Buddy tried to look back, but the diner's sign was no longer in view. He knew neither the restaurant's name nor Leo's last name nor the address of either. How could he mail Leo back his money? Why had he been so careful not to mention the name of the town where he had spent his life? How could he have been so stupid, stupid, stupid?

He would have liked to have blamed his old age, but old habits were as much at fault. Yet other forces seemed to be at work in him, changing him in ways he couldn't name. Would it be better for him to accept or to resist the change? "Poor Jo Ann," he whispered to himself as if speaking in confidence to a stranger.

Nearly as old as himself and wearing a cheap bonnet covered with cotton buttercups, a woman nosily stuck her head over the back of her seat to see what sort of crazy person would be sharing her ride. She shook her head like someone who had seen it all before and settled back into her seat. "Poor man," she remarked to her uninterested companion.

The comment startled him. Was he really a poor man, worthy of her pity? Had he, in saying "Poor Jo Ann," meant to pity her? But pity could only diminish them both. Undoubtedly the end of life impoverished life. But his life with Jo Ann, his and her life together, had been rich beyond their prayers.

Leo had meant no harm. He was just being brash and vain and vulgar in that way so many people were these days. Yet Leo had been kind. His heart, Buddy was convinced, was generous and kind. Restless, Buddy adjusted his seat so it would recline, though he knew his hurting body would not let him sleep. But he did not really want to sleep. Perhaps he could bring Leo the money afterward. "After Jo Ann's death," he said aloud, trying to persuade himself of its imminent reality. What would happen to him afterward? Whatever became of him in the days soon to come, he owed it to Leo not to forget his obligation. More, kindness must be repaid with kindness. He must think of some appropriate gift.

"Old fool," Buddy said to himself. How dare he have such thoughts at such an hour? Would he betray Jo Ann? Once more he wiped the window clear of fog. But he had to go back. And if he were to delay his return to Crescent Beach, Leo's theft, his theft, might already have been discovered. Yet if he were to rush back. He cupped his hands around his eyes, pressed his nose against the pane, and gazed up into the clearing night sky. The stars in their appalling numbers rolled over him like waves.

Surely Jo Ann would understand. After he told her the whole story, she would respond without a moment's hesitation, "Oh, God's in His heaven, Buddy. He brought you back to me. His angel of mercy sounds a little rough around the edges, not someone I would like to chat with just now. But he sounds kind. You'll need someone kind, Buddy."

Then, ready, she would ask him to fill her glass with water. He would be thinking, as he was thinking now, how strangely like death kindness had come to feel to him. But he would bring the filled glass to Jo Ann anyway just as she would expect him to do, placed next to her prettiest napkin on her favorite tray.

The Risk of His Music

THE AUTO REPAIR SHOP and its debris sprawled on a broad knoll. A stern, unkempt, two-storied farmhouse rose out of pine woods a hundred yards behind it. Below the hill, Hebron Road marked one of the borders of a land once given over to small tobacco farms, corn fields, cow pastures, and sheep meadows. But in the last decade much had changed. Recently a second mill had been constructed on the outskirts of Alexandersville, and rumors were rife of a third, enticing many of the remaining farmers whose soil had been slowly dying to seek better-paying work either in the factories or as part of the building boom that followed the new industries' arrival.

When an electronics firm from New Jersey started to erect a plant near the site of the abandoned gravel quarries, even Buck Carmichael decided it was finally time to sell his farm and move his family off the land where Carmichaels had been toiling to no particular advantage for over a century. They settled in a neat, small brick house nestled among other newly fabricated small, neat brick houses squeezed into place among the few remaining trees, close to the new school and public pool the town had built out of its improved tax revenues. Only Orville Earle's service station still blotched the landscape that recent construction had otherwise scrubbed clean of the old shacks and squat farmhouses that for generations had littered the ground through which Hebron Road passed.

Buck Carmichael remained loyal to Orville, who since his own boyhood had worked on all Buck's cars, the two pickups, and the old tractor that, while Orville was in Korea, was constantly breaking down. But Buck had also had to admit to his wife Sara more often than he liked that, now they were living a whole lot closer to the place, he could see why she might consider it an eyesore, though the word she used more often was "disgrace." The repair shop was only a couple of large attached cement block squares crudely painted a watery yellow, with three cracked and almost useless pumps out front and greasy tools scattered all over the place, many of them lying out back among the piles of discarded engine parts and stacks of fenders or hoods or hubcaps. The problem was that, from the road, it looked as if it had been deserted years ago, the packed red clay forty yards or more around the station appearing as barren as if poisons had oozed from the shop itself to destroy all life immediately surrounding it. And what Sara said was true. Orville didn't keep proper care of his house the way a more settled or married man would have, the way his daddy had when the wife was still alive. But right after Orville's mother Katie died the place began looking seedy, though there were few old-timers in Walker County who wouldn't swear by the miracle that Orville Earle could work on just about any motor. His mechanics, the two kids he brought back with him from the last war, were pretty good too, they allowed, though mean looking and too quick to revile the Lord, cussing like the devil himself. All the men in that part of the county, especially those fresh off the land, argued that if you had any sense either you gave the job to Orville or you might as well forget it. Take your vehicle into town and watch them clip you. Let those idiots ruin a perfectly decent piece of machinery that needs only a good ear and a little expert tinkering to put it back right. Go ahead, give it to them, you'll see. You might as well take it to Orville in the first place, since you'll have to sooner or later. Buck

Carmichael had spoken those very words on numerous occasions himself. But times were changing fast. That was the problem. As he kept telling Orville, you can't stop the future no matter how hard you try.

Sometimes, late at night, Roy would imagine dying the way other boys his age, like Nolan, said they thought about sex, as if it alone were the reason and explanation for everything. To his schoolmates, Roy Carmichael was puny, a runt, a shrimp, having managed to grow no higher than five feet two. When he turned sixteen the previous March, he realized that he wasn't going to get any bigger, doomed alone among his blood kin to be little. His father stood several inches over six feet, his mother was tall for a woman, both her brothers were long-limbed men, and his two sisters were just about normal size. Lately, Roy had noticed how it shamed his father to have to verify his son's age, especially to people in authority like the highway patrolman who had given him his driver's test and who repeatedly questioned whether he was old enough to drive without having bothered to notice that he was obviously old enough to have to shave. Yet it wasn't only his size that made him feel peculiar or morbid. There was more to it than that.

During the summer, he had badly wanted to work construction with Nolan at the development that was going up just east of the new stretch of Jackson Street, reaching out toward Cole Lake. But, though Nolan was hired the first day right on the site, Roy was told that he'd be hearing from them in a week or two. After waiting a month, he had to call the company office three times before he learned that his application had been lost or misfiled. In any case, there were no openings left. Luckily, Roy thought, he still had his job at the Food Fair bagging groceries and occasionally helping to unload the trucks, though at that pay he figured it would take him years to save enough money for a decent car.

Sometimes his brother Randy let Nolan borrow his car, and Nolan would drive up the driveway to the Carmichael house and honk for Roy to hurry up so that they could get to the pool before it was too dark, though once there Nolan would never take off his T-shirt even in the water for fear of revealing the worst of his scars from the fire that had burned him so badly three years before. He had tipped his daddy's tractor over on a stump speeding up a hill where he knew he shouldn't have been driving in the first place and the gas tank exploded.

Once it had gotten too late to stay in the water, they'd change, the two of them dressing in a dark corner of the locker room for shame of being seen by the other boys, and drive into the center of Alexandersville to catch a movie or to spend the evening more or less aimlessly wandering, checking out the activities basement at the First Baptist Church or at the Pentecostal Tabernacle or seeing what was happening, if anything, down by the park, then stopping off at the Tottle House or the Krispy Kreme for a snack. During the school year, they would attend all the home football or basketball games together, both of them thinking it was great to have somewhere to go and something to do for a few hours that let them feel part of a group.

"I'm worried about Roy," Sara Carmichael said to her husband after supper in a voice loud enough to penetrate down the hall and through the firmly closed door. Every time his mother initiated this discussion she always raised her voice so Roy couldn't miss a word. He could shut his eyes and see her pouring the endless tablespoons of Hadacol into her mouth.

"Oh, Sara," her husband responded, heaving out a don't-bother-me sigh.

"Well, I mean it, Buck. Never talking. Hiding away in that room. Seeing no one but that misfortunate Nolan Flynt."

"He's just sixteen, Sara. They're both just sixteen."

"I tell you. That Nolan scares me. Doesn't he you?"

"Now, Sara."

"The way he refuses to look at you straight on, with that one eye messed up so bad, you know. And neither of them has another friend in this world. It's not how a boy's world ought to be, Buck," his mother said, slamming the cupboard door closed.

Such prodding made Roy only firmer in his resolve. "I'm going to buy me a car," he proposed to his father the next morning while they were rinsing off the pickup.

His father shut off the water and spat. "You are, are you?"

"A '50 Ford," Roy announced, "over at Bowman's. It's sort of beat up outside and the interior's all torn. That's why it's so cheap, I reckon. But the motor runs pretty smooth. What do you say?"

His father began to wind up the hose and spat again, looking over at Sara where she stood watching them through the window, her arms crossed. "Take it to Orville's. Have him give it a good look. If Orville Earle says it's a fair buy, it'll be OK by me. But, Roy, listen to me now," he added, waving his wife away. "Make some other friends, why don't you? Your spending so much time with that Flynt boy is getting on your mother's nerves."

Since without a big deposit cranky old Dallas Bowman wouldn't let him keep the car past the lot's 6 P.M. closing time, Roy knew how much of a favor he was going to be asking Orville Earle to give the Ford a quick lookover on the spot, plus a test spin out on the road. But he didn't want to waste his hard-earned money on a clunker that might expire over night, dropping all its vital parts on the driveway like old bones. His father was right. If he was going to spend a couple of hundred bucks on a car, he needed some advice.

"My dad says they'll be shutting this dump down one of these days," Nolan remarked as Roy eased the Ford into an open slot near the air pumps. "He says this land's gotten too valuable to waste on a garage." From the crest of the hill, Roy looked down on the new houses being built in every direction along Hebron Road, squeezed in among toppled trees and burned-out brush.

One of the mechanics was lying on a creeper that, dance-like, he was rolling rhythmically back and forth under an almost-new Mercury. Only the heels of his worn black brogans touched the floor. The other was slouching toward the Ford just as Roy hopped out.

"Ain't got no time," he said. He rubbed the knuckles of his right hand across his sooty shirt, one eye shut tight, grease staining his chin, nose, cheeks, and forehead like a soldier's nighttime camouflage. "You boys be wanting some work done on that heap you got to wait until next week."

Nolan squeezed out the passenger's door that would open only a foot before it tipped off its hinge. "I can't wait that long," Roy said. "Where's Orville Earle?"

"Ain't here," the man said and licked his lips. His open eye studied Nolan's scars without surprise, his own face looking as if it had been torn apart more than once. "Upped and took the afternoon off. He does that. Listens to music," he sneered.

"Damn," Roy exhaled. "I'm thinking of buying it, see, if it's not banged up too bad."

"Who from?" The man tugged at the crotch of his dunga-rees as if they were stuck to his skin and scratched to relieve an itch.

"Dallas Bowman."

"You got to be a fool then. I tell you what. Orville's right over yonder," he nodded toward the house. "You can coax him out. Sometimes it works and sometimes it don't. He's right unpredictable is Orville. You sure your legs are long enough to touch the gas pedal, half pint?"

Flushing, Roy turned toward Nolan. "You want to come along?"

"Naw," Nolan said, searching for some change in his pockets. "I'm thirsty. That cooler over there looks more inviting."

Roy didn't hear the music pouring out of Orville Earle's open window until he had passed more than half the distance between the station and the glum-looking house. His mother liked to listen to the local country station while she ironed or did dishes or fixed dinner. His sisters gushed about Elvis and Guy Mitchell or anyone else their gang liked to hear, wasting all the money they earned at Woolworth's on piles of 45s. And Nolan always kept his radio tuned to WAAA because it broadcast nothing but that wild colored wailing that Roy had to admit was more than OK, certainly better than the endless, monotonous hymns they had to sing at church while waiting every Sunday morning for someone to be seized by the spirit of the Lord. Yet these sounds spilling out of Orville Earle's house weren't anything like those he was familiar with. He stood at the door and refrained from knocking, listening until it was quiet and he could hear movement in the hall.

Orville Earle drew up the shade to see who was there, yanked the door open, and bellowed, "Mahler!"

Roy's hands fidgeted in the back pockets of his jeans. "Excuse me, Mr. Earle, I . . ."

"That was Gustav Mahler you were listening to. I saw you," he snorted. "Don't deny it. You liked it, didn't you, you poor kid? Liking Mahler is a bad sign, a very, very bad sign." He tapped his head. "Dementia."

"Mr. Earle, I . . ."

"The adagietto," Orville Earle continued, "from the Fifth Symphony. Bruno Walter conducting. I'm not making much sense to you, am I? But if I don't tell you, who will? Don't be shy. Come on in," he said, shoving Roy inside into a side room that was empty except for bookcases, a badly worn couch, an overstuffed chair, and a maze of electronic equipment that looked homemade, wires twisting and dangling everywhere.

"Here. Sit here," Orville Earle ordered him, "close to these speakers. There, now. I'll set the needle back to the start. I want you to listen from the beginning to the end without interruption. It'll only take ten minutes. Then you can tell me what you felt. Got it?"

"Mr. Earle," Roy started to protest, "I don't have much time. I just want you to . . ."

"What? Look at a car? All right, I'll make a deal with you. You want me to do you a favor, you do me a favor. Just listen. Be quiet and listen." Orville Earle placed the tone arm back to the start of the band.

Roy glanced out the window toward the station where Nolan was leaning against the right fender of the Ford, pop bottle in hand, the left side of his face turned up toward the sun. He wanted to call out to him to come quick and rescue him, but instead he crouched quietly in a corner and tried to listen.

"Did you like that?" Orville Earle asked him after the movement was over, the tone arm returned to its rest.

"Yes. Yes, I did. A lot."

"Who are you anyway?"

"Roy. Roy Carmichael."

"Buck's boy? Of course, I almost forgot. Old Buck called here earlier and said you might be swinging by. Now where's that piece of junk Dallas Bowman is trying to clip you with? Or would you rather listen to some more Mahler?" Orville Earle pulled another record out of its jacket.

Nolan didn't say a word when Orville stooped into the car and started it up, but waited until after he had driven it off down the curving road to the straightaway at the bottom, dark puffs of oil smoking out the tailpipe. "You were gone more than an hour."

"I'm sorry. We were listening to some music."

"We were supposed to drive out to the pond this afternoon."

"He's got hundreds of records. Hundreds and hundreds of classical records. He told me I could hear them. All of them."

"My one day off," Nolan grumbled.

Roy shrugged, kicked a discarded hubcap into the grass, and watched it roll on its rim until it hit a stone, pinging as it fell. The Ford, the front wheel wobbling, curved back up the twisting road.

Once every month or so, Orville Earle would confront himself in a mirror for a few minutes not otherwise spent shaving, never knowing what he expected to find except that he probably wouldn't be surprised by what he saw. Thickset, gnarled, bushy browed, he would poke at his face, its blemished skin the texture and color of unevenly tanned pig hide, with the first two fingers of his right hand. He'd lost their tips to frostbite six years ago while retreating with three thousand other troops, Jake and Ken among them, through blizzards across impassable mountains toward safety south of the thirty-eighth parallel in Korea.

Though he figured he had killed many men there, the only face he could remember clearly was that of a chink who was intending to stab him to death, and who had just knifed his best buddy as he lay next to Orville in his sleeping bag on the frozen ground. During the previous war, in the Ardennes for instance, the enemy's death had been more anonymous, less personal somehow, at least until he saw the bodies afterward. But hand-to-hand combat was common during much of his time in Korea, as if war, having become with the bomb too terrible to contemplate, had regressed to its origins, one brute slaughtering another, beast ripping apart beast. It was what Orville thought fighting ought to be. Yet all he had lost were the tips of two fingers, taken from him by nature not man.

Discharged, he returned at once to the work that the army had been dumb enough to deny him, though he'd repaired more than one balked jeep on one march or another, with or without the appropriate tools. Still gazing into the mirror, he blew on his hands, which felt cold. His black eyes, dark as his hair, stared back at him warily, like a stranger's. "Roy," he had almost said aloud, surprising himself.

His work shirt back on and buttoned, he clumped down the stairs and in the front room extracted a box from the press of other record jackets and boxes, placed one of its discs on the turntable, and carefully lowered the tone arm toward the vinyl. "Brahms," he pronounced out loud, as if that single syllable were by itself capable of magic. He had first heard it uttered over the radio nearly thirty years ago as he waited nervously in an army dentist's office for his teeth to be examined for the first time, a spot having started to cause him grief in the back of his jaw. While the drill ground his tooth, he almost did not feel it, the strains of the music still echoing in his head.

"Orville. Yo, Orville," Jake bellowed at him through the screen of the open window.

"Get lost," Orville hollered back. "This is my afternoon off. Handle it yourself."

"Naw, I think you better come on out now. It's that asshole lawyer again, Orville." The palms of Jake's broad hands pressed against the screen, which twanged under the pressure. "I think Kenny's run after a gun. I ain't seen him this flustered since boot camp, Orville. You know how mad he gets."

"Screw," Orville sighed and tossed the record cover onto the floor.

"See?" Jake pointed to where Ken kept guard on the churning cooler, his rifle lying on his lap as dust clouds billowed up from the car speeding down the hill and hovered like fog near the crest so that it was impossible to see all the way to Hebron Road. Jake shook his head slowly back and forth, like a long-suffering parent. "You gone and done it now, Ken Sharp. Might as well just go ahead and kiss this place good-bye."

"Shut up, Jake," Orville muttered.

"It weren't loaded," Ken growled, tugging like a child at a lock of his curly red hair. "You know I don't keep it loaded no more, Orville. But that fucker's got no rights here. You've said so yourself."

Orville peered over the brow of the hill. "Times are changing, boys. No one respects agreements like they used to do. Every damned thing's got to be in writing these days. No one takes your word for nothing anymore. And what we need I ain't got in writing, you understand? I don't possess the necessary paperwork." He sauntered over to where Ken still sat and took the gun from him, checking for cartridges. "We got maybe six months before they drive their damned tractors and bulldozers and I didn't know what all else up here, hauling their bricks and lumber like this was their land. Say, Jake," he said, turning toward him where he hunkered near a spreading pool of oil. "Didn't you all promise that sweet old Miss Caudle her DeSoto by this afternoon?" He threw the gun back onto Kenny's lap. "Let's see she gets it good as promised," he said and lumbered off.

Back in the house, he picked the tone arm up, the needle having gotten stuck in a bit of gunk halfway through the adagio, and examined the record's surface in the strong light of the corner window, hoping he could clean it sufficiently for him and Roy to listen to it that night when the boy drove over in the zippy Chevy convertible he'd fixed up for him, selling it to him for less than his cost. He'd enjoyed having had it out face to face with the pious crook Bowman for even thinking about trying to sell a gullible kid a hunk of junk like that Ford.

But Orville knew it was risky for him to think about people like Bowman for very long. Ken's outbursts would usually cool in an hour or two, but his own often smoldered for days, until like the flame of sexual desire it had grown into a need so consuming that it demanded relief. But unlike love, hatred had no satisfactory masturbatory substitute but instead required violence without surrogates, the offending thing itself rent apart, destroyed without question forever. Even after he had won a fight his loathing of his victim could last for days more, as if it had not been destruction or victory he had wanted at all.

Only listening to music made him really feel calm, the permanent rage in him temporarily quieted by sounds so beautiful and moving that sometimes even death could not completely anger him. Stretched out on the old couch, the one piece of furniture he could recall his father ever having bought, he listened to the Brahms trio begin again, the noise of a motor occasionally backfiring in the shop interrupting the restful illusion that he was content to call peace.

School over for the week, the pep rally having dispersed at least an hour before, Nolan and Roy sat glumly in the bleachers since they had nowhere better to be, a cool breeze crackling in their ears as sweater-clad cheerleaders previewed their routines for a local TV reporter on the sunnier side of the stands while the marching band paraded up and down the field, still practicing their formations. Nolan kicked the heels of his shoes against the seat in front of him, splintering wood. "Damn it, I still don't know how you could forget about the Randolph game, Roy. It's always the biggest game of the year. You've said so yourself, lots of times."

Roy stuffed his hands deeper into the pockets of his peacoat, which Orville had bought him at the Army and Navy in Winston when they'd gone there earlier in the fall hunting for records. "I don't know. It just sort of slipped my mind, I guess. I said I was sorry, Nolan."

"Where did you say you were going exactly?"

"Over to Monroe County, to that girl's college there where some piano player from up north is going to perform. Orville asked me a whole month ago, Nolan."

"Damn. Double damn," Nolan groaned. "I don't get it. I just don't get it, Roy."

Roy scratched under his nose and stared down toward the field where the band had begun to break up, racing toward the gates, their instruments, like the large buttons on their uniforms, gleaming a bright, polished copper in the setting sun. "I learn things."

Nolan snorted. "What does Orville Earle know about except cars?"

"You're still my best friend, Nolan."

"Sure." He sprang up and started to walk away, his head drooping. "I know."

"You going to the game anyway?"

Nolan twisted around. "Are you kidding?" He bounded down the bleachers toward the sideline, his thick sandy hair, which he wore almost as long as a girl's to help conceal the worst patches of the scarring, blowing like streamers in a gust of wind and exposing his disfigured ear, shrunken and wrinkled like a dried orange peel. He tugged the collar of his coat up higher and held it against his face as he headed toward the small crowd of band members milling about the gate that he would have to pass on his way out.

Since neither of them had ever been even close to the campus before, Orville parked his truck at the first lot he spotted, next to a dorm guarded by a wall of trees. Having walked back up a winding path to the road, he and Roy cut across the quad toward what Orville guessed could be the building where the concert was to take place, brightly lit and crowded with people outside. But it turned out to be only a recreation hall. Ashamed to ask directions, they wandered from building to building. They found each one empty or locked until Orville relented and stopped a nervous-looking girl, hauling an armful of books back to the library. She pointed with her chin toward a chapel where, already late, Roy and Orville had

to wait in the narthex for the first piece to end, listening to
the music with their ears pressed to the cracks between the
doors. After the applause subsided, they were allowed to
squeeze down a long row of tight-lipped, white-gloved, bird-
eyed widow ladies and spinsters, as Orville later described
most of the audience, who wouldn't quit staring at them
even after they'd settled into their space in the pews under
one of the milk-and-caramel-colored windows.

"I didn't know it was going to be in a church," Roy said
on their way back to Orville's truck, "or I'd have worn better
clothes. You never seen me in my Sunday shoutin' suit, have
you, Orv?"

"Never mind about those old biddies. Did you like the
music?"

Roy held the program up toward the streetlight as they
emerged out of the greater darkness of an elm-lined walkway.
"I like the Bar . . . tok," he pronounced hesitantly. "I liked
that best. The suite. And the Allegro Bar . . . bar . . . o. That
was wild. It got me all stirred up. How about you?"

"The Brahms sonata, the Brahms. For me it will always be
Brahms, Roy. The greatest."

"Yeah, that was pretty good too."

"Pretty good?" Orville scowled, halting in the middle of
the campus road. "Pretty good? It was a deep cave," he roared,
"full of terrible spirits and black depths. Outside, a golden
river meanders by ruins of an ancient castle that giants had
long ago carved from the craggy hill on which it perches. A
pale sun sets behind it. Young virgins clothed all in white
linen bow toward a flaming altar in the nearby old oak forest
where stark branches are silhouetted against a full moon that
floats in a now gray, moon-bright sky as . . ."

"Orville."

"As in a faraway town a solitary lover sits in his cramped
quarters, his book lying unread in his lap. Rain splashes
against the windowpanes as it has done for days while the

poor man repeats the name of his beloved over and over to himself like a charm. It was . . ."

"Orville!"

"It was youth," Orville laughed giddily, throwing his arms up in the air. "Youth, Roy, youth, youth, youth, fleeing fastest when it's most your own."

"Yeah, sure, Orville," Roy said, shaking his head. "So calm down, OK?"

Orville slapped him on the back. "I've been reading too many record jackets, kid."

"You sure are something," Roy said admiringly.

They strolled onto the twisting path that led back to the dorm near where the truck was parked. "You're working tomorrow, aren't you?"

"Yes, sir," Roy said. "I got to hustle." But, rushing for the truck, he raced in front of Orville just as a couple leaving the lot turned onto the path. Exactly where the walk was darkest, Roy collided with them at a curve partially hidden by thick bushes and clumps of ivy.

"Oh!" the girl screamed out as she fell, pulling her date down beside her.

Slowly, her boyfriend helped her back up, brushing her off. "Are you hurt, Penny?"

"No. No, I don't believe so. Not too badly," she replied uncertainly, checking her hair with her hands.

Shocked by the accident, Roy stood still, unable to apologize or say anything, gaping at them both. "You little runt," the date yelled at him. "See what you've done?" he said, shoving Roy off the path and forcing him back toward the stone wall.

"Lonnie!" the girl shrieked as her boyfriend suddenly doubled over and fell, struggling for breath, Orville's two punches having both connected exactly where Orville wanted them. "Oh, who do you think you are? What are you doing here?" The girl dropped to her knees to appeal to her date where he lay, clutching his midriff and writhing around on the thin border of grass. "Oh, Lonnie, Lonnie. Why are you always getting me into so much trouble?"

"Haul ass," Orville ordered, tugging on Roy's peacoat. "I mean it, Roy. Now."

Once they'd hopped into the pickup, Orville flew off campus and all the way down to the cutoff that led to the highway before turning on the headlights. But by the time they were safely back on the road to Walker County, he was smiling broadly, satisfied, whistling themes from the Brahms in a kind of shapeless, random medley while, silent and alarmed, Roy sat beside him fidgeting all the way back to Alexandersville, saying nothing even as the truck bounced over the ruts in the road that led through the woods to the back of Orville's house where his Chevy was parked.

Orville cut off the motor and tossed the keys into the glove compartment. "You coming in or not?"

"I don't know."

"That creep back there would have hurt you, Roy."

"But it got violent so fast."

"Life is like that, soldier."

"You think he's OK?"

"Sure. He was just moaning and groaning to impress his girlfriend. Come on in. Let's have us some ice cream."

"It must be close to one now," Roy said as Orville placed the bowl in front of him where he sat at the rough-hewn cabinet near the sink in the kitchen, its top the right height to serve as a table.

"Almost," Orville said. He dragged a stool from across the room to join him. A few minutes later the clock in the hall bonged its single tone.

Above them, they heard a thump and a crash, like the sound of someone falling out of bed and knocking over a chair or a lamp. "Ken," Orville told Roy, who had jumped slightly at the disturbance. "He does that sometimes. He gets scared in the middle of the night. Jake hates it because it wakes him up. Hear?" The two men were arguing overhead in the slow drawl of the half awake. Ken had begun to weep.

Roy sank his spoon into the melting mass of cherry vanilla and waited for the argument to end. Orville touched his forehead with the nub of the last joint of his middle finger. "Bad memories. You better get on home, Roy," Orville said sourly. "It's late."

"Sara," his father said. "Calm down. Just calm down."

"Don't you order me to calm down. He's overslept again. I just got another call from the Food Fair wondering where he's at. He was supposed to be there at 6 A.M., 6 A.M.," she underlined. "It is now well past 9."

"Roy is such a little goof off," Peggy said where she was washing breakfast dishes in the sink. "Really, Daddy, you should talk to him. He was never, ever popular, but it's only gotten worse. You'd think he was a communist or something."

"Boy, is that ever the dismal truth," Carol agreed, wiping a plate with a towel decorated with bright-eyed clown faces.

"He hasn't got a friend in the world, not even that pathetic Nolan," Peggy giggled, wrinkling her nose as she spoke his name. "Not anymore."

"That Flynt boy is just an unfortunate, that's all," their father countered.

"Oh, Daddy," Carol said. "You are so naive."

"Well, say what you will, Buck Carmichael," his wife said, shifting the subject back to her original topic, "that boy is spending too much time with Orville Earle. Classical music," Sara said disdainfully. "Would you listen to that? What's he got on now? Does that make any sense to you? I tell you, it just gives me a headache. Why does he always have to play it so loud?"

"Most likely because he doesn't want to have to listen to you all," Buck boomed. "This house you three made me buy must have been built out of paper. Weeds sprouting in the living room between the cracks and all the floors sinking. It just makes me ashamed. You all make me ashamed. Let Orville and Roy be friends if they want to."

"Oh, Daddy. Really," Carol snickered.

Having shut off his player, placed the record carefully back into its inner sleeve and then the jacket, and buckled the belt on his jeans, Roy carried a chair to the window, opened it, and climbed out, stepping onto three cement blocks he had hauled there for that purpose, turning around to force the window closed again. He'd been sneaking in and out of the house like that for months now, without once having had to explain why he did it. Later at work, he apologized stiffly to his boss and promised he wouldn't be late again, though he knew he probably would be and didn't care.

"It took so much for Nolan to call you, Roy. You don't know how much. I'm so pleased you two boys are going to be friends again." Sally Flynt reached for the church key lying beside her on the tray-like table and released a cap from another bottle. "Sure you won't join me? I won't tell." Roy was standing watchful by the window, an odor like rotting persimmons filling the whole house and irritating his throat. He could taste it whenever he swallowed, the months of undisturbed filth strewn everywhere. "I don't know why he's always so late." She settled wobbily into a dusty overstuffed chair. "Though since the army drafted Randy and sent him to Germany Nolan drives that car every chance he gets just to listen to the music. I never knew a boy so crazy about music, but Joe, he doesn't like for him to play none of it in the house." She clutched a strand of her tawny hair and twirled it around a finger. "Why you been keeping yourself such a stranger?"

Roy edged the frilly curtains back a few more inches, trying to see farther down the road. "I don't know, ma'am. Just been busy, I guess."

"I hear your daddy's still working." She reached for a Chesterfield. "Joe, Mr. Flynt, he got laid off the line the end

of October, I think it was. And I never been able to find anything, not a thing, not since we left the farm." A stream of
smoke poured out of her nostrils and spiraled toward the ceiling. "Then LuAnn ended up marrying that Gordon boy. You
heard about that, I suppose. Practically everyone has by
now," she sighed.

"Yes, ma'am. Stu Gordon and me, we worked at the Food
Fair together for a while, before I got fired. But I found me a
better job at Stillwell's Drugstore. Better pay, too."

"That's good." Sally Flynt brought the beer bottle to her
lips, but set it back down on the tray without taking a swallow. "Your mama and daddy ever regret selling the old place?"

"Yes'm. Every once in a while I hear them saying something like that, especially Pa. Like the other day when the
septic tank broke down again."

"These places is all cheap construction," she said, whirling
one hand around in the air. "But Joe, Mr. Flynt, he's the eter-
nal optimist, saying everything will be peaches and cream
come spring. Well, here it is the end of March already and
I don't see no peaches and cream on the table nor milk
and honey either. Joe swears another bunch of Yankees is
marching down here to build us a spanking new shopping
center over on Hebron Road someplace. As if you can trust a
Yankee," she snorted. "Look what happened over at Keiger
Electronics. Half the locals they'd trained only three years
ago they fired like they was niggers and then shipped down a
trainload of stuck-up Yankees to steal all our jobs. I tell you,"
she declared, taking an even longer drag on her cigarette, "I
don't care what they say. You can't live off hope alone. Nor
promises and expectation, neither. Hilltop Shopping Center
is what they're thinking about calling it. But do you think
the likes of us will ever have enough money to buy the time
of day there?"

"I don't know, ma'am," Roy checked the clock on the
mantle. "You sure Nolan hasn't forgotten?"

"When it's been all he's been talking about, getting you to go to that new drive-in?" She lifted herself weakly out of the chair, almost knocking the bottle off the tray. "That sounds like Randy's car now, don't it?"

"Yes, ma'am, it sure does. Nice talking to you, Mrs. Flynt."

Nolan clapped his hands against his knees in time to the music on the station he had made Roy tune to. "Little Willie John. Just about the best," Nolan informed him, glancing over at the speedometer. "Hey, give it some gas, Roy, or we won't make it on time."

His tires squealed as Roy took the curve heading toward Mendenhall Road too fast, hitting the breaks as he spotted the sign announcing the entrance three miles farther on to the new drive-in theater that, because it was outside the city limits, was spared the stricture of the Alexandersville ban on *And God Created Woman,* showing it as its grand opening feature. "Whoa! Look at that line of cars," Nolan said, whistling as Roy slowed the Chevy down. "Those preachers sure know how to drum up business. You think it's too cool to put the top down when we get inside? I like having the top down, Roy. It's sporty."

By the time they'd paid, they could find a place to park only far to the right in the last row, the corrugated fence alone separating them from the woods behind. In front of them, car horns honked demanding that the show begin while the last few cars to enter the theater wound back and forth, hunting for a spot still open. Just as the title flashed on the screen, a new Packard pulled into the empty space to the right of Roy's Chevy. Nolan watched as the boy lifted the speaker from its stand, hooked it over the window, and cranked the window up again, drawing his girl closer to him.

"Nolan," Roy warned. "The show's that-a-way."

"Yeah, I know." He turned his head back toward the screen.

After about a half hour of the movie, during a dull sequence of plot-making that promised no sex, Nolan rested his head against the back of the seat and looked up toward the cloudless, moonless, star-filled sky whose sparkling, he said, reminded him of the pond on a windy day in summer. He glanced back at the black Packard. "They're sure not wasting much time over there. Look at those windows steam, Roy."

"Nolan, c'mon," Roy muttered.

But Nolan didn't budge. "Before he left, Randy said I should go over to Turner Street by the Bessemer Brickworks there and hire me a colored girl. He said they're used to people with messed up faces and wouldn't mind or say anything, probably wouldn't even notice. That's what my brother said. But I don't know." He looked back toward the picture. "My daddy would skin me alive."

Roy slumped down in his seat, able to see just the tops of the actor's heads, wishing he were at Orville's, his mind wanting no images except for Brahms's or Mahler's and the strange feelings they kept stirring up in him that he couldn't name. "I hate this movie," he yelled into the night air. "I hate it, I hate it." From hundreds of cheap speakers, Bardot's dubbed voice suddenly came alive with longing and words of love buzzed and cracked like nocturnal insects crawling on a window screen.

Strong spring winds tugged at the old house like a creek rushing around a rock, rippling past it. Screens buckled, beams snapped like cooling metal, rope clapped against a long-unused flagpole, tree limbs scraped across the house's siding, a toppled garbage can banged about on the gravel driveway. Close to the porch, a stray dog howled persistently. Orville leaned forward and turned up the volume of the Brahms quartet, distorting the sound of the strings, making them harsh and scratchy. Upstairs, a door flew open. There was a long pause, then a rifle was fired twice in quick succession. Roy leaped out of his chair, dashed to the porch, and stood there, peering into the dark.

"Roy. It was only Jake. Or Ken," Orville called out. "Don't worry. It's only a hungry old hound. They wouldn't hurt it none. Come on back in."

Roy turned toward him, wrapping his arms around his stomach as if he were ill. "How do you know?"

"I know is all. Come on back in, Roy. Sit. Listen."

But Roy didn't move. Instead, he tried to figure out how much more music he would have to listen to before he could leave. All evening it had meant nothing to him, boring him, and he could not keep from staring at Orville where he lay like a black bear stretched on the floor, looking fierce and dangerous if startled or disturbed. If phosphorous glowed black, Roy was thinking, it would look like that, as dark as coal lying in a big shapeless pile, darker than the darkness of night that surrounded them in their unlit room.

"Orville?" he hollered over the quartet turned up so loud that he had to shout to be heard outside.

"Don't worry, Roy. They've gone back to bed."

"It's not that, Orville." He took a deep breath. "I can't go with you to Winston tomorrow. I got other plans."

Orville hauled his body across the room and lowered the volume slightly. Upstairs, either Ken or Jake was striking at a door with an object harder than a fist, something wooden, Roy guessed, like a rifle butt. "Jake," Ken begged. "Jake." When Orville slammed the door to the hall, another door slammed shut above them. The needle on the record player was stuck, vibrating between two notes and hissing. Orville grabbed the tone arm and set it several grooves over.

The wind picked up, sweeping tree branches across the porch roof. The leaves shivered. A loose limb crashed to the ground. Orville followed Roy to the porch and stared up into the sky. "All those stars," he murmured and placed a firm hand on the boy's shoulder, clutching him, drawing him closer. "All those wandering holes."

Roy ducked and swerved. He ran down the steps, making sure he had separated himself from the house by a good hundred feet before he turned around. "Hey," he yelled. "Thanks, huh? Thanks for everything." But Orville had already vanished back into the house.

By the time he had circled around to the garage, Roy could hear that Orville had put on the Brahms First, its timpani pounding in his ears even this far away, though the house muffled much of the power of the strings. A light came on in Jake's room. Standing next to his car, Roy waited and watched as Jake, naked, gazed out into the night, smoking a cigarette, Ken hovering behind him, wearing only shorts. Wanting to see better, Roy took several steps to his right and would have tripped over the dog if he hadn't heard its snarls, its thick fur blown back by the wind so that even in the dark he could see its blood-covered belly. Roy squatted down close to it and placed his palm flat on the warm patch of earth where blood soaked the ground. From its slow, irregular breathing, Roy knew it would be dead soon. Gradually, he became aware that he could hear no more music, not even the wail of Brahms. He glanced back at the house. Orville was standing in the room with Ken and Jake, shouting. Then all the lights went out once more.

With a crowbar, Jake was trying to pry a stuck hubcap off the wreck of a Dodge. "It won't be long now, Orville. It sure won't be long now."

"Shut up," Orville said gloomily, his head hidden by the hood of a Caddy he'd promised the owner he'd have ready that morning, three hours earlier.

Ken rolled the creeper out from under the chassis and sat up, tossing a wrench toward Jake. Jake bent down, found a larger one lying close by on the cement, and pitched it back at Ken who caught it just before it hit the fender. "Two more weeks," Ken bitched. "What we going to do then, Orv? We ain't got the money to buy us another place as good as this one. You heard that asshole yesterday. He called us squatters. On your daddy's own property."

"My daddy was a goddamn fool with fatback for brains. Hand me that screwdriver, Jake. A spineless liar who sold me out while I was serving my country killing commie scum with the likes of you two jerkoffs. Give me that rag," he ordered Jake. "I need to clean a plug. Where's that rich bunghole been driving this thing anyway? Through the swamp?" Orville slammed down the Caddy's hood and wiped his hands off on the bib of his coveralls. "How the hell did you two ever survive five minutes in this hellhole of a world without me?"

Ken wheeled the creeper off toward the bushes. "And we thank you too, Orv. Don't we, Jake? In our prayers," he winked, "almost every night."

"That so?" Orville said. "Well, you'd both be goners long ago is what I'm thinking, locked behind bars or tied down over there at Miz Dix's place. Not that you deserve it any more than anyone else in this world." He spat. "Christians. Why in hell did God ever allow them to take over the Earth?" He opened the lid on the soft-drink cooler, jiggled a bottle down the rack to the dispenser, kicked the machine, and yanked out a bottle of Chocolate Cow. "You'd think it was almost summer, sticky as it is." He finished off the drink, flung the bottle over the cliff, and with this eyes surveyed the whole array of the hilltop. "It sure is a shame," he said.

Jake regarded him suspiciously. "What you thinking, Orville?"

Orville poked a thumb into Jake's cheek. "Well, boys, massive retaliation may be a prerogative of these United States we did our best to protect, since for all our weaponry we don't exactly possess sufficient armaments to fight back. But that ain't no reason we can't have us some fun."

202 | PETER WELTNER

Roy sat quietly on Nolan's brother's bed, listening hard, liking the fact that it was Nolan's music, not Orville's. It had been three months since Nolan had discovered jazz, starting with Parker and Brubeck, then shifting to Johnny Hodges or Miles, now listening mostly to Mulligan and Chet Baker, especially Baker, spending all his leftover money from part-time construction work on album after album, driving great distances, as Roy and Orville used to, to find what he had to have, he and Roy sometimes spending half a Sunday afternoon at Kemp's in Chapel Hill flipping through the bins, reading liner notes, studying the covers as if they were images of a world in which they'd feel welcome.

"Think of the chicks he must get with a voice like that," Nolan breathed.

Without meaning to, Roy stared at Nolan's damaged skin, rippled like plastic after it had melted and cooled, never to be reshaped back into its original form and texture. Chet Baker was crooning about how his love was at an end and that there was no reason for him to pretend and let it linger. The thrill was gone. Roy held the cover in his lap and studied the photograph, which made him feel only more mournful and alone since Baker's face had entered the music and transformed it, inciting in him a desire he could just barely ignore.

"Cool," Nolan enthused. "A very hip guy."

"Exactly, man," Roy tried, but the lingo also made him feel peculiar and ill at ease. What was wrong? Nolan was a good buddy, the best. He really was. On the floor, half hidden under his bed, was a pair of ragged and stained boxer shorts. When he saw Roy noticing them, Nolan reddened. "It's getting pretty late," Roy said, his eyes having fled to the clock on the bureau. "Maybe I should take off. I don't want to be here when your folks get home."

"But it's Friday night. They won't be here for hours yet. And they'll probably be smashed anyway."

"I got to work the counter at Stillwell's tomorrow, remember, with that busybody Mrs. Stillwell watching me every second. Starting at seven."

Nolan sat up in his bed and snapped his finger to the beat. "You know that new Hilltop Shopping Center the rumors been flying about? Well, it's true, Roy. I got my application in yesterday. You ought to apply too. Guess where it's going to be at?"

Lights off, crawling along in his car to make as little noise as possible, Roy wound up the road to the station and left the Chevy just below the ridge, walking the rest of the way to the top. The garage itself was locked and dark, but off in the distance he could see several lights on in Orville's house and through the open windows hear music blaring, Brahms's Double Concerto, second movement, he identified out loud, though from where he stood the violin and cello blended together in a blur. He wanted to walk closer, but hesitated. Once the music stopped a quarter of an hour later and the downstairs light was extinguished, he cut across the grass and through the old peach grove toward the garage where he waited some more, staring up, as if there were something he expected or wanted to see. But soon the upstairs lights also went out, leaving the whole house dark. He breathed out heavily, feeling a fool.

Back in his car, he snuck down the hill as carefully as he had climbed it. Only as he reached Hebron Road did he notice the music playing soundlessly in his brain, a Brahms ballade Orville had forced him to listen to five times in a row that last night. And, no matter how hard he tried, after so many weeks had passed, he still couldn't forget it.

Sunlight splashed onto the pond and rippled across its flashing surface shining like shot silk. Honeysuckle, sumac, sourweed, Queen Anne's lace, and dense brush tangled in thickets among the black trunks of the pine woodland. No

longer accustomed to human presence, crows cawed and repeated warnings from high branches. A flicker drilled in the
taller half of a forked oak. Behind him, Roy listened as
Nolan, his back to him, unbuckled his belt and kicked off his
jeans. With his big toe, Roy tested the water, then slowly
waded out farther, trying not to look back, stepping carefully
so that the larger pebbles or mud-embedded rocks would not
slice into the soles of his feet. As the water reached his navel,
silt oozing between his toes, he started to shiver, his forearms
pricked with goosebumps, and he shifted his upper torso as if
to head back to shore just at the moment when Nolan, now
like him completely naked, ripped his way through the vines
and underbrush and splashed into the pond, diving beneath
the surface as soon as he passed beyond where Roy waited, his
arms clasped firmly to his chest. When his head popped back
up for air, his mouth released an arc of cold water, fountain-
like, onto Roy's buckling back.

Nolan stood up and carefully combed his dripping hair
back into place with his fingers. "You were right, Roy. This is
lots better than that pool. See?" He twisted around. "No one
staring at me like I was some kind of a nigger." He squinted
quizzically at Roy. "You OK? You're shaking."

Taking a deep breath, Roy plunged all the way under the
surface. With quick, deliberate strokes, his eyes still open, he
swam for Nolan's legs, grabbing them and toppling him over
backward onto the dark silence of the pond's bottom where
they wrestled until Roy had to fight his way back up for air.

Once he'd recovered his breath, Nolan laughed. "You're
pretty strong for a pipsqueak." Nolan swam in circles for a
few minutes, then floated on his back, his usually distended
sex, Roy noticed, shrunken by the chilly water.

"Don't you wish we still lived out this way?" Nolan
sighed. "I sure do. I wish my daddy had never sold the farm. I
hated it there, but I miss it, you know?"

Roy paddled around Nolan and stopped to tread water close to his head. "When does the new job start?"

"Next week. Monday. I'm sorry about the way it worked out, Roy. The groundbreaking ceremony's tomorrow if you want to go anyway. Those pissers should have given you a better offer."

"I can't touch bottom here. Can you?"

Nolan dipped down and let his feet sink into the mud, his head and neck still sticking out of the water. "Sure."

"I think I'm going back and get some sun," Roy said. "I'm cold. Aren't you freezing, Nol?"

"I got more meat on my bones, skinny."

As Roy stepped into the woods, two jays swooped onto separate pine branches, nattering and complaining at him in alternation like a team. Roy bent down and took a rock to throw, but, before he got a chance, Nolan had lobbed one at them from the edge of the pond. "I thought you said you weren't cold," Roy laughed at Nolan, his body shuddering, his teeth clacking like two sticks striking one another.

"Maybe we need to wait another couple of weeks."

In a small clearing of the pine, they dried themselves with the single towel they'd brought, passing it back and forth between them, Nolan keeping his scarred side slightly twisted away from Roy's inadvertent glances. He tossed the towel back to Roy, stepped into his droopy boxer shorts, and squatted down on a large, almost flat rock that lay in the path of the sun, shaking his hair every once in a while to free its drying, brightening strands.

Dressed, Roy plopped down next to him on a cushion of decaying pine needles. "I drove up to Orville Earle's again yesterday. You know, just to see it one last time. I mean, I knew no one would be there."

Nolan picked at a scab on the back of his calf. "The sheriff and three deputies had to run him off last Sunday."

"The bastards." Roy drew his knees closer to his chin and wrapped his arms around them. "Everything was all locked up and empty and all the junk and trash had been carted off. It looked dead, Nolan. It made me sad because I think I failed him. He gave me music. He wanted me to listen to Brahms until I'd heard it like he heard it. I couldn't do that but I should have said thanks anyway."

"Forget it." Nolan scratched his armpit and gave it a sniff. "You going tomorrow? Free hot dogs and Brunswick stew. Ice cream too."

"I'd feel like a traitor."

"That's crazy. Hey," Nolan exclaimed, "did I tell you about the great new Chet Baker album I bought last Friday? I had to do something to celebrate the last day of school, right? It's called *Pretty/Groovy*." He reached for the T-shirt he'd hooked over the stump of a branch. "With a slash between the two words. I reckon Chet thinks he's both. And maybe he is. Want to hear it?"

Pine needles clinging to his sweating palms pricked his skin. "Sure," Roy said, eagerly pushing himself off the duff.

An excavator, two bulldozers, three tractors, and a couple of dump trucks waited silently at the perimeter of the site, marked off by stakes that had been pounded into the ground every twenty feet or so, between which taut rows of twine had been strung. Strips of red ribbon had been tied to them as a warning. Bleachers from the high school set up close to the old Earle house held the civic dignitaries and the various executives and future businessmen of Hilltop Shopping Center whose groundbreaking was being honored, the assembled onlookers were being told, by their presence. Close by, in strict formation, stood selected members of the high school band, their instruments gleaming proudly like polished silver in the noontime sun. Cars were parked all over, off the grass and on it, behind the doomed house, around the also-soon-to-be-razed garage and service station, along the two roads that wound up the hill, or off the shoulders of Hebron Road itself. The occupants had had to climb their way to the top where they entered the site close to two tulip trees whose imminent destruction alone a few of them vocally regretted.

By the time the mayor rose to present his speech, the crowd, squeezed together close to the podium, numbered well over a thousand, Roy guessed from where he stood with Nolan, off to one side of the restricted area close to a loudspeaker that faced back toward the people. As the mayor waved and smiled, the band played a medley of "The Old North State Forever" and "Dixie." All the while the crowd cheered or released its various versions of the rebel yell until, the music ended, the mayor lifted his hand for quiet.

"Look," Nolan said, directing Roy's sight to the roof of the house. "Isn't that Orville Earle? What the hell is he doing up there? What's he holding?"

Roy glanced up. Orville was awkwardly crouched by a hole in his roof, balancing himself with one foot shoved into the gutter while both arms clasped what, to Roy's eyes, appeared to be an enormous chicken, its wings flapping wildly.

"Louder," one man in the crowd shouted as the mayor uselessly tapped the microphone that had suddenly gone dead while others slowly began to notice Orville and the squawking chicken on the roof. Many of them raised their arms and pointed until most people's eyes were directed his way. A man in a fancy business suit stepped out of the bleachers to inspect the wires running out of the podium and held up the frayed ends he had pulled back to display to the people, shrugging and scratching his head in puzzlement.

"Ladies and gentlemen, boys and girls," the mayor tried projecting without amplification, "dear neighbors. Today is a proud day for the citizens of Alexandersville and Walker County. This afternoon, our once-struggling community," he continued, his voice thin and piercing. But the subsequent words were all but drowned out by the electric hum of the speakers that had suddenly cut back on, though instead of blaring out the mayor's speech, they played music, deafening, roaring music, full of high-volume distortion, the chorus throbbing to a march. It was Brahms, the second section of the *German Requiem,* Roy recognized at once, where the voices sing that all flesh is grass and all the glory of man as the flower of grass. Orville had played it for him often, more than once joining in the song.

Roy glanced back at the roof toward which everyone was now looking, even the mayor, because Orville had stood up almost to his full, imposing height, his scruffy black hair flailing in the wind as he held the terrified chicken over his head by its feet. He whipped it around like a bola and tossed it, its useless wings flapping desperately, over the heads of the astonished crowd. As it plummeted to earth, a powerful shot from the second floor, right on target, blasted it to bits, its body sundered into fragments of bloodied feathers, carcass, and gore that rained down over shrieking heads. On the other side of the roof, almost beyond Roy's sightline, Jake heaved another poor hen into the air, which Ken also shot while Orville hurled a third.

The crowd, especially those already splattered, began pushing and shoving their way back, screaming, terrified that the madman with the gun might turn on them. One woman, clutching her purse to her breast, turned aside and vomited. Several others had fainted. More were crying or cursing. Above all the other sounds, as most attempted to escape, the Brahms steadily, unrelentingly grieved.

Unable to take his eyes off Orville, as if transfixed, Roy nonetheless saw the crowd surge and grabbed Nolan's hand, jerking him away from that part of the crowd that was headed toward them and the fastest way out by the road down the hill.

Everywhere people were scurrying for cover and safety.

Then, as suddenly as it had begun, except for the cries of the crowd, everything fell silent. The music stopped as if a plug somewhere had been pulled or tripped over. Orville and Jake had vanished. Two cops rushed the porch, weapons out, and kicked the door open.

When he woke up, still dizzy from the beers he hadn't meant to drink the night before, Roy knew with a certitude unlike any he had ever experienced, that he could not go to church with his family that morning or any morning ever again. It was over between him and the Lord without its ever really having begun. If he could, he would have quit his family altogether that instant too, but instead, after dressing, he merely snuck out his window once more and headed straight for Nolan's. If he were lucky, when he got to the house, Nolan's parents would be still sleeping it off so that he and Nolan could be alone.

He parked the car on the shoulder of the road, cut across a neighbor's yard, circled behind and around the Flynt house, and tapped slowly on Nolan's window. Nolan tugged it open and stuck his head out, though, not having dressed yet, almost instinctively he tried to keep most of the scarred side of his body concealed behind the wall.

"Christ," he said, "you see the morning paper yet? Well, you better," he warned, handing the front section to Roy, pointing to the picture of the three of them in custody, their wrists and ankles shackled. Roy read fast, skimming much of it, and angrily shoved the paper back at Nolan.

"You know what 'crime against nature' means, don't you?" Nolan pressed.

"Sure," Roy said. "Sure I do."

"They kept an arsenal out at that place. They found lots more where they were living in that old deserted cabin by Prescott Reservoir. And obscene materials. You know what that means too, don't you, Roy? Pictures of naked guys, I bet."

"Ken's nuts. He was wounded bad in the war. Orville told me so himself. He'd say anything." Roy wished Nolan would put some clothes on or cover himself since his nakedness was making him feel naked as well, his desperation and shame too obvious. "You don't think I knew anything about any of that, do you?" Roy said, knowing even as he asked the question that it was his first betrayal. How many more would follow in his life?

"They already gossip about us," Nolan whispered. "Haven't you heard? 'Yellow on Thursday,' that's what they say behind our backs. Sue Willets told me. Damn, I hate her. I hate all of them."

"So do I," Roy said quietly.

"I've been thinking, Roy. I can't hang around with you anymore. I couldn't stand it. I can't stand anymore stares or dirty looks."

"Yeah. I understand, Nolan."

"Keep cool, man," Nolan said fast, darting back into a dark corner of his room.

Behind the wheel of his Chevy, the motor already on, Roy attempted to contemplate his future—not his future a decade down the road or a year or a week or a day, but his immediate future, the one only minutes away. Brahms, Orville Earle had told him, was his savior and his tormentor. He heard him even when he didn't want to, even as he slept, in the music of his dreams. But, when he thought of Orville now, Roy could hear no music. There was no sound. Rather he saw the bodies of living creatures bursting in the air, torn to thousands of pieces with a single blast and raining down into hungry mouths. The appalled crowd watched and did not run away but instead grabbed for the shreds and gulped them down their throats, the startled, frightened, cruel crowd that for Roy had suddenly become all the world. His hands repeatedly beat against the steering wheel. But, when he glanced up from the dashboard, he saw Nolan sheepishly regarding him from the Flynt porch, wearing only his jeans drooping off his pelvic bones, carrying a towel in one hand as he walked purposefully toward Roy, exposing every scar and wound, as if he knew what it all meant and didn't care. "Let's spend the day at the lake. You and me, we need to talk, Roy. We don't have to stay here. We could drive to L.A. and hear Chet at The Haig. Jesus, that's what I'd like to do more than anything else in this world. I'd die happy if I could just hear Chet Baker in person at The Haig. Do you reckon he still plays there? Let's chance it. Let's leave tomorrow. This car Orville got you, it's in such great shape it'll get us there easy. What do you say?"

Unlike Himself

HIS ARMS OUTSTRETCHED, resting back against the bar, facing Bourbon Street, Brice Landry sat on his stool like a king on his throne, poised to receive the worshipful, ready to dismiss with a flick of his head or hand anyone who might attempt to approach his person without having waited for the subtle sign that granted permission. He was a star who knew he had been born uniquely blessed, as if God had intended him to be always distant from the rest of humanity and radiantly self-luminous. When he was only a toddler in a playground, other children's mothers would pamper him, suspending their chatter among themselves to gush over his dewy skin and blushing cheeks, his wavy sable tresses and sinuous lashes, the amazingly true heron blue of his eyes. In junior high, girls would hush as he walked by them in the halls, then giggle nervously to each other as he turned a corner. A few years later, he was an easy champion on the football fields and basketball courts across the piedmont, much photographed and reported on in the press, president of each of his successive classes, and the boy whom his teachers most gossiped about, pretending they were only comparing notes. Sweethearts yielded to him without a murmur of protest or complaint wherever he chose to take them, whether in the back of his immaculately resurrected '54 Chevy or on blankets deep in the woods behind the stadium or in the rickety frame beds of a motel whose rooms smelled of old dime-store must and decay, where the clerk never refused him a key even when Brice didn't bother to pay. These girls already had convinced themselves, without anyone having to prod them, that Brice Landry would be the most special moment in their lives, however fleeting and sparse the pleasure. For his part, Brice couldn't have cared less about them since what he enjoyed was only the aftermath. Each new conquest added to his long list of victories the special gleam and luster of other boys' envy.

It was that envy which also elevated him during his four-year tenancy into king of the KAs at Chapel Hill, the brother about whom all the other brothers most boasted to prospective pledges during rush. As had become his habit, he lazed his way through school, managing his unearned Cs on dazzle alone. But his spirit was nonetheless restive and dissatisfied. Early in the second semester of his senior year, at his instigation, he and a trio of frat brothers trained down to New Orleans for Mardi Gras. Though the hotels and guest houses were all packed, he secured them a room through simple audacity. The hands of the smitten desk clerk quivered as he slipped Brice the key under the grate. There, in the midst of the Quarter's masquerades and revelries, Brice Landry beheld for the first time the solution to those desires which thus far he had so rarely fulfilled. Having encouraged the brothers to return to the safety of the campus on their own, he stayed an extra week, moving from bar to bar as he followed the path of increasingly higher praise, satisfied to know that it was his nature to deserve it, whatever the source. Watching him undress, one man said it was like seeing a Donatello strip off his armor only to reveal the body of a Michelangelo beneath. Brice understood what he meant and liked the sound of it. It was in fact, he quickly discovered, such words that he seemed to enjoy most, the hymns to his body all others sang. Even when he did not let a man touch him, he nonetheless made him feel almost rewarded simply to be allowed to stand at a distance and adore.

Now, done with school, he sat hour after hour in the Bourbon Pub, music booming through speakers so tall they bumped the ceiling. Brice liked the beat, despite his best friend Mike's complaints that disco was over a decade dead. For nearly six months, almost since Brice's first reappearance in the Quarter, he and Mike had chosen to sit next to each other whenever they were in the bar together, sucking on a beer they'd nurse for hours. The bartenders didn't mind because they knew such guys were good for business, luring others in like an ad with promises of glamour, excitement, sex. Though he was not as experienced as he pretended, Mike taught Brice how to hustle some to earn a little cash he needed that his waiter's job sometimes didn't provide, encouraging him to accept even the paunchy ones with spreading bald patches and age spots blotching their faces and hands because, Mike argued, they already knew he was going to be plenty expensive. What Brice didn't care for were the scenes the tougher ones would throw when, despite his plain statement of his rules, they'd end up wanting more and start to paw or try to kiss him or want him in their mouths or up their hairy butts. Such episodes always irritated him and left him feeling bitter toward the human race.

"Check out that miserable old geezer," Brice said, pointing out to the dark street where a heavyset, jowly man in a too-tight-fitting business suit tottered between the bumpers of two cars, the glaze of inebriation worn like a mask draped over his face, his zipper down as he fondled himself in appeal to the row of boys who lined the street outside the bar, some squatting in defiance, others crooking their legs in provocation against the wall. "I tell you, Mike, if I ever lose my dignity like that you can just go ahead and kill me. I mean that. Just go ahead and shoot me dead."

Before finally deciding, however reluctantly, to attend this year's annual conference on Religion and Literature, Arthur

Loudermilk had never been to New Orleans. In fact, he had rarely ventured beyond the borders of Tennessee, except for two brief tours to Europe when he was much younger—one to the English Lake Country to follow the great poet's steps, the other during a winter vacation to a Mozart festival in Vienna, neither of which was at all spiritually satisfying. While still an undergraduate at Vanderbilt, Arthur had reasoned that the only way to escape temptation was to deny its existence altogether. At least one ought to try. If redemption was to be found at all, a man, especially a man given to damnable impulses, must locate his desert on the map of his soul and then seek some cave to live in alone.

After receiving his doctorate, he was offered a job at a small, conservative Methodist girls' school erected just after the Civil War in a clearing near a wide bank of the Hiwassee River. There he could teach his seminars on T. S. Eliot and lecture his various classes on Elizabethan courtly drama safe from the threats the flesh offered, whether from within or without. He entertained never, refused to own a television set, scrupulously attended chapel at least twice a week, observed the regimen of a vegetarian diet, wrote no personal letters at all to anyone since the loss of both of his beloved parents. When he sensed that he was becoming intolerably stimulated, he forced himself to take long, grueling hikes through the neighboring hills, some lasting much longer than sunlight prevailed.

He was regarded as something of a saint by a few colleagues. Others thought him to be an oddball and a nuisance. When not trekking through the woods, he forced himself to study, and, if he rarely enjoyed what he was reading, he nonetheless pursued it with the commitment of one for whom every foul thought requires the whip of discipline, each word enforced by a brutal necessity. For Arthur Loudermilk had not chosen to devote his life to art but only to sacrifice himself to it, as if he had elected to wear perpetually, instead of haircloth, a painful shirt of words. His one reward would be that no one could ever guess, not even after his death, how thorough his self-denial had been.

In the hotel lobby crowded with noisy conventioneers, standing awkwardly tall above most of the others, he winced when a beady-eyed weasel of a man, studying his name badge distressingly closely, bellowed out his name and insisted on pumping his hand. "Why, Loudermilk," the little man shouted, hurt, "you don't remember me, do you? That conference on the Fugitives when Donald Davidson himself came to speak?"

"I'm sorry," Arthur murmured, shaking his head, for he seldom remembered anyone or anything from his past.

"Listen," the man hollered on tiptoe, tugging him aside from a crowd, "I read that brilliant essay of yours in last spring's *ELR*. It was exciting, I must tell you, to find someone else who took John Lyly seriously. What I want to talk to you about," he continued, shoving Arthur into a corner, "is your contention that Elizabeth was the real or implied incarnational link between mundane reality and transcendence as she sat on the stage during that performance of *Endymion* which you describe so tellingly. I mean, do you really believe that's cogent, Loudermilk? Can you really believe that Tudor propaganda was so effective as to make of her a kind of sacred English virgin? Seriously now, Arthur?"

Had the man been drinking? "As a matter of fact, I do believe that. I believe most of what I write. Don't you?" Arthur inquired, struggling to free himself from the man's grip. "It was visionary theater. Like *Pericles*."

"Ah ha!" the man hooted as if to challenge him. "Paganism! Say, I could use a drink, couldn't you? It's stuffy in here. Too much idle jawing and chitchat. What say we find a cozy little spot and continue our discussion elsewhere?"

Embarrassed for him, Arthur shook his head much too vigorously. "I'm afraid I can't."

"Tomorrow then," the man suggested eagerly.

What could he be wanting from him? "Oh, oh no. I don't think so," Arthur began to apologize, but the man had just spotted another name on a badge and called it out, leaving Arthur uncomfortably in the lurch.

He passed the evening in his room alone, revising his paper for the next afternoon's session. When the curtains were open, the windows looked out on other walls of the hotel, but Arthur nonetheless felt unaccountably free there, as he never did in his little cottage surrounded by dark pine and dense brush. It was an error for him to be in this city, he thought as he studied the bad watercolors of jazz clubs and riverboats that decorated the excessively blue walls. Even the bed was dangerously comfortable, and he had slept, wrapped only in a sheet, on the gritty floor.

His was the last paper of the day. He had not listened to the three that preceded him, absorbed as he was in the disconcertingly asymmetrical arrangement of the fleurs de lys on the maroon papered walls. A voluptuary's mistake, he had decided, after having counted the flowers horizontally, vertically, and diagonally, hoping to uncover some hidden order or numerological obsession. As he heard his name read and a modest scattering of tired applause, he almost failed to rise and move to the podium. But, once there, he managed to ignore his bored audience and glue his eyes to the page. "Nature works her will from contraries," he began, quoting from Lyly's *The Woman in the Moon*, "and this is a moral truth I hope to demonstrate to you today through the visionary art of one of the greatest dramatists of the Renaissance." As he droned on, mouthing words he barely heard himself, he bent ever closer to the lectern until near the conclusion of his talk he had grown stooped as a crone, worrisomely near to licking the sheets as he spoke. Arthur detected disarray around him, unstifled coughs and noisily shuffled chairs, the sound of feet stomping off, making no effort to be discreet. "What is always monstrous in the world," he hastily concluded, sweat dribbling from his temple onto the floor, "is the rigidity of temperament or being that identifies humanity with the unreasonable and leads us, ignoring nature's own spiritual goals, to worship that which we should abhor in the natural world. Man must yield to a sacred love in order to change himself, and he must yield to spiritual change in order to discover that faith in divine transformation that makes him something greater than man."

"The room was much too warm. The earlier papers had lulled everyone to sleep. Nothing could wake them up," the same persistent, ferretlike man who had grievously grappled with his lapel yesterday said to soothe and comfort Arthur. "But yours was the best talk I've heard today, Loudermilk. Really. Now how about indulging in a little nip to celebrate, eh?"

Arthur slapped the manila envelope containing his despised essay against his thigh. "I don't drink."

"A meal then. Surely you eat."

"Not out. No, not ever. Who are you, anyway?" Arthur asked curtly and scurried off.

In the late fall in the hills above the college, when the trees' great, satisfying unleaving had been completed, he would dally amidst the trunks of the pines and the denuded oak, ash, alder, and gum that stuck like spikes out of the earth and note, as the sun disappeared from the earth, how the darkness clarified everything into shapes so bleak and simple that God's rigorous message could not be misread. He would walk to the banks of the Mississippi, therefore, and wait for the sun to decline as the river rushed to join that immensity whose silent roaring was the only voice of God he had ever heard. He prayed he might feel the morning's misguided pride in his paper flow away with those waters.

He waited on a bench on the walk overlooking the river near Jackson Square, clusters of tourists excitedly strolling back and forth before him, people too easily pleased by what they saw, like most travelers. When it was dark enough, he wandered down Decatur, smelling cooking fat and sugar in the air, the sounds of an overamplified guitar and pounded drums violating his ear. A group of men, several of them shirtless though the night was hardly warm, gathered around a lamppost outside a bar, but he squeezed through them without noticing them more closely or looking into the door. Nor did he stop at the shop where the lurid posters hung, black frames enclosing shining silver bodies, too powerfully muscled to be real. Instead, he hurried toward the safety of the greater darkness on the other side of Esplanade, passing onto the less regularly patterned streets of Faubourg Marigny, voices from TVs or radios seeping through old and weathered walls as he began to quicken his pace. Only a large chunk of cement from a cracked and protuberant sidewalk stopped his haste, toppling him forward onto his hands and knees.

His palms and shins hurting, he shivered as a flashlight beam fell deliberately onto his face. "You get up now. You ain't hurt none." The old woman was chewing on something that almost filled her mouth and spat a wad of it into the bushes on Arthur's side of the rail.

He pushed himself back up and brushed off his trousers, noticing a tear in a seam. "That sidewalk ought to be repaired. It's a menace."

"Huh," the old woman snorted, dragging her long skirt down the steps and shining the light more directly into Arthur's eyes. "Watchyou know about it? Watchyou know about anything, fool?"

Arthur shielded his face with his hands. "Do you mind?"

Some juice dribbled down her chin. "I got good magic. Very special. Big surprises. Only ten dollars. You buy it," she insisted as if the transaction were certain.

Arthur defiantly stuffed his bruised hands into his pockets. "You can't be serious."

She reached into a deep fold in her skirt and held out a fist-sized packet for Arthur's approval. In the moonlight, her teeth looked sharp and ratlike, her pawlike hands padded and clawed. "You buy."

"It stinks," Arthur complained.

"Powerful magic."

"Really," he fussed, making motions to walk away.

She summoned him back. "It's a one-time offer only," she cackled.

"You must think that spill knocked out my senses."

"No, man. You the sanest man alive."

"And what exactly is it I'm supposed to do with the noisome substance, assuming that I should buy it from you?"

"You swallow it, hon. Eat it. Whole. Down in one gulp."

"Devour that? I never . . ."

She clicked off the flashlight. "Soon you will taste blood in your mouth. Not your blood. A boy's blood. And you will not want that blood in your mouth. You will want this." She held the packet up to him.

He took it from her and weighed it in his hand, finding it heavy as stone and warm to the touch. Impulsively, he reached into his wallet and handed her a ten-dollar bill. "This is madness."

"Maybe," she grinned. "It's getting cold tonight," she said, huffing back up the stairs. "You go on and get now. I don't want to have to see you again."

"Why, lookie over yonder," Mike said, smirking.

Brice swiveled on his stool away from the door. "Yeah, I saw."

"Seven nights in a row. That's some kind of a record even for you, isn't it?"

"I suppose." Brice squeezed an empty beer bottle between his thighs, having already peeled off its label, and with his thumbnail he made it ping. "I wish he'd catch his plane and go back home to his wife or whatever. Just get him out of here."

"I thought you enjoyed this, dude."

"Yeah, maybe. But this one's too weird."

Mike scratched his cheek. "He sure does look scared, kind of like he was afraid of peeing in his pants. You notice how he keeps wiping his forehead with that big hankie of his. The sight of you is making him sweat," Mike ribbed him.

As the amplifiers throbbed and thumped, a stalky boy a couple of years younger than Brice or Mike pushed in between them to order a Coke, wearing the required, however unseasonal, uniform of baggy Bermuda shorts and brightly colored T-shirt, tight enough to tauten the fibers of the muscles that pulsated and trilled with his incessant movement like plucked strings. "Cool music, huh?" he commented to Brice.

"It sure is," Mike intervened. "This place is hot like this every night. Your first time here?" he asked, appraising the boy up and down as the kid turned to observe the swirl of shirts in the thick of the crowd. "What do you say, Brice? You think he's ready for me? He looks like he just sprouted."

Brice lifted his beer bottle with just the pinkie of his left hand. "He's begging for it."

"You guys," the boy said blushing, retreating back to the crowd of dancers.

Unfazed, Mike stared back out to the corner across the street. "So, what do you think? Maybe he's been following you elsewheres."

"Who cares?" Brice sighed heavily.

"I'd bet he's a preacher," Mike guessed, "probably preparing some terrible curse to chide you with and toss you into the pit of hellfire. After he's done with business, of course. Look at him, buddy. He can weep real tears, just like Brother Jimmy."

"I told you I don't want to have to look at him anymore,"

Brice said annoyed. "It's what I've had to do all goddamn week long practically, look at his ugly face gaping at me, night after night."

"This is much too bizarre," Mike said. "I think I'm going to take a breather and give that kid a second chance. He's a yokel, but he sure is cute."

"Fine," Brice allowed, hoping that his admirer, if that's what he was, might be finally getting worn out. Didn't the man ever rest? The first moment he spotted him he was panting hard, like someone who wasn't used to running or had just had a serious scare. But, when it seemed he would never leave, Brice thought it was maybe because he didn't know how the rules worked and was waiting for Brice to take the first step and demonstrate that he was available—an expectation he'd come to recognize in some first-timers, which in Brice's reading this guy clearly was. But, however long he stood lurking there, he wouldn't budge from his spot on the corner or make his big move. He just moped, every once in a while breaking down like a frustrated child and sobbing, throwing his beat up hat onto the sidewalk, then having to bend over with a heavy moan to pick it up and put it back on his tiresome head. Brice had rarely seen a gaunter scarecrow in his life, like a sad-sack clown, all of whose clothes drooped on him and whose every movement promised a pratfall. If the bastard would only summon his nerve and approach him at last, then Brice could just refuse him with a quick, cutting remark and be done with it, another soul having succumbed. The problem was that until this incident got resolved Brice would continue to feel uneasy, as if he were taking a stupid test all of whose questions he had already answered brilliantly, of course, except for this one, which demanded information he would swear to God he hadn't ever been given and it pissed him off because it wasn't his fault if he didn't know the answer.

He was sensing in himself the development of the uncom-

fortable presence of a doubt and he didn't care for the sensation at all. Over the last two nights he had grown so anxious
that he had nearly broken his strictest rule and made the first
move. But he knew a slip like that would ruin everything, especially his reputation in the Quarter. Only hustlers ever
made the first move, booming invitations into the open windows of a slowly passing car or jumping out of bushes at a
likely prospect or tugging on some fat cat's sleeve. And Brice
was no hustler. He wanted there to be no mistake about that.
He only made himself available on special occasions to earn a
few extra bucks.

Yet once more the old coot was forcing him to go home
early because as long as he stood there lurking nobody else
seemed to matter much. Keeping his sights set straight
ahead, Brice scooted out of the bar without once glancing
back behind him and raced straight for Marigny. As he
neared the house on Chartres where he rented a couple of upstairs rooms, as usual running too fast, he crashed his right
foot into the pitched slab of concrete that for at least a week
had protruded up from the sidewalk, a pain like the stab of a
pin flashing up his leg. "Christ!" he yelled at the wizened bag
who seemed always to be sitting in her ruglike rags, impas-
sively rocking in her swing that hung from creaking chains.
"That's the third fucking time. Can't you even try to get it
fixed?"

She spat a heavy spray of juice over the rail. "It ain't none
of my doing, boy. No law say you can't look where you're
going."

The night air smelled of rotting grass or a fetid pool
steaming under a summer sun. When he breathed in, Brice
became almost woozy and had to cling briefly to a tree
branch. How many beers had he drunk, anyhow, to settle his
nerves? "You're just waiting to see me break my neck, aren't
you, you old witch? You better have that taken out and
repaved soon or I'll get the city after you, you hear?" he

vowed, stomping off to his cottage where, later that night, he would dream he inhabited an even more perfect body that stumbled over nothing, tripped over nothing, but flowed like water through porous stone.

The day the convention ended, Arthur resolved to seek a cheap hotel, finding one that suited his needs well enough far from Canal a few blocks off St. Charles. There he spent most of each day in a dark room, lying immobile on a graying bed-spread that reeked of bleach and detergent, holding his hands stiffly by his side as if he were already safely coffined. On the eighth day, rain from a harsh storm plashed into the pool on the bottom of the light well outside a rattling window that threatened to shatter each time lightning crackled and thunder rumbled. A steady stream from the deluge seeped through the damp plaster above the radiator and trickled to the floor, sopping the rug in an ever-widening ring around the room's only standing lamp. Arthur chose to keep it unlit lest in some way, clicking it on, he might electrocute himself, and, many days after his demise, be discovered by the authorities completely naked, fallen to the floor like some derelict in a flop-house. Cold tears collected in the corners of his eyes and slid down the sides of his head into his ears, but he did not move to wipe them away.

Seven days ago, he had notified the secretary to the chair of his department that he had been struck violently ill with symptoms of a food poisoning, probably from some prawns he had eaten at a restaurant where he ought never to have chosen to dine. Because he was Professor Loudermilk, she did not question him further about the restaurant or the dubious prawns but merely expressed her dismay that he was in pain, reassuring him that all would be taken care of until his awaited return to his classes. Never having purposefully lied like that to anyone before, Arthur was surprised to find his guilt not unmixed with self-satisfaction and pleasure, a sly smile forming itself against his will across his lips as he hung up the phone.

He blamed his lie on his fall, of course. If his foot had not collided with that block of dangerously upturned walkway, he would never have been assailed by that ridiculous old woman and badgered into purchasing her noxious droppings or whatever substance it was that lingered, unopened, in a drawer of his room. Moreover, the incident in its totality had so utterly unnerved him that, heading back to his hotel, he had lost all sense of direction and turned right rather than left on Ursulines, discovering himself against his wishes on Bourbon, headed precisely for where he feared to go in what was undoubtedly the sleaziest part of the Quarter. Unsure of how to escape, he had started to run, but, having quickly begun to lose his breath, he had had to stop to recover it and to lower his speeding pulse. As luck would have it, just as he was reading "St. Ann" on the street sign, his eyes unavoidably dropped. Sitting on his stool, the boy was staring at him as if he were somehow annoyed with him, though why that should be so Arthur could not even contemplate. Yet, despite his recognition that just admiring the boy was a serious kind of idolatry, a sort of spiritual dance around a golden calf, he found he could not take his eyes off him or budge from that spot on the corner.

Thus, night after night, always against his will, he found himself returned to that corner, as if some malicious genie had been repeatedly transporting him there despite the fact that it was not what he had wished for at all, dropping him into a world whose forbidden pleasures he had been compelled to read about, but which he had refused to believe were real, like rumors of pagan rituals in the mysterious East. Arthur loathed the boy at first sight, hating him for making him feel as old, ugly, empty, and weak as he undoubtedly was. But he could not shake himself from him. Standing there in his baggy overcoat, breaking down from time to time into maudlin, adolescent tears, he also could not persuade himself that he would not be there again the following night, still waiting for some sign, however unimaginable it might be.

Once he had forced himself back to his dark room, he would deliberately ponder Leviticus' "abomination" and the curse of the "arsenokoitai" of blessed, vigorous, virile St. Paul. Thus far in his life, as he had persistently regarded as only fitting, his spirit had ruled the flesh, offering him, if not a martyr's blissful release, at least a semicloistered life free from distraction, for the most part solitary and safely unhonored. Yet Arthur suspected that, somewhere in the ruins of his bodily self, he had lately glimpsed a daring or perhaps a courage that made him wonder. Perhaps he had been lied to. Perhaps the whole tradition to which he had given his unequivocal assent had denied him this strength. How else could Arthur explain the strange fact that the boy always appeared to be expecting him, anticipating him night after night as every beautiful springtime thing waits for its death in the fall?

Acutely embarrassed, Arthur was aware that he must look more absurd than usual, with the balcony gutting water onto his head over which he had pulled a rain hat that looked like a sailor's too-big downturned cap, and an unfolded plastic raincoat hanging like posterboards over his spindly shoulders. Despite the absence of dancers because of the lousy weather, music jolted out of the bar, where only a bartender moved, busily arranging glasses in their slots on racks. Yet to Arthur's great distress the boy was there anyway, sitting turned toward the door, an impatient look on his too-handsome face. As Arthur steadied his nerves and slowly strode across the street to where the boy sat, having at last convinced himself that there was no further virtue to be learned in continued struggle, a swirl of water tugged at his feet as if to stop him. When he attempted actually to speak, his tongue stumbled against his teeth and saliva flew out instead of words. The boy, grimacing, ducked and turned away.

Arthur poked his shoulder with two fingers. "Excuse me."

"Go away," Brice ordered.

"Oh, no. I'm afraid I can't. That's exactly what I mustn't do. It's too late."

Brice glided his body back around. "What?"

"I hate to be a nuisance and I can't believe I'm saying this but I think I need to know how much."

"You're joking, right? How much?"

"Please."

Brice rested his elbows on the bar and examined Arthur up and down like a buyer his prospective slave. "Three hundred bucks."

"So much? Must it be so much?"

Brice shrugged. "Take it or leave it. And I don't touch you and you don't touch me, understand?"

"I'm not a wealthy man. Three hundred," Arthur repeated, stunned.

Brice massaged the back of his neck, demonstratively flexing his bicep. "I don't haggle, friend."

"No, of course not, of course not. All right then. But you'll go with me now, please, before I lose my nerve."

Brice hopped off the stool. Honoring Arthur's elaborate, whispered instructions, he followed him no less than ten yards all the way to his hotel, pretending to be no more mindful of the man than a detective would be of a petty crook he was trailing on an unimportant case. Close to his quarters, Arthur begged that he hide outside the entrance, thrusting a slip of paper on which he had jotted down his room number into Brice's hand, imploring him to let no less than five minutes pass before Brice walked through the lobby past the desk clerk to the elevator. The elevator swayed, striking the sides of the shaft as it clanked its way up, its doors straining to open at Arthur's floor. Without knocking,

Brice entered the dimly lit room where Arthur, wringing his hands, hovered near the head of the bed.

"I find this deeply humiliating. Don't you?"

With a flick of his head, Brice tossed back his sleek wet hair. "No. Why should I?" He immediately started to un-buckle his belt.

"Wait," Arthut cried out. "Would you mind telling me your name? I'm Arthur. Arthur Loudermilk. And it would mean a lot if you would tell me yours."

"Sure. Why not?" He dropped his dripping T-shirt onto the clunking radiator. "It's Brice Landry."

"I think I'd better sit down," Arthur said as Brice kicked off his shoes, tugged his socks off and draped them on a chair, zipped down his fly, and let his clinging Bermuda shorts slither onto the rug.

Brice snapped the band of his briefs. "You going to just sit there or what?"

"I don't know. I'm not sure. What do men like me usually do in these circumstances?"

Brice teasingly inched down his underwear. "Most guys like to jerk off."

Arthur looked astonished. "Oh, no. No, I can't."

"Suit yourself. It's your bread." Brice poked a fist into the pouch of his briefs to shove them down further, stepped out of them, kicking them toward his shorts, then positioned himself at the foot of the bed, directly in the line of Arthur's worried eyes. "You know, this all really would feel a whole lot better if you could work up a little excitement or enthusiasm, Arthur. I like to get them real excited. Do you understand?"

"I'm ugly," Arthur suddenly cried out, blocking his sight with his fists that pounded against his eyes. "I've always been ugly."

"I've seen worse."

"Please go away. Please, boy."

"A deal is a deal. You owe me the three hundred no matter what. So you might as well enjoy yourself, Arthur."

"Perhaps if I just took off my jacket," Arthur said, relenting slightly.

"Sure. But hurry it up, OK?"

"I think, I'm sure I need to go to the bathroom first," Arthur said, having carefully folded his sports coat on the seat of a chair.

When he walked back out, he was wearing only his old man's baggy, snap-up boxer shorts. His hairless skin, especially on his pole-like legs, was the color and texture of parchment. He lay back in the bed, propping his head up on two pillows. "I feel like such a fool."

"You're supposed to be excited. What do you think this is all about? You're supposed to have a hard-on. It's part of being alive."

"I've never liked being alive," Arthur confessed.

"Don't talk crazy. Stare at me. Go ahead. Admire me. Tell me how good my body is making you feel."

"I can't."

"You've got to."

"I can't. I thought my chastity would keep me safe. But it's failing me. Oh, how it's failing me. Look," Arthur said holding up his wrist for Brice's inspection. "Do you see this watch? It belonged to my father and before that to his father, their only extravagance. It's yours."

"That's good, Arthur," Brice said. "Give me things. Give me lots of things."

He drew it off his wrist and flung it at Brice. "It has five diamonds and a pearl and the band is platinum." Arthur snapped open his shorts and wriggled out of them. "I've never felt this naked in my life."

"I believe you, Arthur."

"Please, Brice. Please touch me."

"I don't do that, Arthur."

"Leave part of yourself in me. Let me possess some small part of your beauty."

"No. I don't do that. Never."

"Please."

"No," Brice barked.

"But I love you," Arthur wailed.

"Oh, Christ!" Brice swore. "But you damn well really better be a virgin," he shouted, violently wedging himself between Arthur's knobby knees.

"I don't fucking believe it," Brice said afterward. "Look at my goddamn shoulder, you creep. It's bleeding."

"I know. I'm sorry," Arthur whimpered. "I don't know what came over me. Perhaps it was the pain."

"Where's the damn money? All of it," Brice demanded, already half-dressed. "You got some Band-Aids or something?"

Arthur swung his racked body over the edge of the bed and veered toward the bathroom, removing from it both his wallet and a first-aid kit he always carried with him. "I didn't mean to bite you. Only I was in such torment, you see. Let me clean it with this cloth."

"You're a menace, you know that?" Brice said, pulling the tabs off the bandages as Arthur swabbed his shoulder.

"I'll be leaving in the morning, Brice. Back to Tennessee."

"Well, that's a blessing at least."

"Please don't be mean."

"Right," Brice agreed, snapping the watchband in Arthur's face. "I'm going to miss you, Arthur. Now where's that three hundred?"

Shortly after Brice had departed, Arthur collapsed on the bed, but the unpleasant taste of blood in his mouth kept him from thinking about anything else and wouldn't go away, not even after several glasses of water. Outside, the rain had ceased

and in the stillness he remembered the old woman and her
instructions for her noxious package. Rolling over the twisted
sheet, he pulled open the drawer and unfolded the ends of the
envelope, extracting the dark, brownie-like square. Pinching
his nose closed, he bit into it, managing to swallow more
than half of it before the sickening taste and a fear of vomit-
ing made him dash to the bathroom and flush the remainder
down the commode. Only after he had brushed his teeth repeatedly did the taste of both Brice's blood and the terrible
food he had just devoured begin to disappear.

Why was he not more afraid of the death to which he had
just doubly exposed himself? He suspected a need to evacuate
his bowels, but hesitated since he did not want to rid himself
of Brice too quickly. For there was now perhaps no virtue left
in Arthur Loudermilk, he was thinking, except the rapidly
expiring sperm of a rare and unforgivably beautiful youth,
whom only a truly desperate God would substitute for His
grace.

"You don't look so hot, champ," Mike commented, plopping
down next to him at the bar, having momentarily left his new
boyfriend, the tall boy, bobbing on the dance floor. "We've
been expecting you ever since the rain quit. Where you been?"

Zombie-like, Brice regarded him vaguely. "I don't feel so
good, Michael."

"There's blood on your shirt."

"Yeah, I know. From a trick. I got him too excited. The
fucker bit me."

"Not that dried-up old string bean?" Mike guessed,
astounded. "You can't be serious, Brice."

"I don't want to talk about it."

"No kidding."

"It doesn't make any sense."

"Boy," Mike whistled, "it sure doesn't."

"Three hundred bucks though," Brice told him as an attempt at self-justification. "And this." He held up the watch for Mike to admire.

"But he was a complete horror."

"All right, then, fuck you," Brice screamed out. "Here, take the goddamn watch, if that'll shut you up. Maybe I liked the guy, all right? Maybe I grew to like him. And who are you to talk anyways? I've seen you bought by lots worse."

"Sure," Mike said placatingly, "sure. Lots worse." He examined the watch's jewels in the glow from the streetlight. "But . . ."

"No 'but's," Brice hollered back as he stormed out of the bar.

At exactly 3:30 in the morning, the eye of the full moon looking down over the city suddenly blinked. Most of the scattered carousers who still lingered in the streets noticed nothing or sensed only that a roving cloud had again passed over head, though one tourist, bleary from drink, swore that he'd just seen a flying saucer or maybe just a huge black hole cut into the sky. But the lovers who strolled nearby on the river walk that late at night paid no attention to him, careful only to keep their distance.

Straying from the bed where his boyfriend of two days lay, Mike Hand thought for an instant that the winds had blown the shutters closed in the outer room, though, when he checked, they were still firmly hooked in place and the room for once looked almost clean in the fresh wash of light. But, surprised at how coarse his skin felt and how creaky his bones were when he pulled up the covers in bed, Brice Landry clenched his teeth at the sudden cold and rubbed his hands together for warmth, guessing that the old guy must have been stronger than he looked. And, in the midst of an otherwise obscure slumber, Arthur Loudermilk suddenly believed he was a boy, a friend beside him drifting down an aimless river as together they lazily basked in the sun, though when the moon returned, without even knowing it, he swiftly lapsed into his old dreamlessness once more.

Only an old woman, puttering restlessly about her trash- and food-littered kitchen, understood the implications of the split second's loss of light, having prophesied to herself exactly what would happen and when, by reading cards and throwing bones. As the light paused and the expected sharp pain began between her dugs, she tried to reach a chair, but, once the seizure had gripped the whole of her chest, she grasped the edge of a table instead, pulling it down on top of her as she collapsed onto the floor, the plug of tobacco she was always chewing lodging in the back of her throat so she couldn't breathe.

Though he had buried his head under three pillows, the buttons of his flannel pajamas jabbing his skin prodded him awake as Arthur Loudermilk slowly climbed back up to consciousness like a worker testing each rung of an old wooden ladder before stepping onto it with his full weight, worried once he'd reached the top that it still might crack or break. He felt peculiar, almost uneasy, thinking how simple it had been to get that pathetic geek to hand over his watch last night. All the tricks were like that, wanting him so bad they'd almost die for it, pleading and begging and trying to bargain their way into being loved. Touching his shoulder, he tested for any scabs where his teeth had penetrated his skin and was relieved and a little surprised to find none. Mike sure as hell would envy that watch though, he found himself grinning, so maybe it was worth it. Toward the back of his head, almost muffled by pillows, he could hear loud cheering and some girl's simpering tears that always made him laugh.

Frightened, Arthur flung the pillows off his face and onto the floor, his heart racing like that of someone who had just avoided a terrible accident. During the night, something serious must have gone wrong with his brain, he was sure of it. Keeping his eyes tightly shut, he sprang up in bed and forced the tips of his fingers to explore down his smooth knees across his strong thighs and stomach to his marble-carved chest. A statue? Brice? No, it couldn't be, he muttered as he groped his way toward the bathroom before whose full-length mirror he reluctantly placed himself. He flicked the switch on and, when they had gotten accustomed to the light, not his own dark eyes but another's coruscating blue ones flashed back at him. "A Gentle Knight was pricking on the plaine," he recited to himself to prove he was still himself, still Arthur, "Y cladd in mightie armes and silver shielde." The tip of his tongue stabbed at the tongue in the mirror. "Brice Landry?" he wondered out loud, cupping his hands over his newly heavy genitals to test their heft and weight.

He forced up another line, one of his favorites from John Lyly. "Our thoughts shall be metamorphosed," he bellowed out, "and made hail fellows with the gods." So part of him, he was relieved to confirm, must still be Arthur. But many other memories, especially physical ones, could not be his at all. A boy named Steve was lying naked and a little loggy from beer on a bench in a locker room, his half-lidded eyes regarding him with something like longing. Arthur pushed Steve out of his mind, but others followed, their actions increasingly pornographic, and he could sense himself becoming irreversibly aroused. He felt like a man standing up to his waist in flooding waters, losing his balance. Self-denial had been his whole life, all that Arthur could ever really claim, however secretly, as truly his own. How could he abandon that way now simply because his body had been inexplicably transformed into the image of all he had ever desired and suppressed?

As usual when he was greatly upset, he drew himself a lukewarm bath, but once he had stepped into it, he discovered that he wanted the water to be much hotter, almost scalding. And he had to release some of it down the drain because of his now greater bulk and weight, despite the fact that he was several inches shorter. He tried to calm himself in the tub, but more pictures kept developing in his mind. A girl he loathed lay under him groaning, moaning Brice's full name as lingering birds twittered on pine branches. Some boy was swiftly stripping for him in a motel down the highway from Chapel Hill. A wrinkled man, soused to the gills, a globular black booger poking out each nostril, was stuffing a wad of twenty-dollar bills into the tight back pockets of his jeans. Men standing around a gas station were saying as he passed, "There goes Brice Landry. A real star," he heard them say, "the best." Yet, watching it all with his own heart, Arthur felt only shame and humiliation at what he had become.

Drying himself off, he began to worry about clothes since none of his own could possibly fit him. Yet he would have to wear what he had until he could purchase others, no matter how much like a clown he might look in rolled up trousers and a button-popping shirt. But the clerk at the store paid him little attention, and, dressed in his new T-shirt and 504s, he passed the desk clerk without inciting suspicion or inquiry about what that hustler was doing traipsing back through the lobby.

He lay back in bed, confused and brooding. Some combination of blood and semen and the old witch's offal must have done this to him, he conjectured, but it was a gift he did not want. Such beauty was a moral burden his soul refused to bear, believing that it was unacceptable for any mortal thing to attempt to pretend, however alluringly, that it was to be spared from corruption and death. He crossed sinewy arms over a chiseled chest and sighed. He would have to find Brice Landry and give him back his body, even if that meant that Arthur would be left with nothing. Getting up, he twisted his wrist to check the time but his watch, of course, was gone. Back on the streets, though, he could tell from the sky that it was well past noon.

On Canal, a few blocks down from Bourbon, a black man was playing a couple of tourists in two games of chess, a third board set up awaiting another challenger. Arthur remembered how he had once been reasonably proficient at the game, despite the fact that he was most often his own opponent, and, though he was running low on cash, considered risking the five dollars the man required you to wager on each game in order to play him. But a pulse in his loins like the compulsive throb in that modern music he so detested urged him elsewhere, the lure of less disciplined games filling his head.

At the Bourbon Pub he took his usual seat, spreading his arms out wide behind him as, yawning, he rested his back against the bar. A few guys huddled in various corners inside and out, several of them stealing quick glances at him, lustful or envious, he didn't care which. A bartender, mopping the floor, passed in front of him and looked up. "You're on display a bit early today, aren't you, Brice?" he teased. "What's up? Or do I have to ask?"

Arthur stretched in his seat and smiled. "It's just such a beautiful afternoon, Roy. That's all."

"Sure," Roy winked, pushing his mop toward the silent speakers.

"Hey, Brice," a guy hollered at him from across the street, but Arthur ignored him, his interest having been grabbed by a blond kid, much more his type, who was fast approaching him, like a messenger with urgent news, from the sunlit corner on the other side.

In a series of tantrums, Brice had broken every mirror in his rooms. The last one, the one over the washbowl, now lay scattered in dangerous shards and slivers over the floor and basin. No calmer, he stood by a window to inspect his skin, gaping in disbelief at how white and wrinkled it had become overnight, flaking at the slightest contact, its few thin hairs either mouse brown or old-lady gray. His jowls drooped like a toothless dog's, he could barely lift a pillow, much less the lightest chair, his shrunken muscles ached, though no pain was greater than what he experienced in his joints when he tried to bend them, and his vision blurred whenever he attempted to focus on anything close or far away. Worst of all, his cock had shriveled to a disgusting segment of a squirming larva, hooded by wrinkled flesh. And his head was full of absurd phrases and pompous sentences that made no sense to him, as if his brain had been taken over by one of his dottering, mumbling profs in college whom he couldn't stand listening to on days when he was in the best of moods.

He grabbed a Japanese jar, very valuable some grateful old goat had assured him, and hurled it across the room at the air conditioner, on which it shattered into hundreds of pieces that littered the floor. Less than thirty seconds later, the hunk from downstairs pounded his door. "Brice? What the hell is going on up there, Brice?"

"Nothing, go away," Brice croaked like an old man.

"What? Where's Brice?" Steve demanded through the crack.

"Out, goddamnit," Brice screamed back.

"Right. I get it. I told that asshole not to bring you old queens home," Steve said, shaking the door handle.

"Oh, Lord. Please, please go away," Brice moaned.

"Sure. You bet. You just tell that hustler I want to see him pronto when he gets back. He can't treat this place like his personal whorehouse, you hear?" Steve yelled as he thudded back down the stairs.

"I don't deserve this," Brice sobbed as he glanced down at his shorts, which were dangling off his thigh bones like a wet cloth suspended from a wire hanger. His hollow, flabby stomach rumbled with gas that nipped at his guts until at last he farted. Driven from one room to the other by his own stench, he oozed back into bed as he heard a noise like the door of a cell being slammed shut in his brain and men singing strange, monotonous chants that sighed and whistled like wind over sand. Sweat beading feverlike on his forehead, his spirit strained defiantly against its confinement in Arthur Louder-milk's body, blotched with scabs and patches ruddy with sores. "In my beginning is my end," he muttered without meaning to, Arthur's senseless words like the taste of shit on his tongue.

In a few minutes, Steve would be leaving for work. Then he could sneak down there to steal some clothes to fit this new absurd size and dress himself so that he could hunt for that evil creep Arthur who had done this to him, killing the bastard if he had to. Nothing would come easier to him at that moment than to slit the throat of the monster who had made him monstrous like himself and sip his blood just as he had tasted Brice's last night. They dragged you down, people did, and made you as ugly and common as themselves. What they claimed to be love was really nothing but envy and hate. He had seen it lots himself. Humanity was always trashing its gods.

The nightly barricades across Bourbon halted the steady pro-gression of a large covey of tourists, men and women dressed alike in nothing but grays and browns whose deliberate drab-ness seemed meant to oppose the carnival colors of the strip through which they had just passed like missionaries trek-king through a heathen jungle. Though they wore their con-ventioneers' badges as proudly as military ribbons, the sight of the bar where Arthur sat made them visibly uneasy and they huddled together, not knowing whether to proceed or retreat. Two cabs honked angrily at them and squeezed past down St. Ann toward the square, one stopping at the corner to emit a fastidiously, elegantly graying man who regarded the world into which he had just had himself delivered with something like suspicion, if not complete contempt—one more colonialist, Arthur thought, in search of liberating savage rites who would soon vanish, never to be seen again, like many other ill-prepared explorers. Like himself, Arthur grimaced, still stunned by his own transformation, the excitement of his afternoon's romp having sufficiently diminished by nightfall to reveal to him again how utterly and bewilderingly he was lost. Get more, more, Brice urged like a phantasm in his ear. And Arthur did indeed sit on his stool as enticingly as he could manage.

Shoving his way through a crowd that was patiently waiting outside to get in, Mike hopped up the bar's steps and whipped his hand hard across Arthur's thigh. "You sure do get them riled, champ. Look at that bunch over there."

"To hell with all of them," Arthur grumbled.

"You said it."

Arthur frowned, wondering if it was he or Brice who was blushing and whether Mike could notice in the dark bar. "You're wearing my watch," he remarked.

"Well, you gave it to me, buddy."

"My father's watch?"

"Your father's? You said last night it was that old . . ."

"Give it back."

"Jesus, you're not acting normal, dude."

"I said, 'Give it back,' Mike."

"OK, OK, calm down. You earned it. You keep it. What do I care?" Mike said, tugging the band loose and thrusting the watch into Arthur's waiting hand. "But I wouldn't turn around right about now if I was you, Brice baby, because that precious timepiece's real owner has just showed up again, looking more ridiculous than ever. Where in hell did he ever pick up those stupid threads? You must have really turned his head to make him dress like that."

Arthur whirled around and saw, of course, himself, only a little more haggard than usual, his eyes flickering with a desperate loathing that had not quite focused on anyone yet, a

monkish hatred, Arthur thought, random and complete, de-
spising all the world.

The line of boys waiting to get into the bar parted with
embarrassment as the old man stumbled up the first step,
grabbing onto the door frame for support, his chest heaving
as he struggled to lift legs that seemed to be mired in deep
muck.

"Jesus," Mike whooped. "I'm out of here." He leaped for
the safety of the dance floor.

"Give it back," he wheezed at Arthur, his arms flailing the
air between them. When, at first confused, Arthur made motions to hand him the disputed watch, Brice only shook his
head more vehemently. "No, damn you. My body. I want my
body back."

"You think I want it?" Arthur said astonished. "You think
I can live with your incessant desires. With your needs. Do
you really?"

"I want to kill you," Brice forced through clenched teeth,
as the crowd looked on delighted by so much drama, poking
each other to keep still.

"It would be like perfect peace," Arthur said, jumping off
his stool and heading for the street where Brice pursued him,
the row of gawkers outside the bar still guffawing and snorting like vicious children at the withered old man they thought
he was.

"You don't know where you're going," Brice hollered after
him.

"Of course I do," Arthur shouted back, walking steadily
faster.

The nearly full moon shone over Marigny like a vast iris-
less eye over which a gray film had grown, obscuring its
sight. Leafless tree limbs shook in the breeze, twitching like
fingers of an ancient hand, pointing up. When, unnerved,
Arthur glanced to see at what, he tripped once more on a
chunk of cement protruding from the cracked sidewalk.

This is where you fell ten days ago, Arthur thought as Brice spoke the words out loud. They studied one another and shifted their gaze toward her house.

"I always hated her," Brice confessed. "You could always smell her. You can still smell her. The whole house stinks."

"She made me buy a package," Arthur said.

"Yes, I know."

"Nothing else explains it."

"No, nothing."

"We should visit her, don't you think?"

On the floor of the kitchen, they discovered a good part of her body already nibbled away by the rats that they had had to scare off by stomping on the floor and shouting before they could enter the room, their hands covering their faces to allay the powerful, nauseating odor. One remained unafraid, squatting emaciated by the sink, its long whiskers quivering as it menaced them with its scarlet eyes.

"I'm going to be sick," Brice said, darting from the kitchen onto the back porch.

As he heaved, Arthur tried to ignore the noise and desperately explored all the drawers and hiding places he could think of, but to no avail until, his foot caught on a rip in a rug, he spied in the far corner of a rotting cabinet a single package like the one he had purchased from her. Picking it up, he took it to the porch to show Brice. "It's still warm."

"How could you ever swallow that stuff, Arthur?" Brice whined.

"You're going to have to find out, aren't you?"

"What?"

"There's only one thing to do. Reverse the witch's hex. Here," he said, placing the package in Brice's hands. He checked his watch. "Meet me back at the pub in three hours. But," he added, handing him the watch, "you'll need this of course, too. To give me later. And I assume you still have the three hundred dollars. I'm expensive, you know," he leered.

"I understand, Arthur. I understand exactly. We must remember."

"Everything," Arthur emphasized. "To the last detail."

Shortly after midnight, on the way to the hotel, Arthur followed Brice just as Brice had followed Arthur, keeping himself hidden in shadows and around dark corners. He waited by the entrance for Brice to enter his room, he rode up the rocking elevator, he forced open the door, and found Brice hesitating in fear and humiliation by the head of the bed. All the words flowed from their mouths like dialogue they had diligently memorized. Only the sense was changed, transformed. Brice pounded his eyes and screamed out, "I'm ugly." Arthur urged Brice on, saying "It's part of being alive." Brice, twisting the band of his watch preparing to give it to Arthur, carefully repeated, "It's yours." "Please," Brice was pleading and Arthur barked back, "No!" "But I love you," Brice whimpered. And Arthur boomed, "You damn well better really be a virgin," as he drove Brice's body into his own. But it was not Arthur's body that Brice felt inside him, of course, but his own, just as, his teeth having pierced Arthur's shoulder, he tasted only his own blood and the semen shooting into his bowels was his own semen, rushing to its own dark source. And the excitement Arthur had felt wasn't Arthur's. It was Brice's, so unlike his own, expanding no further than the circle of his self where it had always moved.

As Arthur was screaming, "Look at my fucking shoulder. I'm bleeding, you bastard," they both already knew that the play was unlikely to work its magic since the sense of what they spoke was so different from what the other had meant the previous night. Arthur in particular stumbled bady over his exit line, calling Brice 'Brice' instead of 'Arthur.'

"Damn," Brice lamented in bed alone. He had devoured the whole horrible mess by mistake and miserably experienced no nausea at all. When Arthur arrived back at the bar to deliver the watch to Mike he could find him nowhere, it being unlikely in any case, Arthur glumly admitted to himself, that Mike would have ever accepted it once more anyway. It was all completely different really. Neither of them could ever be only himself again.

Brice suffered a night of sadly dreamless sleep, no arms reaching out to touch him, no eyes pursuing him, no feet turning as he passed. Though the pain he experienced upon waking confirmed his and Arthur's failure, when the telephone rang he still did not dare open his eyes, but blindly brought the receiver to his ear. "Don't say it, Arthur."

"It's true for you too, then. It didn't work," Arthur sobbed.

"All I have to do to check is wiggle a toe or crook a finger. If I ever get out of this body of yours, Arthur, I'm never going to let myself be old again. I can promise you. I'd rather be dead."

"We'd both rather be dead then."

"I don't know what you're bitching about. You're the one who lucked out."

"Yes, I suppose you would think so. But I didn't want to 'luck out,' and only your vanity could presume that I would. A body like yours is too spiritually dangerous. But I don't expect you to understand that. Or me."

"Listen to this nonsense, Arthur. It's been in my brain ever since I woke up. 'When she whose figure of all is the perfectest, and never to be measured, always one, yet never the same, still inconstant, yet never wavering, shall come and kiss Endymion in his sleep, he shall then rise; else never.' What the hell does that mean, Arthur? Is it some kind of idiotic charm or what?"

"In a way. It's from a sixteenth-century play actually. *Endymion*. I've written on it."

"I hate crap like that, Arthur. I hated it in school, I hate it now. I want out of this. I want out of your ruined body. I want you and your stupid quotations out of my head. Pronto, you understand?"

"Do you think I enjoy your memories, Brice, or your impulses? I am at every instant assailed from within by temptations that would prostrate a saint. And I am hardly a saint. My spirit is failing. I can feel it fading, succumbing to you and your quite outlandish self-regard. I'm dying too, Brice, and facing ruin. That's why this morning I've devised an audacious plan. We've learned that we can't simply reverse the spell or whatever it might be, right?"

"Correct."

"So what's next? What's left?"

"Hell on earth," Brice snarled.

"Exactly," Arthur agreed. "Or else we have to keep trying again and again, without all the ritual repetition we tried last night, without all the reliance on the magic or voodoo or whatever, until we get it right. We were emphasizing the wrong thing. Now we must try it the other way. Don't you see?"

"No, I don't see," Brice said irritably.

"By making love."

"By fucking?" Brice said savagely.

"If you prefer. Until we get it absolutely right since obviously neither of us is any good at it. Until our bodies change, completely change, restored to what we were before this embarrassing transformation in truth occured."

They found a cheap furnished room for rent by the week near the river in a dilapidated converted warehouse where they knew no one would ask any questions. Toward sundown, they sat on the edge of the sagging bed and ate stale sandwiches and packages of cheese crackers, and drank lukewarm sodas bought from vending machines at a neighboring gas station. After their meal, Arthur was the first to strip, but when Brice looked at him bathed in the beige light that seeped through worn shades he wanted to weep for the glory he had lost. And Arthur saw in Brice's tattered nakedness the destitute body that, even in its youth, had daily stretched out its hand like a mendicant, begging only for spiritual release. Each made love as if tormented by his need to possess his own being again, their flesh mingling in sexual turmoil only because they yearned so fervently to become themselves once more. When they had failed to realize their desires and disentangled their sweating limbs, they lay side by side on the dank bed, sharing at least their grief and disappointment, their bodies shivering as chill air whistled through broken windows.

Then they would dress and part in silence. Arthur returned to his hotel where every day he would phone the college to assure them that, though he was still feeling unlike himself, he was recovering nicely, albeit slowly, and should be able to travel soon, while Brice escaped to his mirrorless room where, careful to avoid Steve, he would lock himself in for hour after hour, watching without attention endless TV— both of them doing nothing but anxiously waiting for the time until their next encounter, expectant still and desperately hopeful that the next late-morning struggle or skirmish in the afternoon or evening's thrashing would free them from the prison of the other's body, in whose cells their trapped selves lay dying like a wounded animal caught in a cage.

On the evening of the fifth day, Brice sat up on the corner of the bed and stared off into a corner. "We have a rat. Or rats."

"I noticed," Arthur said gloomily. "I'll buy some traps in the morning."

"I can't screw in a room with a loose rat," Brice announced. He dressed himself and knocked on neighbors' doors, expressing his dismay at conditions in the building in hopes of eliciting sympathy. At the fourth try, a bedraggled old woman with beady, almost-red eyes rummaged around in her closet and extracted two traps, one of which seemed to be almost in working condition, and gave Brice a dollop of peanut butter for bait.

"This had better work," Brice said, setting the trap and placing it where he'd last spotted the vermin, to the left of the door to the john. He lay back in bed. "I can't stay here in New Orleans much longer, Brice. I have to go back to work. I have to return to the college and my students."

Arthur flinched, then relaxed, wondering if Brice's confusion might be a sign. "Yes. I understand. They must miss you. They must be worried."

"I lied to them. I told them I took sick. They believed me. They always believe me. They may not like me, but they would never think badly of me. I must meet my Eliot seminar next Thursday, you see. On the *Quartets*," Brice explained. "'In my end is my beginning.'"

"What about this mess you got us into? What about me?" Arthur demanded.

"I'm sorry, Brice, but I have to leave. This . . . arrangement . . . has been a terrible mistake. It was my duty to remain always celibate, to have lived my life without bodily pleasure. For this error, this mortal lapse, I blame only myself, of course." He rolled over to question Arthur who was stirring restlessly, poking around on the floor for his clothes. "Where are you going, Brice? Or do I have to ask?"

"You're so feeble you can't even get it up anymore, can you? Can you, old man?" Arthur taunted him. "Well, look at me. Look at this. See? No problem. Any time I want."

Brice bent toward the window sill and picked up the watch. "Have I shown you this? It was my father's and my father's father's. It is precious to me. But now it's yours."

Arthur expanded the band to test its fit. "Yeah, it's all right, I suppose. But before I take it you better tell me what I have to do."

"Say you love me. I don't expect you to mean it. Just say it. Pretend it's a play, a masque, and we're both in costume."

"I won't. It's bullshit. And you know it, Arthur. You're

just a pathetic lonely old queen without any memories to keep you living. I'd hate to be like you."

"What you say is true, in its way. I should mind terribly. But I don't, because I do love you, Brice. Oh, I know it's foolish and sentimental of me. But I do."

Angrily yanking the watch off, Arthur pitched it to the floor. "Christ, am I ever sick of toothless fairies bribing me to lie to them."

"Just this once, Brice. Then I'll depart from your life for good. Haven't I paid you well, night after night?"

"Shit. All right then, if it'll get rid of you. 'I love you.' How's that?"

"Insincere and badly delivered, but effective nonetheless." Brice opened his arms toward him. "Now hold me."

"Did you hear the trap spring?" Arthur asked when it was over.

"Yeah. But I thought it was just you coming again," Brice teased.

"Brice?"

"What?"

"Bend a finger or a toe. Try stretching."

"Huh?"

"Do as I say." Arthur reached over him and drew up the shade. "Open your eyes, Brice. It's morning."

"My God!"

"Yes."

"It's happened, Arthur. Jesus fucking Christ. I'm myself again."

"We're both ourselves again, my lad. So I must truly be off to my faraway study where this decrepit Faustus belongs. And you, my beautiful Mephisto, you must return to your vocation as a seducer of souls. But you'll not have mine. I've won."

"Arthur?" Brice said, pushing the old man's hand off his thigh so he could get up. "How can you be so sure? How can we be sure? Really sure? That you're you and I'm me?"

"Sure? How can I not be sure? Look at us. You are Brice

Landry and I am Arthur Loudermilk, no doubt about it. There's no confusion. Not a bit."

"Yes, I see what you mean. And yet perhaps . . ."

"No, no," Arthur insisted, wagging a finger. "No 'perhaps's,' Brice. We must be certain, certain of everything about ourselves henceforth and hereafter. It would be a spiritual disaster not to be absolutely clear on so necessary a point. Believe me, neither of us is so brave that we'd be likely to suffer this transformation yet again. One shudders to contemplate the consequences," Arthur concluded, stretching with a pain-filled grunt to reach for his clothes.

When, dressed, Arthur had disappeared into the john to douse his whiskered face with water, he glanced down onto the tile floor and let out a little shriek that brought Brice scurrying in. "Look," he said pointing down at the bloody trap, a bloody trail stretching behind it.

Brice squatted down to inspect it more closely. "It must have dragged itself in here from the other room, trying to free itself from the trap. Or to escape the pain."

"How horrible!"

"Look how skinny it was. And it doesn't appear to have touched the bait. And here, Arthur. Do you see?" Brice said, freeing the watch from the rat's claws. "It must have gotten caught on it while it was crawling across the rug." He handed the bejeweled timepiece back to the old man. "Go ahead, take it. It's yours."

"Is it? I mean, I can't recall, can you? Which one of us was wearing it last, do you suppose?"

Everybody is always another's body and no one is ever only himself.

Several days later, having fully recovered what he regarded as his senses, Arthur Loudermilk was back at the college busily lecturing to his seminar on the gnostic sources of T. S. Eliot's *Four Quartets* with customary lucidity, as if nothing inexplicable had ever happened to him in his life, when out of nowhere it occured to him that one day, as he stood positioned at the blackboard to establish some point, he would turn to face the astonished classroom of young women like a man transfigured, glorified, perfect, wonderful to behold. The thought made him, speechless, drop his chalk on the floor. What should he do then? What should he ever do?

And, while having sex with a new guy in town who had confessed to having fallen in love with him at first distant glimpse, Brice Landry, without meaning to, imagined how surprised the kid would be when he opened his eyes and found not Brice but some dried-up old codger grasping him, wheezing and sputtering, his breath vile, spit seeping between his lips like slime. The thought of it at first made Brice laugh out loud because it was so ludicrous. He would never let himself be tricked like that again, not ever, no matter what. Yet, unlike himself, he clasped the wayward, startled boy almost lovingly in his adoring arms.

PETER WELTNER grew up in North Carolina, graduated from Hamilton College, and, after receiving a Ph.D. from Indiana University, moved to San Francisco where he teaches modern and contemporary American poetry and fiction in the English Department of San Francisco State University. His previous books are *Beachside Entries/Specific Ghosts*, a collection of stories with drawings by Gerald Coble; *Identity and Difference*, a novel; and *In a Time of Combat for the Angel*, three novellas. His work has been included in *Men on Men 4* and *Prize Stories 1993 The O. Henry Awards*.

This book was designed by Will Powers. It is set in American Garamond by Stanton Publication Services, Inc. and manufactured by Edwards Brothers on acid-free paper.